I0831788

Experimentation and Versatility

Experimentation and Versatility:

The Early Novels and Short Fiction of Fred Chappell

By

Casey Howard Clabough

MERCER UNIVERSITY PRESS
MACON, GEORGIA
25TH ANNIVERSARY

ISBN 0-86554-945-1
MUP/H681

1400 Coleman Avenue
Macon, Georgia 31207

First Edition.

The paper used in this publication meets the minimum requirements of American National Standard for Information Sciences—Permanence of Paper for Printed Library Materials, ANSI Z39.48-1992.

Library of Congress Cataloging-in-Publication Data

Clabough, Casey Howard, 1974-
Experimentation and versatility : the early novels and short fiction of Fred Chappell / by Casey Howard Clabough.— 1st ed.
p. cm.
Includes bibliographical references and index.
ISBN 0-86554-945-1 (hardcover : alk. paper)
1. Chappell, Fred, 1936—Criticism and interpretation. 2. Experimental fiction, American—History and criticism. I. Title.
PS3553.H298Z63 2005
813'.54—dc22

2005007424

Contents

Abbreviations

Commonly cited writings are abbreviated in the following manner:

DAG *Dagon*

INT Author's Interview with Chappell (appendix pages 159-167)

ITL *It Is Time, Lord*

MOL *Moments of Light*

MSO *More Shapes than One*

GP *The Gaudy Place*

INK *The Inkling*

Preface

Experimentation and Versatility considers Fred Chappell's first four novels chronologically and his short fiction thematically, attempting to demonstrate the uniqueness, range, and literary importance of his fictional prose. Although it references several poems, it does not make critical assertions about his poetry—the subject of *Dream Garden* (1997), a compilation of critical essays. Nor does it consider in detail the Kirkman novels or Chappell's literary essays, both of which merit specific, self-contained critical studies. Chappell says of the four Kirkman novels and four books of *Midquest*, "I hope to have some sort of unspoken commentary between fiction and poetry," underscoring the unmistakable interrelatedness of those eight works and the necessity of their being discussed together—perhaps in some future book-length project.[1] This study also is not biographical: it does not seek to identify or speculate upon Chappell's childhood publications in pulp magazines, why he was suspended from Duke University, what dialogue he may have contributed to *Frankenstein Meets the Space Monster*, or what intriguing events he may have witnessed or participated in at the 1970 Hollins Writers Conference. Like the Kirkman/*Midquest* books and his criticism, Chappell's biography is a promising topic for future scholarship.

Unless otherwise noted, all of Chappell's papers cited here are located in the Duke University Library. Each unpublished source is footnoted in the following manner: title, box, series, subseries, page number (if available).

---

[1] "Fred Chappell," *North Carolina Book Watch*, PBS, North Carolina Public Television, 1997.

Acknowledgments

Several sections of this book were published previously in scholarly journals. I am indebted to the following periodicals and their editors for allowing me to reintroduce my essays in book form: *Appalachian Heritage*, *Journal of Appalachian Studies*, *Lovecraft Studies*, *Mosaic*, *South Carolina Review*, *ALCA-Lines*, and *The Southern Quarterly*. Several individuals contributed to the researching, writing, and overall development of this project. Joyce Pair promptly read the manuscript at each stage of the process; I am thankful for her ongoing editorial attention to my work. Several of my students at Lynchburg College were required to read *Dagon*, and I thank them for the various enlightening conversations that followed. I am particularly indebted to Brittany Darden, Josh McCrowell, and Jacquline Marien for assistance in preparing the index. Ariel Myers, Eleanor Mills, and Jim Pollock aided me in research—finding and acquiring important and sometimes evasive scholarly materials. Also supportive of my research were my colleagues in the English Department at Lynchburg College, especially Thomas Allen. My final and largest debt is to Fred Chappell, who consented to an interview, permitted me to quote from his unpublished work, and offered valuable corrections and advice on the manuscript.

Introduction

Experimentation and Versatility

His work displays thematic range and venturesomeness.
—Review of *The Fred Chappell Reader* in *Publishers Weekly*, 78

A detailed critical study of Fred Chappell's fiction is probably long overdue, especially in light of the recent appearance of valuable book-length scholarship on his work. Patrick Bizzaro's excellent edited retrospective collections of essays, *Dream Garden* (1997) and *More Lights than One* (2004), contain provocative samples of scholarship on Chappell's poetry and fiction from several decades, constituting a history of Chappell criticism while also celebrating his work in the present. Equally significant, John Lang's *Understanding Fred Chappell* (2000) provides a much-needed introduction to his work as a whole. Although Lang offers valuable background information and close readings of Chappell's fiction, the aim of his book is to summarize all of Chappell's writing, fiction and poetry. As the editor of the *Understanding* series, Matthew Bruccoli, explains, such books function as "companions for students as well as good nonacademic readers."[1] Comprising an informative general introduction to Chappell's novels and two short story collections, *Understanding Fred Chappell* establishes a sturdy groundwork for a more detailed and encompassing consideration of his prose fiction.

Norman Mailer maintains that writers, or at least male writers, are like pole-vaulters: "The man who wins is the man who jumps the highest without knocking off the bar. And a man who clears the stick with precise

[1] Matthew Bruccoli, "Editor's Preface," in John Lang, *Understanding Fred Chappell* (Columbia: University of South Carolina Press, 2000) iv.

form but eighteen inches below the record commands less of our attention."[2] If Mailer had his way and writers generally were viewed as track and field competitors, Chappell might best be described as a decathlete, competing not only in pole-vaulting, but in numerous other events with equal skill and success—novels, stories, poems, essays, reviews, teaching, and so on. As one reviewer of *The Fred Chappell Reader* (1987) summarizes, "He is a writer rich in intentions and gifts."[3] When Chappell humorously introduces a fictional projection of himself in "Snakehandling" (1997)—his short prose contribution to the multi-authored serial book *Pete & Shirley: The Great Tar Heel Novel*—he relates, "The bleary- eyed instructor poured words—'Aristotle,' 'syllabic achronicity,' 'Cthulhu,' 'Homeric simile,' 'grandmother'—upon his bemused audience like a man slopping Pulitzer Prize-winning hogs."[4] Although Chappell's tone is comically self-mocking, his description of the fictional Chappell's random, pedagogical language points to the range of both his learning and art—Aristotle and Homeric simile (his classical education and literary applications of it), syllabic achronicity (the complexity of his aesthetic forms), Cthulhu (a name from H. P. Lovecraft, reflecting his fondness for fantasy and science fiction), and grandmother (his use of autobiographical, Appalachian materials).

Not unlike the precarious relationship between the fictional Chappell and his bewildered writing students in "Snakehandling," considering Chappell's wide-ranging fiction runs the risk of "bemusing" both the scholar and the scholar's readers. As this chapter's epigraph states, Chappell's "work displays thematic range and venturesomeness," and thus resists most ready-made, restrictive, and reductive scholarly categorizations of his work. Instead of inserting Chappell's fictional variables into a convenient theoretical formula for literary meaning, this book traces and celebrates the creative, chaotic elements—his fiction's experimentation and versatility—that make both him and his fictional output so difficult to categorize.[5]

---

[2] Norman Mailer, *Cannibals and Christians* (New York: Dial, 1966) 202.

[3] Review of *The Fred Chappell Reader*, *Tri-Quarterly* 71 (1988): 217.

[4] Fred Chappell, "Snakehandling," *Now & Then* 14/1 (Spring 1997): 31–33.

[5] Review of *The Fred Chappell Reader*, *Publishers Weekly* 231 (13 February 1987): 78.

Chappell's unique, experimental approach to writing fiction manifests itself in several respects. For example, he says of the intricate symbolic structures of his early novels:

> Well, the novels are symbolic, I suppose. But not in the ordinary way that novels are symbolic, not like a novel by Mr. Faulkner or a novel by Thomas Pynchon, for example. But more like a poem's symbolism in which the intellectual structure is outside and behind, and the narrative takes place, I hope in its own terms. And so that you can figure out the novel, if you have a little information, you can figure out symbolic structures, the other symbolic structures; but you don't need it to enjoy the book.[6]

Reluctant to allow his symbolic structures to dominate his books' literal narratives, Chappell attempts to separate them from the narrative, allowing the reader the choice of either ignoring them or applying them poetically as a means of enriching the book's meaning. Chappell's distinctive use of symbolic frameworks evokes the term "mysticism," as employed by Olaf Stapledon, the great science fiction writer of the 1930s and 1940s: "[I]t is an immediate acquaintance with the hidden essence of a 'reality' which is said to lie behind all ordinary and illusory experience."[7] Based on the relationship between everyday life and Stapledon's mystical hidden reality, Chappell's use of narrative and poetic symbolic structures echoes the interplay of the "real" and "imaginative" worlds in which we live. Chappell maintains, "I figure the symbolism and all that kind of structure can go hand in hand, because the reader has to read from sentence to sentence, and my thinking in a novel has always been to give a narrative drive to it so people will finish the damn thing."[8] Chappell's idea of "narrative drive" echoes Michael Boyd's definition of the reflexive novel: a work that "is about itself. In order to avoid tautology, it must make its *action*—not its subject or object, which duplicate each other—its theme. The reflexive novel is *about* 'bending back.'"[9] Establishing a strong, reflexive narrative tone, Chappell proceeds to

---

[6] In David Paul Ragan, "Flying by Night: An Early Interview with Fred Chappell," *North Carolina Literary Review* 7 (1998): 112.

[7] Olaf Stapledon, *An Olaf Stapledon Reader*, ed. Robert Crossley (Syracuse: Syracuse University Press, 1997) 180.

[8] Ragan, "Flying by Night," 112.

[9] Michael Boyd, *The Reflexive Novel: Fiction as Critique* (Lewisburg: Bucknell University Press, 1983) 36.

shade it with enriching, though not indispensable, symbolic and allegorical functions.

Chappell's early novels are also experimental and reflexive in terms of their characterization. He asserts, "They're novels...that believe very strongly in original sin. It seems to me to be a theme in all the books. An original sin may be figured often in the books not as original sin in the garden, but as a condition of things that exist before the character shows up."[10] Having constructed and introduced a lingering history of past events, Chappell forces them upon his protagonist, the qualities of whom—Appalachian background, scholarly predisposition, etc.—are often autobiographical. As R. T. Smith says of Chappell's technique in regard to his first three books, "[He] begins with fictionalized autobiography and works toward parable and character mosaic."[11] One of the most important elements that goes into Chappell's character mosaics is psychology. In fact, James Justus maintains that a central concern of contemporary Southern fiction centers on "the psychologically wounded seeking healing rituals to overcome familial incoherence."[12] Throwing protagonists such as James Christopher, Jan Anderson, and Peter Leland into historical circumstances beyond their control, Chappell dramatizes their anguished reactions to seemingly inevitable, debilitating events. In doing so, he practices Jung's psychological mode of artistic creation, which "deals with material drawn from the realm of human consciousness—for instance, with the lessons of life, with emotional shocks, the experience of passion and the crises of human destiny in general—all of which go to make up the conscious life of man, and his feeling life in particular."[13] Investigating his own psyche, Chappell projects aspects of the undertaking onto his protagonists, who are attempting to become themselves just as Chappell seeks to realize a defining fictional voice.

---

[10] Ragan, "Flying by Night," 118.

[11] R. T. Smith, "Proteus Loose in the Baptismal Font," in *Dream Garden: The Poetic Vision of Fred Chappell*, ed. Patrick Bizzaro (Baton Rouge: Louisiana State University Press, 1997) 38.

[12] James H. Justus, foreword, in *Southern Writers at Century's End*, ed. Jeffery J. Folks and James A. Perkins (Lexington: University Press of Kentucky, 1997) xii.

[13] Carl Jung, "Psychology and Literature," in *Modern Man in Search of a Soul* (New York: Harcourt, Brace, 1933) 155.

The reflexive, psychological quests of Chappell's protagonists often have meaningful destructive consequences. As Louise Gossett observed of Southern literature in the 1960s, the period in which Chappell produced his first novels, "Vehemence, passion, excitability turned inward may immobilize the normal capacities of the person in confusion and tension; turned against another these powers may violate and destroy both the aggressor and the victim."[14] Such inward violence often has repercussions for the overall narratives of Chappell's books, which occasionally take on qualities of the grotesque. William Van O'Connor's solid, seasoned definition of the term *grotesque* characterizes it as "merging tragedy and comedy, and seeking, seemingly in perverse ways, the sublime."[15] With the exception of *The Gaudy Place*, Chappell's early novels possess little humor, flirting with the sublime almost exclusively through the existential tragedies and traumas of their young protagonists. In his foreword to Marion Cannon's *Another Light*, Chappell summons G. K. Chesterton's morbid assertion, "A novel without any death in it is still to me a novel without any life in it," and this view is evident in Chappell's first three novels, in which visceral violence and murder, and the accompanying psychological tragedies, lay the groundwork for unusual life-changing epiphanies.[16]

In addition to experimenting with characterization, Chappell's early novels also served as testing grounds for fictional forms and techniques. For example, over the course of his first three books Chappell found the literary use of dreams to be unsuccessful:

> I used to keep a little journal of dreams. I used to try to borrow ideas and imageries, and especially transition passages from dreams, which interest me—how do you get from one place to another in a dream. But now I don't do that much anymore. I don't care much for dreams in literature, except as an obvious literary device that has nothing to do with dreams. I think it's a weakness in my early books, the use of dreams, because I think the story should tell itself with events and not with dreams."[17]

---

[14] Louise Gossett, *Violence in Recent Southern Fiction* (Durham: Duke University Press, 1968) x.

[15] William Van O'Connor, *The Grotesque: An American Genre and Other Essays* (Carbondale: Southern Illinois University Press, 1962) 3.

[16] Fred Chappell, foreword, in Marion Cannon, *Another Light* (Charlotte: Red Clay, 1974) 8.

[17] Irv Broughton, "Fred Chappell," in *The Writer's Mind*, ed. Broughton, vol. 3 (Fayetteville: University of Arkansas Press, 1990) 116.

As Ralph Ellison maintains, "Every serious novel is, beyond its immediate thematic preoccupations, a discussion of the craft, a conquest of the form, a conflict with its difficulties and a pursuit of its felicities and beauty.[18]

Having pursued the formal utilization of dreams, Chappell ultimately found the technique detrimental to his craft and sought to attain Ellison's "felicities and beauty" by moving on to other aesthetic methods.

According to Goethe, "Criticism is either destructive or constructive. The former is very easy; for one need only set up some imaginary standard, some model or other, however foolish this may be, and then boldly assert that the work of art under consideration does not measure up to that standard and therefore is of no value."[19] As he did with the literary application of dreams, Chappell frequently employs and then discards literary forms and techniques, making the establishment of what Goethe would call a "Fred Chappell fictional standard" exceedingly difficult. In fact, Chappell has no grand fictional design in the tradition of Hugh Vereker in Henry James's "The Figure in the Carpet." Instead, he is the weaver of many small designs that come together and overlap at various points. Chappell articulates his avoidance of one single set of fictional ideas in a comment on the composition process: "The artist is constrained to hold allegiance to his ideas for the length of time it takes to bring his work-in-hand to a successful conclusion. No longer. As far as the writer is concerned, the ideas in a short story or novel exist in a closed system, and as soon as that system is completed, finally enclosed, the ideas no longer have validity."[20] Taking note of the variation in Chappell's work and his belief in the philosophical autonomy of his texts, this study does not endeavor to seek out the writer's dominant aesthetic impulse, as Georges Poulet attempts in *Etudes sur le temps humain*,[21] a monolinear approach to a collection of important French writers. For if Chappell has a guiding directive for fiction it would seem to consist of the simple rule that the author and his narrator be "dispassionately engaged." He asserts: "We feel that the person who tells

---

[18] Ralph Ellison, "Society, Morality and the Novel," in *The Collected Essays of Ralph Ellison*, ed. John F. Callahan (New York: Modern Library, 1995) 695.

[19] Johann Wolfgang von Goethe, "On Criticism," in *Goethe's Literary Essays*, ed. J. E. Spingarn (New York: Ungar, 1921) 140.

[20] Fred Chappell, "Visible Allegiances," *Abatis One* (1983): 62.

[21] Georges Poulet, *Etudes sur le temps humain* (Paris: Plon, 1956).

us a story ought to have a reason for doing so, he ought to be engaged. But if he is too closely engaged, if he is caught up in the heat of the action, he cannot report carefully. His attention will be otherwise employed, and reporting will have to be of secondary concern to him. We expect a great deal from our I; he has to be dispassionate enough to be trustworthy, but passionate enough to have a stake in the action."[22] Deferring a work's ideas to the even-handed method through which they are rendered, Chappell places his dedication to the craft above the philosophical concepts he wishes a given work to convey.

Although Chappell is a versatile writer—his novels and stories containing forays into genres such as historical fiction, fantasy and horror, and academic fiction—he is often categorized or explained as a Southern or Appalachian writer. As one reviewer of *The Fred Chappell Reader* summarizes, "Chappell is a regionalist who speaks with the unmistakable authority of the native son."[23] Whereas such evaluations credit the unique perceptiveness with which Chappell dramatizes Appalachian settings and themes, they are limiting in the sense that they ignore the achievement of his numerous and important non-regional narratives. To be sure, much of Chappell's writing possesses commonalities with the work of traditional Southern writers. For example, Chappell himself asserts, "The charge that Southern literature is a backward-looking body of writing is probably a fair one"—an accurate observation in terms of his first three novels, in which the protagonists are haunted by past events beyond their control.[24] However, although Chappell is interested in the effects history can have in the present, he does not dramatize or sentimentalize the past as an end in itself. As Walker Percy maintains, "The Southern novelist can't go back now, back to the wilderness, back to the small Alabama town in *To Kill a Mockingbird*. He'd better not even look back. Because if he does, he'll turn into something worse than Lot's wife—a bad novelist."[25] Earlier in the same notable essay,

---

[22] Fred Chappell, "Powers of Observation: the Stone, the Hawk, and the Solitary I," *An Open World: Essays on Leslie Norris*, ed. Eugene England and Peter Makuck (Columbia: Camden House, 1994) 181.

[23] Review of *The Fred Chappell Reader*, *Publishers Weekly*, 78.

[24] "'Not as a Leaf': Southern Poetry and the Innovation of Tradition," *Georgia Review* 51/3 (Fall 1997): 477.

[25] Walker Percy, "Novel-writing in an Apocalyptic Time," *Signposts in a Strange Land* (New York: Farrar, Straus and Giroux, 1991) 167.

"Novel-writing in an Apocalyptic Time" (1986), Percy explains his objection to the label "Southern novelist": "What I object to is the undue attribution of a particular sort of regionalism which the expression invites—regionalism in the bad parochial sense, not the good universal sense in which the best writers are all regionalists. Even William Faulkner is generally thought of as a Southern novelist. But Hemingway and Bellow are not thought of as Northern novelists. Cervantes is not thought of as an Andalusian novelist. Cézanne is not thought of as a Provence painter."[26] Implied in Percy's important observation is the danger that a writer possessing universal themes may be pigeonholed or undervalued when, like "Ol Fred" (the affectionate, regional nickname often attributed to Chappell), he is limited by critics to a particular province or tradition.

For Chappell's own part, he does not shirk regional labels, although he realizes the detrimental connotations they potentially carry.[27] In discussing his identity as an Appalachian writer, Chappell cites the courage of Lee Smith, a Virginia novelist whose career began long after his: "She was the first person I ever met who admitted to being an Appalachian writer rather than a Southern writer, and I admired her a great deal for it."[28] As Olaf Stapledon points out, a writer's dominant national/regional allegiance is important, if for nothing other than compositional purposes: "[W]ithout daily intimate contact with some particular social tradition he cannot write anything but banal generalities."[29] Although much of Chappell's work is utterly removed from Appalachia, the region still serves as the wellspring from which flows his predispositions with regard to community and individual character. And when he does literally employ regional historical narratives, he does so in the tradition of writers such as Faulkner or Ivo Andric, dramatizing local characters and events in order to make universal claims.

---

[26] Ibid., 154.

[27] For a collection of Chappell's opinions and anecdotes regarding Appalachia, see Gene Hyde, "'The Southern Highlands as Literary Landscape': An Interview with Fred Chappell and Donald Harington," *Southern Quarterly* 40/2 (Winter 2002): 86–98.

[28] "Fred Chappell," *North Carolina People: with William Friday*, PBS, North Carolina Public Television, 1985.

[29] Stapledon, *Olaf Stapledon Reader*, 198.

In *After Southern Modernism: Fiction of the Contemporary South*, Matthew Guinn says of interpreting contemporary Southern literature: "One looks for the stock motifs of history, place, and community (as established by Louis D. Rubin and others) in new works, finding them sporadically in such contemporary writers as Fred Chappell, Wendell Berry, and Lee Smith."[30] While Guinn's general observation is accurate, I would add the caveat that in Chappell's particular case, he usually presents and explores modernist Southern motifs in decidedly unconventional ways. Yet, in citing Chappell's manipulation of traditional Southern literary tropes I am hesitant to label him a postmodernist. As Paul Maltby asserts, "Postmodernism today is a hypertrophied and unstable term that is fought over and selectively appropriated on behalf of various theoretical projects."[31] Whether or not the term is appropriated here seems largely irrelevant. More important is the general recognition of elements of experimentation in Chappell's fiction, beginning with his early novels, that reflect the intellectual spirit of the period in which they were written. In the mid-1960s, for example, Louis Althusser and Michel Foucault were trying to reconcile the most up-to-date social science research with an effort at philosophical renewal that came to be known as "structuralist." Like these independent French philosophers, Chappell was experimenting with various strands of philosophy in the hopes of hitting upon new modes of expression, writing an "innovative" brand of fiction in Michael Boardman's sense of the term: "The discovery of a form perfectly expressive of some new way of seeing the world."[32] Although his background material generally was not new, his methods of expressing it were. Nabokov writes, "Time and space, the colors of the seasons, the movements of muscles and minds, all these are for writers of genius (as far as we can guess and I trust we guess right), not traditional notions which may be borrowed from the circulating library of public truths but a series of unique surprises which master artists have learned to express in their own

---

[30] Matthew Guinn, *After Southern Modernism: Fiction of the Contemporary South* (Jackson: University Press of Mississippi, 2000) x.

[31] Paul Maltby, *Dissident Postmodernists: Barthelme, Coover, Pynchon* (Philadelphia: University of Pennsylvania Press, 1991) 4.

[32] Michael M. Boardman, *Narrative Innovation and Incoherence: Ideology in Defoe, Goldsmith, Austin, Eliot, and Hemingway* (Durham: Duke University Press, 1992) 1.

unique way."[33] Attempting to establish new forms of literary expression, Chappell reconfigured numerous familiar Southern motifs and introduced a few of his own while striving for a distinctive mode of expression.

As Chappell maintains, a work's method of utterance is important only insofar as it is faithful to its material. He articulates his theory of style at great length:

> I think the prose style of any particular piece should conform to the material or subject matter being treated. So when I come across a highly individualistic style, highly mannered style, I sometimes suspect that the writer is more interested in the sound his voice makes than in presenting what he or she is dramatizing or thinking about. So I become very suspicious sometimes of overwrought passages of prose—even Mr. Faulkner seems to me self-indulgent, here and there, in this matter. On the other hand, I understand a writer has a certain style and that he sees and feels the world in terms of this style. So that a great deal of it is not self-indulgent in the least but absolutely necessary: that's the temperament of the artist speaking and interpreting. But sometimes there's a line of distinction that might be drawn perhaps, and the more chances you take in prose style the more likely you are to cross the line and become a little ridiculous, and sometimes a little obtuse. But look at the achievements that can be made by following your own genius to that extent. So it's a trade-off, like most things in art, and I would rather be an artist like Mr. Faulkner than some sort of more measured artist. On the other hand, there's something at bottom that's a little suspicious about it. I don't know. (INT)

Leery of practicing style for style's sake, Chappell interprets and employs narrative form as an integral *part* of a work's larger apparatus. Both in the wide-ranging subject matter and structural forms he applies, Chappell reflects Donald Hall's general observation that "American literature is a literature of synthesis. For an American writer, to use the foreign is not to lose nationality, which is as difficult to lose as your fingerprints, but precisely to be American."[34] One of the results of such experimental synthesis—throwing together "foreign," unconventional subjects and traditionally disparate forms—is the creation of formal structures and

---

[33] Vladimir Nabokov, *Lectures on Literature*, ed. Fredson Bowers (New York: Harcourt Brace Jovanovich, 1980) 2.

[34] Donald Hall, "A Literature of Synthesis," *To Keep Moving: Essays 1959–1969* (Geneva NY: Hobart & William Smith, 1980) 21.

philosophical statements the writer otherwise might not have foreseen or produced. Paul Ricoeur articulates the common theory that "with written discourse, the author's intention and the meaning of the text cease to coincide...the text's career escapes the finite horizon lived by the author."[35] With his courageous and often unorthodox matching of numerous fictional styles and subjects, Chappell occasionally is able to transcend his "finite horizons," practicing what Baudelaire calls "pure art": "The creation of a suggestive magic containing both the object and the subject, the world outside the artist and the artist himself."[36] Their conflicting elements brought together by Chappell, his fictional works often go beyond his compositional formulas to produce unanticipated meanings—the unexpected fruits of his unique experiments involving versatile variables.

Discussing Chappell's novels chronologically and his short fiction thematically, the book's chapters attempt to articulate the particular types of experimentation and versatility with regard to the works in question. Howard Nemerov states, "The writer attempting for the first time a short novel must face, I should think, nothing but problems," and chapter 1 records the challenging composition of *It Is Time, Lord* before interpreting the book in terms of temporality.[37] Chappell harshly evaluates his first novel as a "terrific failure. And the reason for it is I had an enormous amount of material there, a great deal of material, which I really didn't cover."[38] Although Chappell is unduly critical of his initial book, his comment goes a long way in explaining why he returned to almost identical milieus in *The Inkling* and *Dagon*, addressing several related elements his first novel neglected or left unsolved. Like the first chapter of this book, chapters 2, 3, and 4 all consider their individual novels in terms of the themes that make them experimental, versatile, and generally unique fictional works. Part 2 of the book, chapters 5 and 6, discusses Chappell's short fiction

---

[35] Josef Bleicher, *Contemporary Hermeneutics: Hermeneutics as Method, Philosophy, and Critique* (Boston: Rutledge & Keegan Paul, 1980) 230.

[36] Charles Baudelaire, "Philosophic Art," *Baudelaire as a Literary Critic*, trans. Lois Boe Hyslop and Francis E. Hyslop, Jr. (University Park: Pennsylvania State University Press, 1964) 187.

[37] Howard Nemerov, "Composition and Fate in the Short Novel," *New and Selected Essays* (Carbondale: Southern Illinois University Press, 1985) 56.

[38] Ragan, "Flying by Night," 107.

thematically—chapter 5 considering his initiation, Appalachian, and academic narratives, and chapter 6 examining his stories involving historical and fantastic elements. Each of these chapters includes in its discussion references to and summaries of previously unpublished and unknown Chappell stories, several of which shade and even constitute important transitional events in his writing. The concluding portion of the book, part 3, serves as an appendix, containing a previously unpublished short story, "The Two Ministries," and an interview in which Chappell answers specific questions about various aspects of his fiction. Throughout the book, I make reference to Chappell's unpublished notes, manuscripts, and letters—previously uncited documents that helped me develop a much fuller perspective on Chappell's fiction, and should prove useful to scholars.

Part 1

Early Novels

Chapter 1

Temporality: *It Is Time, Lord*

> Man's misfortune lies in his being time-bound. —Jean-Paul Sartre, *Literary Essays* 79

More than one initial reviewer saw in *It Is Time, Lord* "an investigation into the nature of time and of memory."[1] Subsequent considerations of the book generally have not deigned to elaborate on the observation.[2] Yet time, literal and symbolic, pervades the novel, including its title, taken from the first line of Rilke's poem, "Herbsttag": "Herr: es ist Zeit. Der Sommer war sehr Gross."[3] In the book's first paragraph, Chappell's protagonist James Christopher records, "On the mantel above the iron stove there was a large clock" (*ITL*, 3), establishing time's obvious importance, as well as suggesting the memorable time-haunted opening passages of novels such as James Gould Cozzens's *By Love Possessed* and Chappell's own *Farewell, I'm Bound to*

---

[1] Richard Gilman, "Someone Else Is Living My Life," *New York Times Book Review* (8 September 1963): 43.

[2] For additional early reviews that address the importance of time in the novel, see "Review of *It Is Time, Lord*," *Virginia Quarterly Review* 40/1 (Winter 1964): xii; and Granville Hicks, "Thirty Years with a Stranger," *Saturday Review* (10 August 1963): 17–18. More recently, in his summary of the book, John Lang briefly addresses the thematic importance of time before interpreting *It Is Time, Lord* and Chappell's three following novels in terms of will and appetite (*Understanding Fred Chappell* [Columbia: University of South Carolina Press, 2000] 17–19).

[3] "Lord: it is time. The vast summer has passed by" (*The Selected Poetry of Rainer Maria Rilke*, trans. and ed. Stephen Mitchell [New York: Vintage, 1989] 10).

Leave You—the third Kirkman book, published thirty-three years after his first novel.[4] While the use of clocks in anointing time a theme may seem a self-evident or worn literary convention, the theme itself often turns out to be exceedingly rich and complex as a result of the many and often conflicting readings to which it gives rise. Spinoza interprets time in the way things move at different rates than other things, fixed or unfixed, and this simple distinction is applicable to fictional events themselves as well as representations and readings of those events.[5] In his study, *Structures and Time*, Cesare Segre remarks, "Time, as an irreversible order of succession, is thus the basic element of discrimination between various modes of linking events: a sort of ideal 'measuring rod.' ...An interlacement of some complexity exists among reading (or discourse) time, plot time, and fabula time."[6] Segre's "interlacement of complexity," the fruit of temporal analysis, underscores what valuable interpretive knowledge ultimately may be gained in coming to recognize the various time signatures of a text. As Virginia Woolf writes in *Orlando*, "This extraordinary discrepancy between time on the clock and time in the mind is less known than it should be and deserves fuller investigation."[7] Attempting to distinguish the book's various kinds of time and their diverse implications, this chapter investigates temporal discrepancies as the central avenue for reading Chappell's first novel.

"Time in narrative fiction can be defined as the relations of chronology between story and text," writes Shlomith Rimmon-Kenan in *Narrative Fiction*.[8] In *It Is Time, Lord* the temporality of story and text is skewed from the novel's beginning. The first forty pages of the book are from James Christopher's manuscript biography, a text no one in the novel ever reads in

---

[4] "Love conquers all—*omnia vincit amor*, said the gold scroll in a curve beneath the dial of the old French gilt clock" (James Gould Cozzens, *By Love Possessed* [New York: Harcourt, Brace and Company, 1957] 3). Chappell's *Farewell, I'm Bound to Leave You* begins with the sentence, "The wind had got into the clocks and blown the hours awry" (New York: Picador, 1996, 3).

[5] Harry Austryn Wolson, *The Philosophy of Spinoza* (New York: Meridian, 1934) 353–54.

[6] Cesare Segre, *Structures and Time: Narration, Poetry, Models* (Chicago: University of Chicago Press, 1979) 4.

[7] Virginia Woolf, *Orlando: A Biography* (New York: Harcourt, Brace and Company, 1928) 91.

[8] Shlomith Rimmon-Kenan, *Narrative Fiction: Contemporary Poetics* (New York: Metheun, 1983) 44.

its entirety. Although the manuscript has its own internal chronology and the outside reader spends time perusing it, it has no overt temporal presence in the non-manuscript, "real" time events of the book. As in R. V. Cassill's *Clem Anderson*,[9] the novel's narrative structure includes a transition from a fictional text (a book within a book) to actual or "real" fictional events, each possessing its own respective temporalities. After addressing—as a preliminary distinction—the novel's composition, its "author time," I turn to an examination of manuscript time versus "real" time, focusing on the conflicting representations of memory and James Christopher himself. This consideration, in turn, reveals that the central schism in the novel between manuscript time and "real" time is interwoven with Christopher's obsession with the duality of self as a means of escaping temporality. I conclude by addressing Christopher's ultimate inability to reconcile himself to the pressures and responsibilities of "real" time, as evinced primarily by his recurring dreams—symptoms of traumatic anxiety that underscore his lingering apprehensions.

Author Time and Composition

John Barth once attributed to Ernest Hemingway the claim that "every writer owes it to the place of his birth either to immortalize it or destroy it."[10] Nearly all of Chappell's novels take advantage of his childhood background in mountainous Canton, North Carolina, in constructing milieus and cultural conditions as the operating backgrounds for various plots, and Chappell seizes upon the idea of the writer's origin in his own way in one of his essays on Southern fiction: "The individual recognizes an obligation to transform the history, personal or local or cultural, that he or she is burdened with. That is why the characters in Southern fiction can be so loudly violent or so dreamily passive, why they keep digging at the roots of situations; they are trying to hammer the circumstances of the past into a future that transcends these circumstances."[11] Chappell's observations on

---

[9] R. V. Cassill, *Clem Anderson* (New York: Simon and Schuster, 1961).

[10] John Barth, "The Spirit of Place," *The Friday Book: Essays and Other Nonfiction* (New York: G. P. Putnam's Sons, 1984) 127.

[11] Fred Chappell, "The Good Songs Behind Us: Southern Fiction of the 1990s," *That's What I Like (About the South: And Other New Southern Stories for the Nineties)*, ed. George Garret and Paul Ruffin (Columbia: University of South Carolina Press, 1993) 1.

backward-looking Southern protagonists certainly are applicable to his own "dreamily passive" James Christopher, whom reviewer Granville Hicks characterizes as "searching his past in order to find some guidepost for his future."[12] However, Chappell's initial comment on transforming personal history is more closely directed at the writer in general, who often endeavors to generate aesthetic creation through meditations on specific intervals of personal experience. In summarizing Michel de Certeau's conception of historiography, Michael Bechler describes how the "desire to forget temporality itself is connected to representation and to the knowledge of the 'past' produced by the historiographic text."[13] This distinction, with its focus on the writer's disruptive relationship with time through text, is applicable to James Christopher and his manuscript, but perhaps also to the young Fred Chappell and his first novel. The implication is that whereas Christopher attempts to reconcile and conclude events of his childhood through writing, Chappell sought to develop and bring to fruition a specific piece of short fiction—an early literary event—that had continued to fascinate him since the time of its composition.

The germ for *It Is Time, Lord* is a two-and-a-half page short story called "January," which appears in William Blackburn's *Under Twenty-five*, a collection of fiction and poetry by writers Blackburn taught at Duke University.[14] The story's rich and various potentials for further development, including Christopher's familial relationships and an explanation of the ambiguous rape scene, led Chappell to use the piece as the catalyst for his first novel.[15] By the time the story appeared in the

---

[12] Granville Hicks, "Thirty Years with a Stranger," *Saturday Review* (10 August 1963): 18.

[13] Michael Bechler, "Speaking for Nothing: Michel de Certeau on Narrative and Historical Time," in *Signs of Change: Premodern, Modern, Postmodern*, ed. Stephen Baker (Albany: State University of New York Press, 1996) 148.

[14] Fred Chappell, "January," in *Under Twenty-five: Duke Narrative and Verse, 1945–1962*, ed. William Blackburn (Durham: Duke University Press, 1963) 191–193. The story appears intact in *It Is Time, Lord* (6.22–8.34) with only minor inconsistencies. Christopher's sister, for example, is named Sandra rather than Julia in the story.

[15] Despite the compelling nature of the event, Chappell decided not to develop the rape scene. He explains, "Well, it's intimated, more or less tenuously, in the first novel, that there's a child rape that takes place, that he's raped by those convicts. But that's never made clear. The reason it's not made clear is because, as a matter of fact,

Sewanee Review as the sixteen-page "For the Time, Being,"[16] it had grown to constitute, with minor differences, the first chapter of *It Is Time, Lord*. Chappell's first book then is based on a short fictional fragment that manifested itself in various forms before finally growing into a novel. In its development, *It Is Time, Lord* suggests Walter Benjamin's concept of "now-time," in which the shocking authentic moment of an innovative present interrupts the continuum of history and breaks away from its homogeneous flow.[17] Haunted by the authentic and innovative "January," Chappell was unable to leave the story alone or behind, invoking it and its accompanying ideas again and again in the present as he composed a novel around it.

Memory and Christopher's Manuscript versus "Real" Events

Freud says, "A strong experience in the present awakens in the creative writer a memory of an earlier experience (usually belonging to his childhood) from which there now proceeds a wish which finds its fulfillment in the creative work. The work itself exhibits elements of the recent provoking occasion as well as of the old memory."[18] Just as "January"—an early fictional event—preoccupied Chappell to the point that he reconciled it with a novel, so James Christopher seeks to bring closure to his childhood traumas through his biographical manuscript. In *The Art of Fiction*, W. Somerset Maugham puts forth the familiar assertion that often "an unhappy experience in childhood is the determining force of creative instinct," and this is applicable to Christopher in his attempts to recall and then "write away" his past.[19] Like Marcel Proust and Thomas Wolfe, Chappell and his fictional writer seek to recapture and reconcile their pasts through conscious and unconscious memory, and to demonstrate the power that recollections of the past evoke in the present. Chappell recounts, "One of the major themes in my first novel, *It Is Time, Lord*, was that the human will is as

---

at one point it was. And then I just cut it because it seemed to me that it lessened the impact of the work" (Ragan, "Flying by Night," 116).

[16] Fred Chappell, "For the Time, Being," *Sewanee Review* 71 (Spring 1963): 251–67.

[17] Walter Benjamin, "Theses on the Philosophy of History," in *Illuminations*, trans. Harry Zohn, ed. Hannah Arendt (New York: Schocken, 1969) 253–64.

[18] Sigmund Freud, *The Freud Reader*, ed. Peter Gay (New York: Norton, 1989) 442.

[19] W. Somerset Maugham, *The Art of Fiction* (New York: Arno, 1977) 310.

helpless as a foetus under the ruthless pressure of time itself. Time, especially past time, presented itself to the protagonist as an always changing, always dangerous, force. To illuminate this point, I caused him to keep a journal of his past and present life, which though he momentarily thought it true, was in reality stuffed with lies."[20] In his consideration of the novel, Shelby Stephenson maintains, "James Christopher is a poet," and in being a poet he is also a liar.[21] Perhaps the most tragic aspect of Christopher's character is the manner in which he disingenuously—though often unconsciously—attempts to fix time, both to remedy and limit it, through the writing process. According to Santayana, "Memory itself is an internal rumor; and when to this hearsay within the mind we add the falsified echoes that reach us from others, we have but a shifting and unseizable basis to build upon."[22] Shifty and poetically manipulated, Christopher's manuscript gives the reader an ideal picture of his past, the realities of which become evident only through the "real" time memories of the chapters that follow.

Chappell recalls that his decision to give the book both a traditional and manuscript narrative was purely a result of practical and stylistic considerations: "It's a novel in two distinctly different styles because of the double time-scheme. The present time-present tense is a much faster kind of story than the more deliberate past-time story. The reason for that is that when I picked it up again after that initial week of writing, I had no idea where I was going, and I couldn't get back into the original style."[23] Perhaps the most valuable result of the double narrative is the fullness it gives to Christopher's character, one narrative portraying him as he ideally would like to see himself, the other revealing him through genuine interactions with other characters and actual events. In this way the book echoes novels such as Italo Svevo's *Confessions of Zeno*,[24] in which the main narrative is written by a man named Zeno who is giving an account of his life as part of a

---

[20] Fred Chappell, "Six Propositions about Literature and History," *New Literary History* 1 (Spring 1970): 517.

[21] Shelby Stephenson, "Vision in Fred Chappell's Poetry and Fiction," *Abatis One* (1983): 33.

[22] George Santayana, *The Life of Reason* (New York: Scribner's, 1932) 40.

[23] Tersh Palmer, "Fred Chappell," *Appalachian Journal* 19/4 (Summer 1992): 404.

[24] Italo Svevo, *Confessions of Zeno*, trans. Beryl De Zoete (New York: Alfred A. Knopf, 1930).

psychological treatment. However, Zeno's account is prefaced by an amusing preemptive introduction by his doctor, whose prognosis anticipates and calls into doubt many of the claims Zeno later makes. In a similar manner, the "real" time events in *It Is Time, Lord* cast doubt upon Christopher's manuscript, which, in turn, reflects back on Christopher himself. As Henry James explains, "There is one point at which the moral sense and the artistic sense lie very near together; that is in the light of the very obvious truth that the deepest quality of a work of art will always be the quality of the mind of the producer."[25] In its fraudulence, the manuscript reveals the shortcomings and apprehensions in Christopher's mind, setting them in relief against the harsh truths of reality.

Over the course of the "real" time narrative, Christopher drives away from a traffic accident, gets drunk, commits adultery, and ignores his wife and children. Yet, he says of himself in the manuscript, "I am a very prudent person, and do not make decisions easily" (*ITL*, 27), as if he hopes to write himself into being a different person or to use his fictional self as a model for moral behavior. In the manuscript he fraudulently maintains, "I remain fascinated by my profession: I am a Methodist minister" (*ITL*, 27). Christopher's manuscript logic functions beneath the assumption that to be good is to be Methodist and to be Methodist is to be good—a distinction that aligns his fictional self with a virtuous sign and its accompanying moral associations. Attempting to further engage the reader's sympathies, Christopher couples his moral signposts with literal portrayals of himself as a victim. For example, he describes himself at great length as physically diminutive, effeminate, and fragile (*ITL*, 26), and remarks more than once on his abuses at the hands of Hurl—a small, young, morose boy. Of course, in the "real" time narrative it becomes apparent that Christopher is as much a hard selfish hustler as a victim. For example, he snakes Preach's love interest, Judy, and then leaves town when her violent husband, Jack Davis, fresh out of prison, learns of Judy's philandering. Whether or not Christopher consciously comprehends his actions, they have real effects: namely, Preach's death at the hands of Judy's jealous husband.

Christopher never fully acknowledges his actions and responsibilities because he is trying to live an ideal and unrealistic life, reminiscent of the

---

[25] Henry James, "The Art of Fiction," in *The House of Fiction*, ed. Leon Edel (Westport: Greenwood, 1973) 44.

one in Evelyn Waugh's humorous essay, "A Young Novelist's Heaven": "One makes a lot of new friends in Heaven; all encumbering relationships such as marriage and parenthood are instantly broken at death. Love affairs are frequent, terminable at will and mutually satisfactory."[26] Like the protagonists in Isak Dinesen's "The Old Chevalier" and Guy Owen's earnest first novel, *Season of Fear*, which takes place in a rural community during the 1930s, Christopher is confronted with a conflict between moral principle and personal inclination.[27] He flees from the turmoil, and a major component of the reason for his flight is his inexperience with adversity, stemming from his largely edenic and ideal childhood. Like the young protagonists in Chappell's Kirkman novels and much of the work of James Still and Welsh writer Leslie Norris, Christopher is the shielded beneficiary of a strong traditional value system functioning in a country milieu. The land is open and pastoral, by turns benign and stern; reflecting also the strong familial value and support systems of the people who work it, exuding both love and discipline. In an essay on the farming family, Wendell Berry holds that "by elaborating household chores and obligations, we hope to strengthen the bonds of interest, loyalty, affection, and cooperation that keep families together."[28] With its partial focus on farm life and the accompanying development of a family or individual, *It Is Time, Lord* fits into a certain genre of literature, traditionally attributed to Appalachian writers, that stretches back to Elizabeth Madox Roberts's *The Time of Man* and beyond.[29]

---

[26] Evelyn Waugh, "A Young Novelist's Heaven," in *The Essays, Articles and Reviews of Evelyn Waugh*, ed. Donat Gallagher (Boston: Little Brown, 1984) 66.

[27] Isak Dinesen, "The Old Chevalier," in *Seven Gothic Tales* (New York: H. Smith and R. Haas, 1934); Guy Owen, *Season of Fear* (New York: Random House, 1960).

[28] Wendell Berry, "Family Work," *The Gift of Good Land: Further Essays Cultural and Agricultural* (San Francisco: North Point, 1981) 155.

[29] Elizabeth Madox Roberts, *The Time of Man* (New York: Viking, 1926). Other notable examples of this kind of writing appear in William Hoffman's *The Dark Mountains* (Garden City: Doubleday, 1963), which follows the fortunes of the coal-mining MacLauglin family; Sylvia Wilkinson's *Cale* (Boston: Houghton Mifflin, 1970), tracing the Lemirt family from its early beginnings in North Carolina to its place in the modern South; Robert Morgan's long short story "The Mountains Won't Remember Us" (*The Mountains Won't Remember Us* [Atlanta: Peachtree, 1992] 177–250), which portrays an Appalachian mountain family from World War II to the 1990s; Jim Wayne Miller's *Newfound* (New York: Orchard, 1989), a bildungsroman involving a Tennessee mountain boy; Wil Hickson's *A Bitter Thirst* (Chapel Hill:

Christopher's family shelters and nurtures him through childhood, and he is never plagued or scarred by poverty or the prejudices of class or race. However, one negative result of his snug and bucolic upbringing is that he is never made to be responsible. As in Chappell's poem "The Farm," Christopher's mind wanders idly while his grandfather tranquilly "snorts / and nods and the chessboard idles while whiskey / nudges his elbow."[30] Entirely alien to Christopher would be the corresponding Appalachian childhood of Brad in Robert Morgan's "The Sal Raeburn Gap,"[31] who is dispatched on an unsavory errand to fetch his debauched grandfather from the clutches of the local whore. As an adult Christopher embraces inebriation and adultery on his own, because even with a strong family background and loving wife he feels he is lacking in genuine experience—the love and security he has always enjoyed are not enough. He struggles at length with John Mill's concept of utilitarianism, which "holds that actions are right in proportion as they tend to promote happiness, wrong as they tend to produce the reverse of happiness. By happiness is intended pleasure, and the absence of pain; by unhappiness, pain, and the privation of pleasure."[32] Christopher, though, as a result of his irresponsibility and naive selfishness, confuses the connection between happiness and pleasure, believing that massive amounts of the latter necessarily lead to the former. Like Alice in Donald Barthelme's story of the same name, Christopher's lover Judy promises pure pleasure, yet their relationship constitutes anything but happiness: "It doesn't feel like a sin; it feels like punishment" (*ITL*, 99).[33] Predictably, Christopher's utilitarian experiment in sex and unabashed drunkenness fails, and he flounders home accompanied by a phantasm of guilt instead of the fulfillment he sought.

In an effort to flee reality Christopher attempts to displace his guilt and time itself in his biographical manuscript, a process of escape foreshadowed and confirmed in the epic poem he writes as a boy, "The Ironbird." He

---

O'Possum, 1998), the first volume of a six-part mountain epic involving the Carlton and Haney families; and various novels by Lee Smith.

[30] Fred Chappell, *The World Between the Eyes* (Baton Rouge: Louisiana State University Press, 1971) 20.

[31] Robert Morgan, "The Sal Raeburn Gap," in *The Mountains Won't Remember Us* (Atlanta: Peachtree, 1992) 39–52.

[32] John Mill, *Utilitarianism* (New York: New American Library, 1974) 257.

[33] Donald Barthelme, "Alice," in *Unspeakable Practices, Unnatural Acts* (New York: Farrar, Straus and Giroux, 1968) 115–23.

initially recounts the poem after Hurl gives him yet another beating, using the manuscript to work through his feelings of frustration and impotence. He writes that the great mechanical avian protagonist of the poem "could see into the far past and the far future, prophesying in unintelligible language" (*ITL*, 71). Even as a boy then, Christopher appeals to his writing as an illusory means of altering and gaining control of his "real" life. However, his approach becomes problematic when he begins to invest nearly all of his thought and energy into his fictional world. He says, for instance, "The only way I could measure time then was by the weight of my epic poem" (*ITL*, 149). In fact, his ardent involvement with his escapist narratives retards his development in dealing with reality. He remarks, outside of the manuscript, in "real" time, "It seems to me that I am younger than everyone I know. I don't know why I think about this older-younger idea" (*ITL*, 42). After Christopher burns the house down his father tellingly comments, "I'm going to believe that you don't understand the feeling of having a real past that you can remember and remember hearing about" (*ITL*, 77). Withdrawn into the dynamics of his fictional world, Christopher is unable to comprehend sufficiently the complexity and importance of the real. Outside of the manuscript, just before his grandfather's death, he recalls, "Back then it was a time when everything was yet to happen. For although everything did happen, was already happening in my sight, I did not realize it" (*ITL*, 93). Distracted by his constructed fictional world, he fails to interpret fully the significant events—such as his grandfather's passing—of the real, the pain and negativity of which threaten to push him progressively further from reality.

Christopher's Duality of Self and Intertextuality

Christopher says, "The truth is that I want to fight back at my past life" (*ITL*, 95). The implications of this statement form the center of his split between the real and fictional narratives in which he participates. Christopher realizes he partially gave up on the "real" narrative as a boy: "I succumbed in an instant, although there is now no way of locating this instant lost in the interminable row of little boxes which enclose all instants" (*ITL*, 115). He ponders, "To begin again, and to go straight forward and never to surrender: isn't this the purpose of the self?" (*ITL*, 115), yet his past actions leave his half-hearted resolution in doubt. In his insightful essay on

Chappell's early novels, R. H. W. Dillard evokes Gemini and the twins in observing, "James Christopher is more than one man," an allusion to the split worlds in which he functions. Gemini also becomes symbolically important when Christopher claims those born beneath the sign are fond of "acting and oratory" (*ITL*, 3).[34] Near the end of *Truth and Method*, Hans-Georg Gadamer asserts, "Language is the single word whose virtuality opens up the infinity of discourse, of discourse with others, and of the freedom of 'speaking oneself' and of allowing 'oneself to be spoken.'"[35] In his manuscript, Christopher attempts to construct a different self through language—his own "self-building" attempt by means of transcribed "acting and oratory." Central to his dilemma is the desire, reminiscent of Sinclair's in Hermann Hesse's *Demian*, to be someone else and, in the process, to escape time—an empty wishful condition Stephen Spender labels the "Nostalgic Fallacy."[36]

One way in which Christopher deflects attention from his own situation and hints at potential alternate selves is through the multiple and wide-ranging intertextual sources to which he frequently refers. One early reviewer laments, "There is a great deal of symbolism clotting up the works," while another observes "a torrent of allusions that often seems purposeless."[37] However, Christopher's literary and artistic references do, in fact, have a significant function. In addition to directing attention away from himself, each intertextual allusion contains dynamics that fall into a specific category for negotiating personal adversity. Models for self-analysis and personal improvement, the three most crucial intertextual types fit beneath the designations of escaping, conquering, and analyzing/solving problems through art.

The escape sources, with their focus on men forsaking civilization for the wilds of the unknown, suggest the traditional "runaway males" of American novelists such as James Fenimore Cooper, Jack London, and Hemingway. Significantly, it is Christopher's sister Julia who introduces the

---

[34] R. H. W. Dillard, "Letters From a Distant Lover: The Novels of Fred Chappell," in *Hollins Critic* 10/2 (April 1973): 6.

[35] Hans-Georg Gadamer, *Truth and Method* (New York: Seabury, 1975) 498.

[36] Hermann Hesse, *Demian* (Berlin: S. Fischer Verlag, 1925); Stephen Spender, *The Struggle of the Modern* (Berkeley: University of California Press, 1963) 20.

[37] John Hall, review of *It Is Time, Lord*, in *Books and Bookmen* 10/11 (1965): 36; Larry Vonalt, "Five Novels," *Sewanee Review* 73/2 (April–June 1965): 333–39.

first escape text in the novel, picking up his copy of H. G. Wells's *The First Men in the Moon*. Julia comes to Christopher in the hope of reconciling him with his wife and reminding him of his responsibilities (*ITL*, 37–39), but the Wells novel, in which an inventor builds a super spaceship similar to that of Joe Robert Kirkman in Chappell's *Look Back All the Green Valley*, foreshadows both the failure of her visit and Christopher's impending flight from home into the arms of debauchery. Later in the novel, Christopher recalls reading Dillon Wallace's *Ungava Bob* right before his father approaches him about learning Latin: "Holding the book [*Ungava Bob*] spread in his left hand, he suddenly popped it shut. 'This is a good time for you to start learning Latin,' he said" (*ITL*, 80).[38] Wallace's book, an escapist action narrative centered on trapping and exploring in Alaska, offers the elder Christopher cause for concern, especially given his son's already dangerous penchant for ignoring reality. Hoping to replace Christopher's interest in reading such books with a desire for "useful" academic knowledge, he resolves to instruct him in the dead classical tongue.

Both of Christopher's escape books comment directly on separate "real" time events in the novel. The same is true of some of the texts containing conquering protagonists, each reinforcing Christopher's desire to take control of his life. For example, he begins reading Wells's *The Island of Doctor Moreau* immediately after cursing his manuscript's inability to motivate or help him: "I pull at random a sheet from the typed manuscript. *Take yourself up*, it says. *My sermon*...'Shit.' I jerk a novel out of the jumble. Here is *The Island of Dr. Moreau*" (*ITL*, 66). Realizing he lacks the efficacy to "take himself up," he draws out the Wells novel as an alternative model for achieving agency in his life. Just as Moreau monstrously attempts to control natural selection and evolution in order to mold the world to his liking, James endeavors to manipulate his past through writing. However, both fail and it is significant, in his moment of frustration, that Christopher selects a sympathetic narrative that, like his manuscript, aims at control only to be ultimately foiled.

While Christopher is cleaning his room and deciding what books to throw out, Sylvia asks him if H. G. Wells is a literary figure compared to the writers in Christopher's pulp fiction collection. He replies, "You've got me. A book is a book" (*ITL*, 113). Christopher's comment is most likely tongue-

[38] Dillon Wallace, *Ungava Bob* (New York: Grosset and Dunlap, 1907).

in-cheek, for his references show him to be exceedingly well-read, yet he alludes to a great many pulp books over the course of the novel, and at least two of them speak to his desire for control. During her visit, Julia notices an open copy of *Doc Savage* that Christopher is in the process of reading (*ITL*, 39). The protagonist of Kenneth Robeson's series, Doc Savage, is a virtuous, brilliant, and physically powerful hero who time after time succeeds in conquering his antagonists while, in the obligatory superhero tradition, translating his visceral triumphs into reductive moral sermons. In issues such as *The Thousand-Headed Man*, Savage seizes treasure from villains and bestows it upon victims and civic-minded organizations—a physical and intellectual *ubermensch* adhering to Christian morality and influencing the world accordingly.[39] Just before she notices the volume of *Doc Savage*, Julia picks up another symbolic control text, *The Blue Atom*, a futuristic science fiction novella that centers on the reawakening of a "Great Race" whose emperor, Jared, threatens to enslave earthlings.[40] As the book's cover reads, "Who controls it [the Blue Atom device], controls all," and Chappell places the text in Christopher's room to further buttress his character's symbolic desire to achieve command of his life.

Although *Doc Savage* and *The Blue Atom* constitute important narratives of order and control, they are both fantastic and unrealistic to the degree that Christopher cannot ultimately apply their formulas to himself and his immediate surroundings. While he reads these books for wishful inspiration, he must look elsewhere for sources that come closer to the essence of his situation, sources that generally fall under the categories of literature and art. When, for example, he mentions Stendhal's *The Red and the Black*, he symbolically likens his own situation to that of Stendhal, who, beginning with that novel, attempted to understand and solve in fiction the problems he had found insoluble in life.[41] Christopher's taste in visual art ("Three pictures on three walls: Matisse, Klee, Max Ernst" [*ITL*, 104]) also speaks to his aesthetic leanings and ambitions in the novel. Matisse's group was called *les fauves* because of the extremes of emotionalism in which they seemed to have indulged, their use of vivid colors, and their distortion of shapes. The first and last aesthetic traits of Matisse's circle, acute emotionalism and

---

[39] Kenneth Robeson, *The Thousand-Headed Man* (New York: Bantam, 1964).

[40] Robert Moore Williams, *The Blue Atom* (New York: Ace, 1958).

[41] Stendhal, *The Red and the Black: A Chronicle of the Nineteenth Century*, trans. E. P. Robbins (New York: Richmond, 1898).

distortion, apply respectively to Christopher's sensitive emotional states as well as his attempt at obfuscating the past in his writing. In small-scale paintings, drawings, and watercolors, containing as many if not more intertextual references than Christopher's manuscript, Klee incorporated allusions to dreams, music, and poetry with a complex language of symbols and signs of arrows, letters, words, commas, and musical signs in a form of writing. However, the artist most useful to Christopher from the trio is probably Max Ernst, who, with frottage drawings and decalcomania, used nontraditional methods to make a work of art—frottage with scraping and decalcomania a transfer process. Both techniques serve as versions of automatism or automatic writing in which the images are not planned but discovered through the process. The desired results of Ernst's method, authentic discovered images, suggest Christopher's manuscript in its attempt to ascertain and articulate his life's meaning through a creative retelling.

A specific subcategory that functions beneath the distinction of intertextual aesthetic self-analysis involves a sequence of Wells novels and their running commentary on the book's narrative. In addition to Wells's *The First Men in the Moon* and *The Island of Dr. Moreau*, Christopher alludes to three other Wells novels in articulating his mental outlook at given intervals. Near the novel's beginning, he quotes the first sentence of *The War of the Worlds* after making the comment, "This was the summer which was in winter" (*ITL*, 13). Christopher refers to the novel because its title articulates his developing ability to reshape the world as he likes, resulting in a conflict between the world as it is and the world as he has constructed it. He also reads *The War of the Worlds* after his grandfather's death (*ITL*, 96), as if he is trying to comfort himself with the belief that in his constructed world the death has not really occurred. Later, he tries to console himself along temporal and historical lines when he brings to bed a copy of *The Time Machine* and a textbook containing the writings of Tacitus. Whereas the title of *The Time Machine* alone represents an obvious desire to go back and remedy events of the past, the Tacitus book is significant for its pronouncements on history and morality. Writing to his granddaughter, Thomas Jefferson asserts, "His [Tacitus's] book is a compound of history and morality of which we have no other example."[42] Tacitus proclaims, "I consider it the chief function of history to ensure that virtue be remembered, and to terrify evil words and deeds with a fear of posterity's damnation."[43] Tacitus's condemnatory historical perspective has obvious ramifications for Christopher, who has performed questionable actions and wishes to write them away. The last Wells novel, *When the Sleeper Wakes*, suggests the possibility of an approaching epiphany for Christopher and a shift to responsibility. He selects the book from his shelf of Wells novels before making the long trip to visit his parents (*ITL*, 153), which leads the reader to anticipate that a tangible transition in Christopher's character is on the horizon.

Before Christopher can effect any lasting change in himself, he must first solve the problem of his fragmented selfhood, which is inextricably bound to temporality. Existentialists generally define time as "the measure of the flow of consciousness."[44] Christopher drunkenly whispers to Preach, "For a long time now, someone else has been living my life. Or living in my life, inside. It's clear to me that I have been completely usurped" (*ITL*, 50). In making the distinction "for a long time now," Christopher hopes to defer responsibility for his previous actions to another while escaping into a different life—displacing his consciousness. Borges says, "Denying temporal succession, denying the self, denying the astronomical universe, are apparent desperations and secret consolations."[45] Craving a "secret consolation," Christopher desperately denies both the authority of time and his authentic self; yet in doing so he can never (a temporal distinction) truly be who he is. Hegel maintains, "Time is the externally envisaged pure self not as yet apprehended by that self. In so far as the latter apprehends itself, it supersedes the form of time, understands what it envisages, and becomes intuition understanding and understood. Time therefore appears as the

---

[42] Thomas Jefferson, *The Writings of Thomas Jefferson*, ed. Andrew Lipscomb. (Washington, D.C.: Thomas Jefferson Memorial Association of the United States, 1905) 255..

[43] Cornelius Tacitus, *The Annals of Tacitus*, book 3 (New York: Cambridge University Press, 1996) 65.

[44] Wesley Barnes, *The Philosophy of Existentialism* (Woodbury [New York]: Barron's, 1968) 223.

[45] Jorge Luis Borges, "A New Refutation of Time," in *Labyrinths: Selected Stories and Other Writings* (New York: New Directions, 1962) 233.

doom and the necessity of the Spirit that is not yet perfected in itself."[46] Only by achieving self-consciousness through a temporal process can self-conscious Spirit come to be, a process Christopher remains wholly unable or unwilling to undergo.

Dreams, Death, and Failure

During Christopher's visit with his father, the older man says, "I've just about stopped reading, and only just now I've started hoping that I've stopped in time" (*ITL*, 158). The relationship of Christopher and his father, like that of Paul and his father in Olaf Stapledon's *Last Men in London*, has long been strained and tumultuous. Yet the elder Christopher's comments to his son are both sincere and perceptive. Comprehending Christopher's dual lives, he suggests that his son banish or subordinate his debilitating imaginative existence as a means of both negotiating time and stabilizing the self. However, Christopher either ignores his father's advice or fails in attempting to carry it out. Near the novel's "real" time conclusion, just before the dream sequence, he reads again in *The War of the Worlds* and speaks to Judy about Preach's death on the phone, twice asserting, "It's not my fault" (*ITL*, 170), as if he is trying to convince himself.

Although he has given up on his manuscript, at the book's conclusion Christopher is not far from where he was at its beginning, and his "*deus ex machina* conclusion" via recurring dreams remains unconvincing. As Chappell holds, "Now, there's the final ruination of that novel—the attempt to bring it to a conclusion by means of dreams."[47] Christopher's dreams are interesting in the way they mix and cross-reference people and events from different times and symbolically reassert his fears, providing the reader a window into his unconscious mind through his psychological associations. However, they remain dissatisfying because they are unable to articulate a pronounced change in Christopher's conscious self. In fact, psychologically, the recurring dreams tend to suggest that Christopher more than ever is a slave to his past, his guilt, and his imaginary life. According to psychologist Lenore Terr, "The traumatized dreamer may be granted a month's rest or even a year's respite. But sooner or later the post-traumatic dream will come

[46] Georg Hegel, *The Phenomenology of Mind* (New York: Macmillan, 1910) 612–13.

[47] Ragan, "Flying by Night," 117.

back. Traumatic anxiety apparently does not spontaneously dissipate during one's lifetime. Once this anxiety has been set into motion, it may recur with new life stresses, especially those that carry echoes of the old helplessness and loss."[48] Rather than overcoming or reconciling himself to his anxieties, Christopher merely locks them in dream, a twilight realm from which they will continue to haunt him.

Meditating on time in his manuscript, Christopher writes, "To wish a past instant returned is to wish for death. The past is an eternally current danger, in effect, a suicide" (*ITL*, 34). Living in the past and haunted by its dreams, Christopher has no avenue for meaningfully moving forward or existing. His friend Preach at one point confesses that he "wishes he was back again in high school" (*ITL*, 40) for the purpose of screwing girls. Preach's literal desire for temporal return is accompanied later, and not without irony, by his literal death. Lost in the vast complexities of the past, Christopher suffers a mental or psychological death—he himself calls it a "suicide"—of which his dreams constitute an important symptom. His plaintive cries to Julia on the book's last two pages, "You won't leave me, will you?" (*ITL*, 182–83), reflect his ongoing desperate fear of reality. Attempting to console himself, he maintains that "event will cover itself over again with my mind like an old man pulling the blankets about himself in a winter night" (*ITL*, 182). Shrouding reality in the blanketed fraudulence of his fictional interpretations and unconsciously reducing its complexities into dream, Christopher lives in perpetual fear of the life he is living, has lived, and the one that lies ahead of him; and pervading his fear and misfortune, presiding over it all, hovers the inevitable and ubiquitous specter of time.

---

[48] Lenore Terr, *Too Scared to Cry: Psychic Trauma in Childhood* (New York: Basic, 1990) 214.

Chapter 2

Will, Appetite, Alchemy, Faulkner, and Two French Poets: *The Inkling*

Just love me, protect me and trust me. I am very weak, and very much in need of kindness. —Letter from Verlaine to Rimbaud, in Rimbaud, *Complete Works*, 170

What I mostly ripped off from Rimbaud was the notion of fire,/As symbolic of tortured, transcendent-striving will. —Chappell, "Burning the Frankenstein Monster: Elegiac Letter to Richard Dillard," in *Bloodfire*, 31

Although Chappell's second book, *The Inkling*, is a more challenging and complex novel than his first, it is cut from the same aesthetic stone in several fundamental ways. At one point in *It Is Time, Lord*, Christopher confesses, "But now I keep two bloody red apes chained to myself. Named Will and Appetite, these beasts tear and bite me. When my heart is at last eaten away, they will quarrel and fight over my bones" (*ITL*, 103). As we shall see, will and appetite constitute the dominant, though buried, conflict that fuels Chappell's second novel. In an unpublished autobiographical essay, Chappell comments at length on the development of his second book while tracing its roots to his first:

> My larger ambitions for the novel were the same as for the first: to produce a daring and even experimental novel which would not look or feel experimental, and to keep a story going with such force that a reader would

be led on from first paragraph to last whether he actually liked the book or not.

The Inkling was another, and almost the last, work that came to me as a whole, almost as a vision. In my mind's eye, I could see the book in print, a perfect novella, and even the words on the pages. Short and savage and serious, a book that took no prisoners.[1]

Beyond Chappell's similar ambitions for his first two books—constructing gripping narratives accompanied by disguised experimental techniques—the novels have many of the same literal characteristics. Both narratives, for example, contain settings in rural western North Carolina, involve dysfunctional families, include central violent acts, and follow confused and tortured male protagonists. One practical reason for the close surface similarities is that Chappell simply did not have time between the books to research and devise new background materials. Having published his first novel in 1963, written a mammoth concordance of the poems of Samuel Johnson for his Duke M.A. in 1964, and accepted his first teaching position at the University of North Carolina-Greensboro the same year, Chappell admits he had little space in which to prepare his second book: "With *The Inkling* I was under real pressure to get it done in a hurry. It was my last summer before I came to teach at UNC-G, my last summer of graduate work. I had no other choice but to write it in six weeks."[2] In terms of its composition then, as well as its literary form, the novel is decidedly "short and savage and serious."

Whereas *The Inkling* possesses many literal and surface similarities with Chappell's first book, it remains very much its own novel, especially in terms of the deep, hidden symbolic structure it contains. In 1985 (before he had written the Kirkman sequence), Chappell fondly labeled it his preferred work of extended fiction: "I tend to favor my second novel, *The Inkling*, because it's kind of neatly done and because the intentions are hidden; it's kind of a secret novel in a way, one nobody ever bothered or should bother to figure out."[3] Ignoring Chappell's counsel, this chapter attempts to make some headway in "bothering" to figure it out, investigating the book's

---

[1] "Fred Chappell," box WM-1, writings by Chappell, miscellaneous subseries, 16–17.

[2] Tersh Palmer, "Fred Chappell," *Appalachian Journal* 19/4 (Summer 1992): 404.

[3] Ian McDowell, "Fred Chappell," *Coraddi* (Winter 1985): 34.

hidden symbolic intentions and various levels of meaning. I begin by identifying the novel's central obscured historical allegory, its relation to the lives and work of the French poets Rimbaud and Verlaine. Ignorance of this oblique allegorical distinction led to the host of misreadings that greeted the book when it initially was published, and I go on to consider several of the misguided reviews that conveniently dismiss the novel as a reductive Faulkner imitation and a Southern cliché. I then turn to the book's central symbolic tension, its meditation on the forces of will and appetite, discussing the multiple ways in which it shapes the novel's literal and metaphysical agenda. Finally, I consider the book's identical beginning and conclusion, its foiled symbolic union via alchemy, disclosing its implications for the philosophical concerns of the novel.

Allegorical Shadows: Rimbaud and Verlaine

Few readers and none of the book's initial reviewers recognize *The Inkling* as a heavily disguised historical allegory. Chappell recalls, "*The Inkling* was very experimental because it was my first attempt at doing the kind of Thomas Mann kind of thing, using historical characters as prototypes for fictional characters."[4] Although Chappell has published numerous short stories involving diverse historical figures, *The Inkling* was his first attempt at historical fiction, which partially explains why the historical narrative remains buried to the point of nearly going unremarked. As Chappell notes, there were specific reasons for why he did not flesh out the historical dimension of the book: "I lit upon the very famous figures of Rimbaud and Verlaine, but I didn't know anything about France of that period, though I know the work of those poets fairly well. I felt defeated. I could not have made a historical novel out of them. So I decided to put it in an allegorical setting, a fairy-tale setting in the mountains of western North Carolina and choose a family to act out the drama" (INT). Lacking both the necessary historical knowledge of nineteenth-century France and the time to master it, Chappell set the story in a familiar milieu while symbolically infusing the characteristics of Rimbaud and Verlaine into the characters of Jan and Timmie Anderson, respectively. Like their intellectual countrymen Sartre and Merleau-Ponty, Rimbaud and Verlaine were by turns passionate friends

[4] David Paul Ragan, "Flying by Night: An Early Interview with Fred Chappell," *North Carolina Literary Review* 7 (1998): 109.

and bitter enemies, and this powerful conflict between two brilliant personalities fuels *The Inkling*'s central tension as seen through Jan and Timmie's unusual sibling relationship. Furthermore, at the core of the poets' tempestuous personalities Chappell identified two powerful archetypal forces: will and appetite. He explains: "Rimbaud always seemed to me a figure of pure will—just sheer willpower transforming the world in so far as possible to its own ends, absolutely shaping the world as perhaps, say, modern science does, to that degree. And the other side of the coin is a kind of languid passiveness, a kind of television-watching attitude, perhaps, but more than that, that is extremely—well, it's appetite in the sense, taking whatever comes—and to its own end."[5] Like the characters in Gladys Swan's *Of Memory and Desire*, who are haunted and consumed by the disparate terms in the book's title, Jan and Timmie, via Rimbaud and Verlaine, play out the conflict between will and appetite.[6] Propelled by hidden historical and philosophical agendas, the characters and the book amount to much more than they initially appear to be.

Although the novel contains a rich buried symbolic structure, it is often obscured to the point that readers cannot identify it without Chappell's help. He says, for example, "A great deal of the material in those weird internal monologues are my wild translation of Rimbaud and Verlaine," yet this is difficult to perceive without reading passages of the book alongside Rimbaud's and Verlaine's poetry.[7] In other words, on one level, the book is not altogether fair to the general reader, since a more than rudimentary knowledge of Rimbaud and Verlaine is required in order to recognize its allegorical richness. On the other hand, Chappell expects the book's literal narrative to be powerful enough to satisfy readers without any allegorical knowledge. He recounts, "For *The Inkling* I talked a fair amount to my French translator Maurice-Edgar Coindreau about French symbolist poets and the symbolist movement in France, because I needed that background for that novel, which you wouldn't think, because it takes place in a little town in the mountains of North Carolina."[8] Expecting that most readers

---

[5] Ibid., 110.

[6] Gladys Swan, *Of Memory and Desire* (Baton Rouge: Louisiana State University Press, 1987).

[7] Ragan, "Flying by Night," 110.

[8] Carmine Palumbo, "Folklore and Literature: The Poetry and Fiction of Fred Chappell" (diss., University of Southwestern Louisiana, 1997) 194.

"wouldn't think" the book had anything to do with French symbolists, Chappell seems comfortable in having camouflaged the novel's symbolism to the extent that he did. Yet, ignorance of the book's obscure central allegory generally led to unsatisfying and even frustrating reading experiences among early reviewers. Blind to the novel's secret agenda, reviewer Ervin Gaines comments, "Chappell lacks the talent to infuse his plot with the insights to elevate it to art."[9] Of course, the irony in Gaines's reading is that he fails to detect the artistic allegory Chappell renders in the book. Another early reviewer also condemned the novel on the basis of its overly simplistic artlessness: "How predictable [Chappell's] book's development is once the setting and characters have been grasped."[10] Basing their readings purely on the book's readily available literal narrative, reviewers generally found the novel unsatisfying and incomplete, even though the aesthetic thing they believed it lacked was ironically hidden inside it, lurking in the shadows just beyond their perceptions.

"A Tumor of Misunderstandings": Early Reviews and "Faulknerism"

Surface readings that found the novel artless and predictable generally proceeded to catalogue its Southern clichés, usually tracing them to the work of William Faulkner. Orville Prescott suggests, ironically it seems now, that imitative writers like Cormac McCarthy and Chappell are induced to "slavishly copy Faulkner's literary mannerisms."[11] Clearly, with their considerable output and originality, McCarthy and Chappell have forged significant literary legacies of their own; however, in 1965—as young and relatively unknown Southern writers dealing with violence and the grotesque—unfair comparisons to Faulkner perhaps were inevitable. Part of the reason for this condition is that what constituted "Faulkner" was almost indistinguishable from what comprised "Southern literature" in the 1960s and, to a lesser extent, in the ensuing decades. Kenneth Lamott does not bother summoning Faulkner's name, listing instead some of his themes, in

---

[9] Ervin J. Gaines, "Review of *The Inkling*," *Library Journal* 90/14 (August 1965): 3308.

[10] Review of *The Inkling*, *Times Literary Supplement* (10 November 1966): 1028.

[11] Orville Prescott, "Brilliant, but Unsatisfying," *New York Times* (11 August 1965): 33.

confessing, "I cannot promise to keep the peace if I am exposed to another bright young Southern writer who is hooked on incest, barnyard sadism, imbecility and domestic bloodletting."[12] Chappell recalls, "When the comparisons to Faulkner came along I was surprised. I partly discounted them because a Southerner can't write a book without some reviewer saying, 'Well, Faulkner is present here.' And that's simply because Faulkner is such a famous and pervasive writer" (INT). Faulkner's "pervasiveness" is obvious in the sense that he seized upon and skillfully explored conventions of Southern culture—historical tropes, race relations, class conflict, the feeble-minded family member—in an unprecedented penetrating and comprehensive manner. When other writers chose to investigate these themes for their own purposes, reviewers naturally associated them with and compared them to the groundbreaking master.

To be sure, "Faulknerisms" do pop up in *The Inkling*, though certainly more subtly than the emblazoned "Faulkner shirt" worn by Harry Crews's memorable protagonist in *Karate Is a Thing of the Spirit*.[13] However, what separates Chappell's book from imitation or literary redundancy is his use of traditional Faulknerian themes—such as Southern familial strife, madness, and violence—for his own innovative purposes. As Octavio Paz maintains, "To learn to speak is to learn to translate; when the child asks his mother the meaning of this word or that, he is really asking her to translate the unknown term into his language."[14] Whereas Chappell addresses several of Faulkner's motifs, he translates rather than mimics them, shaping and shading them to his own intellectual ends. Although Chappell may not have been completely, as Fred Hobson says of the Southern writer, "out of the shadow of Faulkner," he certainly was not eclipsed by it.[15] Reynolds Price, another North Carolina writer whose work on occasion reductively has been labeled "Faulknerian," remarks that the use of the word "influence" is "an unmistakable symptom of a tumor of misunderstandings of the narrative

---

[12] Kenneth Lamott, "Deja Vu, Ya'll," *Book Week* (15 August 1965): 10.

[13] Harry Crews, *Karate Is a Thing of the Spirit*(New York: Morrow, 1971).

[14] Octavio Paz, "Literature and Literalness," *Convergences: Essays on Art and Literature*, trans. Helen Lane (New York: Harcourt Brace Jovanovich, 1987) 184.

[15] Fred Hobson, *The Southern Writer in the Postmodern World* (Athens: University of Georgia Press, 1991) 9.

imagination, the purposes and strategies of an individual novelist."[16] Just as early reviewers neglected to detect the allegorical dimension of *The Inkling*, so they also failed to appreciate Chappell's use of conventions traditionally associated with Faulkner for his own singular philosophical designs. When Chappell remarks, "I hadn't thought the least bit about Faulkner when I was writing that story" (INT), he underscores his total and exclusive involvement in his book's fictional universe during its composition. Largely oblivious to the novel's complex philosophical and allegorical vastness, the reductive comparative readings of early reviewers constitute an unfortunate "tumor of misunderstandings."

Appetite

Instead of thinking about Faulkner, Chappell was pondering the archetypal significance of will and appetite as expressed through the relationship of Rimbaud and Verlaine and, by translation, Jan and Timmie. The theme of appetite in the novel begs initial consideration since it is more primal and fundamental. After all, without overwhelming irrational desire there is little need for a governing will. Appetite or desire (I will use the terms interchangeably) calls to mind a host of varying definitions and references, many of which have little to do with Chappell's interest in the term. Chappell's particular understanding of desire for the purposes of the book resembles Wittgenstein's use of the word in his definition of intentionality: the fixation of the mind towards an object that may or may not exist.[17] In the novel, Timmie is fixated on Jan and the various hallucinatory elements she believes he represents. As eventually becomes evident, Timmie's very obsession with Jan comes to threaten Jan's existence. However, in the beginning we only know that Timmie, weak-minded and fearful, compulsively looks to Jan for security and reassurance. At one point in the novel, Timmie is described as being "completely without responsibility" (*INK*, 119). Although this distinction becomes dark and foreboding when Timmie's post-puberty madness turns violent, early in the book it merely underscores her imperative need for Jan's care, while allegorically echoing Verlaine's obsessive desire for Rimbaud: "Just love me, protect me and trust

[16] Reynolds Price, "The Thing Itself," in *A Common Room: Essays 1954–1987* (New York: Atheneum, 1987) 9.

[17] Ludwig Wittgenstein, *The Blue and Brown Books* (Oxford: Blackwell, 1958) 22.

me. I am very weak, and very much in need of kindness."[18] In fact, Timmie's worship of Jan mirrors that of the speaker in Verlaine's "J'allais par des chemins perfides…": "Your dear hands led me, guided me. / Over the far horizon, night / Glowed with the pallid hope of dawn. / Your eyes' glance was my morning light."[19] The eventual result of Timmie's overwhelming dependence on Jan and his peculiar gaze is that it evolves to the point where nothing he gives her can constitute enough: "Unthinkingly, she wanted more and more of the comfort that was in Jan, more of his sureness" (*INK*, 28). Like Verlaine, who shot Rimbaud when their relationship went sour and Rimbaud threatened to leave him, Timmie becomes dangerous once she exhausts the comfort Jan provides.

When Jan is away from Timmie, she is easily afflicted by deep dread and dark woes. The calming effect of Jan's will gives out and her mind races, her thoughts and imagination in limbo. Timmie's hallucinatory reveries—which Hal McDonald interprets as a kind of "metaphysical magic realism"—though occasionally nonsensical, often comment on her relationship with Jan.[20] When, for instance, her mind fancies strange birds, they possess "Jan's kind eyes instead of the mean glassy bird eyes. They did not really fly, but floated about like balloons, and they were not really real birds because in some way they were responsive to her desires, her fears" (*INK*, 53). Like Jan, the birds comfort her with the gentleness of their gaze and responsiveness to her needs. In Rimbaud's court testimony he relates, "There was no sense in [Verlaine's] thoughts," and this is true of Timmie in the sense that her thoughts are largely irrational and impressionistic.[21] However, her helplessness and retardation serve only to boost her importance in the novel. Like Fyodor Dostoyevsky's *The Idiot* and Faulkner's *The Sound and the Fury*, *The Inkling* is remarkable in the way it reflects the whimsical consciousness of an interesting imbecile who in many ways holds the key to the book. Like Prince Myshkin, Timmie simultaneously possesses both a penetrating childlike intuition and the

---

[18] Arthur Rimbaud, *Complete Works*, trans. Paul Schmidt (New York: Harper & Row, 1976) 170.

[19] Paul Verlaine, *One Hundred and One Poems* (Chicago: University of Chicago Press, 1999) 73.

[20] Hal McDonald, "Fred Chappell as Magic Realist," *North Carolina Literary Review* 7 (1998) 128.

[21] Rimbaud, *Complete Works*, 184.

pitiable stupidity of a simpleton. For example, despite her cognitive shortcomings, she repeatedly reads Jan's thoughts and possesses an inexplicable way of knowing when she is about to be locked in her room, utilizing this knowledge with destructive consequences near the novel's conclusion.

Timmie's rather harmless visions as a child develop into a dangerous psychosis as she passes through puberty, which triggers and is triggered by her evolving desire for Jan. As Sartre maintains, "Even the feeblest desire is already overwhelming. One cannot hold it at a distance...."[22] When sexual desire is added to her already arduous need for Jan, her precarious pleasure principle is devastated and her psyche cannot cope. Yet Timmie's madness is necessary to the book, since it frees Chappell to explore her consciousness without restriction. On a small scale, Chappell's intention is akin to that of Shoshana Felman in her study *Writing and Madness (Literature/philosophy/Psychoanalysis)*: "To examine in what way literature and madness are informed by each other, in the process of informing us each about the other."[23] Consisting of impressionistic poetry, free association, and carnal symbolism, Timmie's deranged reveries provide an alternative point of view through which to interpret events and ideas in the novel.

Timmie's madness becomes acute with puberty, her changing body informing the alterations in the hue of her dreams. From a purely physical standpoint she resembles one of Verlaine's fecund peasant maidens—fleshy, immense, and full of passion. Yet her sexuality is inextricably bound with her hallucinatory fantasies, as seen both through her festive, lustful episodes with Jannie the giraffe and her masturbatory dream about living with Jan in a cave in the woods (*INK*, 51–53). The imagery of Timmie's orgiastic fantasies is also allegorical in the way it resembles the sensual poems "Printemps" and "Été" from Verlaine's *Parallèlement*. However, her visions ultimately function as subtle foreshadowing for Jan's destruction. After Timmie goes through puberty, Jan becomes a lost and manipulated figure in her dreams, and her conscious response to his presence turns malevolent: "She smiled: it was like that; whenever Jan was sad she smiled, and when his face was happy hers became mournful. He planned to keep every emotion

[22] Jean-Paul Sartre, *The Philosophy of Jean-Paul Sartre*, ed. Robert Denoon Cumming (New York: Vintage, 1965) 214.

[23] Shoshana Felman, *Writing and Madness (Literature/philosophy/Psychoanalysis)*, trans. Felman and Martha Noel Evans (Ithaca: Cornell University Press, 1985) 16.

away from his features" (*INK*, 83). She begins to toy with Jan; yet, out of love and habit, he still attempts to comfort her, making himself vulnerable. Timmie's new relationship with Jan comes to resemble that of the speaker in Rimbaud's "Lines": "Let me penetrate all of your memories… / Let me be *that woman* who can bind you hand and foot… / I will strangle you."[24] Having been the object of Timmie's desire for so long, Jan continues in his attempts to comfort her, even though her appetite for him has shifted permanently from love to destruction.

Will

Tragically confronted with a retarded sister, problematic family, and lonely and unhappy childhood, Jan hones his will in an effort to negotiate and master the difficult and unpleasant world that surrounds him. Schopenhauer believed Kant had identified the transcendental self with the will, conceiving it to be the true substance behind appearances, and Jan attempts to transcend his surroundings by utilizing his will power.[25] He stares at objects as if endeavoring to see through their surface images and force their true natures to reveal themselves to him—the penetrating power of his gaze linked symbolically to his will. Like the figure in Verlaine's "Pierrot," Jan's "eyes are two deep holes of phosphorus," burning with the intention of defining and mastering all they behold.[26] As Chappell says of *The Inkling* in his poem "Burning the Frankenstein Monster: Elegiac Letter to Richard Dillard," "What I mostly ripped off from Rimbaud was the notion of fire, / As symbolic of tortured, transcendent-striving will."[27] Fueled by Rimbaud's blazing aesthetic, the incendiary element of Jan's character is revealed through his will and gaze, as well as his explosive act at the novel's violent conclusion.

Like fire itself, Jan's will remains largely elemental and solipsistic, and he never reconciles it with human conventions like social law, as Hegel

[24] Rimbaud, *Complete Works*, 221.

[25] Roger Scruton, *Kant* (Oxford: Oxford University Press, 1982) 93.

[26] Verlaine, *One Hundred and One Poems*, 123.

[27] Fred Chappell, *Bloodfire* (Baton Rouge: Louisiana State University Press, 1978) 31.

proposes in *Philosophy of Right*.[28] He also makes the mistake of attempting to utterly divorce will and desire; Hegel, for example, believed that the Rational Will cannot be accomplished without personal interest and passion.[29] The lack of morality, feeling, and direction in Jan's will constitutes the seeds of its inevitable unraveling. Wittgenstein regards the will as the potential "bearer" of both "good and evil,"[30] and, with his obsessive reductive focus on inhuman will, Jan withers within himself all human hope and becomes a prisoner of his own dark reason. He attempts to construct a will-driven intellectual system by which to negotiate the complexities of a violent evil world but in the process becomes an agent of evil and violence himself. As Thomas Mann says of the willful and world-shaping Nietzsche, "The mind was compelled to violate its own nature, to become the mouthpiece and advocate of blatant brute force, of the callous conscience, of Evil itself."[31] Speaking of Jan in "Burning the Frankenstein Monster: Elegiac Letter to Richard Dillard," Chappell asserts, "It is Henry, as everyone knows, who's really the monster, / Not the innocent wistful crazy quilt of dead flesh."[32] In seeking to do battle with a monstrous reality, Jan becomes monstrous, destroying Buddha the cat (*INK*, 15–16), frightening the principal's secretary, terrorizing a classmate, and killing Uncle Hake. Having adopted and shaped his will for the purpose of protecting Timmie and himself, his binding resolve becomes synonymous with death and destruction, eventually even for himself.

Jan develops and exercises his will through his materialistic manipulation of physical objects. When he steals Uncle Hake's bullets he aligns himself with Rimbaud's young protagonist in "The Boy Who Picked the Bullets Up." Like the boy in the poem, Jan forsakes childhood objects for those possessing the power to shape reality and life: "[His] toys are all

---

[28] Judith N. Shklar, *Freedom and Independence: A Study of the Political Ideas of Hegel's Phenomenology of Mind* (New York: Cambridge University Press, 1976) 174–79.

[29] J.N. Findlay, *The Philosophy of Hegel* (New York: Collier, 1958) 309.

[30] Wittgenstein, *Blue and Brown Books* (Oxford: Blackwell, 1958) 21, 24.

[31] Thomas Mann, "Nietzsche's Philosophy in the Light of Recent History," in *Last Essays*, trans. Richard and Clara Winston and Tania and James Stern (New York: Knopf, 1959) 142.

[32] Chappell, *Bloodfire*, 31.

forgotten, now he only dreams / Of things that are forbidden."[33] Jan's focus on material objects also aligns him allegorically with the Gaelic ancestors of whom Rimbaud speaks in *A Season in Hell.* At the beginning of the novel, long before he steals the bullets, Jan's interest in using objects as agents of will is obvious: "[H]e had designed something important to build with the Tinkertoys" (*INK*, 10). As he gets older, he begins constructing curious simple mechanisms, baffling Mrs. Boggs, the good-natured housekeeper: "She would come upon him laboring over some contraption—he was always making strange little devices of some kind" (*INK*, 57). Serving as literal projections of his will, Jan clings to his objects and mechanisms even as his will begins to fail: "He kept all kinds of things...anything that might be conceivably be useful at any time.... The solidity of the wood was almost gratifying; it indicated that the world of things, of everything, wasn't so tenuous as he was now continually perceiving it" (*INK*, 104–105). As he progressively loses his grip on the world around him, Jan turns to his familiar objects in a misguided effort to center and reestablish his existence.

William James delineates free will through his insistence that consciousness is an agency that selects and fights for ends.[34] The aim and end of Jan's will is to protect Timmie, a fact he comprehends early in the book with the vague intuitive knowing of a child: "He realized at that moment that he would have to look out for Timmie, to take care of her. Though she was larger and taller than he, and a year older, he was much stronger in a way that seemed to be important" (*INK*, 19). Jan protects Timmie by creating a world she can understand and be comfortable in, while simultaneously infusing it with elements of his will. For example, Jan gives a fanciful account involving a balloon and a straw man when he tells Timmie how the Indians willed the sun into being (*INK*, 48–49). He mixes childish images with Rimbaud's fiery will in constructing his own explanation of nature for Timmie. Like Rimbaud, Jan poetically reinvents the world as if summoning his will from a logic beyond all imagining. When his will begins to be compromised, Jan loses his ability to define the world for Timmie and himself, becoming vulnerable both to his own developing desires and those of the people around him.

---

[33] Rimbaud, *Complete Works*, 129. As with the boy in the poem, in Jan's "blood flows the memory of an exiled / Father," his father having died at Pearl Harbor.

[34] Gerald E. Meyers, *William James: His Life and Thought* (New Haven: Yale University Press, 1986) 164.

Will and Appetite

Jan rejects Aristotle's view that will is determined in part by its relation to desire or appetite. He attempts to keep the terms separate, even when they begin to overlap and fuse as he passes through puberty. He wants to believe, like Spinoza, that will is identical to intellect, that it makes claims about things in regard to good or evil and truth or falsehood; while desire, on the other hand, merely advances an inclination.[35] Yet his faith in will's triumph is a kind of desire in itself, and it is interesting to watch how Chappell slowly and subtly confuses Jan's perceptions. Like the artistic protagonist, Goldmund, in Hermann Hesse's *Narziss und Goldmund*, Jan never suspects or admits that his will may go stupid, even as he unknowingly surrenders more and more completely to the hegemony of the senses.[36] He knows his will is not functioning properly but remains uncertain of the reason: "And his will, that mechanism he had fashioned so intently and so finely to see with seemed now to be blocking the clear sight of another better perceptive faculty within him that he knew nothing of" (*INK*, 105). Jan's concrete world of things and objects begins to give way to a dim sphere of desire, the shadows of which obscure its complexities and implications.

In *The Phenomenology of Mind*, Hegel defines Desire (*Begierde*) as the attitude that seeks to make external things conform to our requirements.[37] Whereas appetite constitutes a confusing and disruptive force for Jan, Timmie masterfully utilizes it to manipulate the world around her, especially through her relationship with Jan. For instance, their docile mother, Jenny Anderson, notices that Timmie is involved "in too violent a symbiosis with Jan's will" (*INK*, 75), but is powerless to do anything about it. Jan too is both unwilling and unable to disrupt the potent bond between his carefully crafted will and Timmie's overpowering desire. As Simone de Beauvoir maintains, "Man is free; but he finds his law in his very freedom."[38] Having developed his will as a purposeful instrument of personal strength and liberation, Jan watches as it becomes, in the end, an ironic doctrinal implement for his own self-styled bondage through its interaction with

---

[35] Harry Austryn Wolson, *The Philosophy of Spinoza* (New York: Meridian, 1934) 164–65.

[36] Hermann Hesse, *Narziss und Goldmund* (Berlin: S. Fischer, 1931).

[37] Georg Hegel, *The Phenomenology of Mind* (New York: Macmillan, 1910) 141.

[38] Simone de Beauvoir, *The Ethics of Ambiguity* (New Jersey: Citadel, 1948) 156.

Timmie. Rimbaud wrote to Verlaine, "I'm the only one you can be free with," and this tragically becomes the case for Jan and Timmie, each needing the other in order to be themselves.[39] When his mother mentions sending Timmie to an institution, Jan genuinely is shocked and frightened as if he cannot conceive of an existence without Timmie (*INK*, 79). Like the figures in Verlaine's "En sourdine," Jan and Timmie tragically "blend their souls as one," though their union can bring no happiness.[40]

Jan stubbornly worships Timmie whatever fate may bring, which proves to be his undoing. As her madness grows and deepens, Timmie begins to consider Jan, like the damsel in Verlaine's "Colombine," with "cat-eyes" and "callous looks."[41] Mirroring the dark evolving relationship of Verlaine and Rimbaud, Jan's and Timmie's bond becomes progressively manipulative and violent. Yet Jan still cares for Timmie in spite of her cruel air of evil, which puts him in jeopardy. When her insanity worsens, one of the first things she does is stick a safety pin deep into Jan's hand (*INK*, 82). Yet the intensity of his vigilance and concern only increases. Like the speaker in Verlaine's "Tu fus souvent cruelle...," Jan remains devoted despite the abuses he suffers, and his obsessive and self-destructive care ominously suggest the narrator in Verlaine's "Tu crois au marc de café...," "You are all I live for now."[42]

Although she clearly wishes to injure him, the physical danger Timmie represents to Jan pales in comparison to the psychological trauma to which she submits him. When Timmie goes mad Jan begins to lose his facility for planning: "He tried to plan, but nothing sensible would come clear in his head" (*INK*, 83). In terms of power and perception Jan and Timmie trade places: "He was intensely troubled. Why was it that he didn't understand anymore? The tighter his will got, the more easily she was able to evade its grasp. The closer his surveillance of her became, the more he felt, though obscurely, that she was watching back" (*INK*, 85). Having zealously cultivated his will-driven worldview, Jan becomes lost and unsure when Timmie turns it against him. He realizes that his will has reached a point where it is "blocking his own view" (*INK*, 106), but lacks utterly any alternative method for interpreting reality. In her madness, Timmie

[39] Rimbaud, *Complete Works*, 178.
[40] Verlaine, *One Hundred and One Poems*, 61.
[41] Ibid., 55.
[42] Ibid., 209.

understands that Jan is "willing himself out of being" (*INK*, 116), while Jan can only marvel at the dissipation of a thing he thought immutable.

Although she constitutes the central force of his undoing, Timmie is not alone in unraveling Jan's will. Despite her feeble, wraith-like presence throughout the book, Jan's mother has a stabilizing effect on him. When she dies, his confusion becomes amplified: "It was as if his mother's death had opened, not closed, a door, a portal entering maze upon maze of blind queasy corridors he could not escape. Every extrapersonal object seemed flimsy, gelatinous. He moved hesitantly and slowly, as if the air itself weighed too much, a breathable water. In his mind things were in pieces" (*INK*, 129). Coupled with Timmie's psychological manipulations, the death of Jan's mother helps render his once rock-hard, definite perceptions flabby, uncertain, and fragmented, making him easy prey for Uncle Hake's scheming and seductive young wife, Lora Bowen. Taking advantage of Jan's faltering relationship with Timmie and his mother's destabilizing death, Lora functions as the final variable that pushes Jan into madness. Succumbing to his physical desire for her, Jan becomes Lora's perverse plaything: "Now she had him, he couldn't stir without her allowing. He was like an empty eggshell that she kept rolling gently to and fro under her instep. Everything at last—his whole being—had betrayed him into her hands" (*INK*, 141). Lora ignites Jan with mad desire, accompanied by an intense omnipresent migraine, which consumes his brain and from which he never recovers. Chappell comments, "Now the characterization of Lora [*sic*] is drawn after a sonnet by Rimbaud called 'La Maline'.... [O]ne recognizes...in that sonnet, a little bit of Poe's 'Imp of the Perverse,'...which became your erotic id later on."[43] Destroying the last vestiges of Jan's will and even the rational capacities of his mind, Lora functions as a symbol of the conquering id. The result, however, turns destructive in ways Lora cannot predict: "All this unlooked for desire had kept working at, had sapped, Jan's vigilance, which had come to feel to him unnecessary and, at last, onerous. He had forgot to lock Timmie's door after a session with her and Peter Rabbit" (*INK*, 144). Having helplessly traded vigilance for dalliance, Jan neglects his duties and Timmie, like Rochester's mad wife in *Jane Eyre*, bursts in and attacks him—a foreboding episode that triggers the novel's final bloody sequence of events.

---

[43] Ragan, "Flying by Night," 111.

Alchemy and the Failed Union

One finishes reading *The Inkling* with a vague sense that something just beyond Jan's reach has failed to come into his grasp. Instead of achieving a balance between will and appetite, he recklessly shifts from one extreme to the other—a traumatic, overwhelming transition that destroys him. Chappell comments tellingly and at great length on the book's conclusion, relating it to alchemic symbolism:

> The yellow color, of course, in *The Inkling* is related directly to the other allegorical strand. The novel is finally about the marriage that doesn't come off, of sulphur and quicksilver, the great thing that would produce a philosopher's stone, cause time to stand still. So that Jan is identified with a sulphur color, with yellow. As Timmy is supposed to be identified with a kind of dead whiteness throughout the book....
>
> Well that wedding there, which doesn't happen, doesn't truly take place, is supposed to be the golden wedding of the alchemist, which transmutes the philosopher's stone, which transmutes elements, but also another thing, causes time to stand still and the New Jerusalem to take place on earth. But because of various circumstances the book is a perversion of time standing still. In fact time doesn't stand still; it kinda turns backwards and sideways. It's disrupted at the end of *The Inkling* rather than coming together.[44]

Alchemy, then, provides a small symbolic substructure through which to interpret events in the novel. Yet it also relates to the book's allegorical use of Rimbaud and Verlaine—alchemy appears, for example, in the "Second Delirium" section of *A Season in Hell*. Jan is delirious and everything is yellow—his hair, the whiskey, the field, the sun—at the book's beginning, which also serves as its end. As the speaker explains in Chappell's poem, "The Autumn Bleat of the Weathervane Trombone," "[Y]ellow is the color of time," and this is true in *The Inkling*'s opening and closing scenes, in which the murderous, insane elder Jan believes that he encounters himself and Timmie as children through a miraculous temporal warp.[45]

As Chappell says of the book's conclusion, time is "disrupted" rather than reconciled, the potential union between Jan/Rimbaud/will/sulphur and Timmie/Verlaine/appetite/quicksilver having failed to take place. Correspondingly, Chappell writes at the conclusion of his poem "The Rose

---

[44] Ibid., 112.

[45] Fred Chappell, *Wind Mountain* (Baton Rouge: LSU, 1979) 16.

and Afterward": "And then there was no knowledge of what the world / Had ever been besides the thing it was, / Whatever that might be: the history of desire / Had found its red fulfillment, the longing / That made us animal at last had made us human."[46] Such an epiphanic reconciliation—the use of desire as a humanizing and world-defining force—is precisely what does not occur in *The Inkling*. Instead, having cultivated his will to a perverse extent, Jan is overwhelmed by its opposite, ushering in his destruction. At one point in the book, Timmie accurately perceives Jan as "willing himself out of being" (*INK*, 116). Heidegger interprets the will's attempted destruction of existence as a kind of vengeance: "the revulsion within the will itself...constituting the essential nature of revenge."[47] In using his will destructively, Jan destroys it or causes it to betray itself. He becomes a victim of unfettered depraved desire, and near the book's conclusion he desires only death. He repeatedly asks Timmie and his younger self, "What if you was to die?" (*INK*, 152–53), for at the very end the elder Jan is already dead, staggering down the road like "a man who had been hanged" (*INK*, 153). Yet he laughs as he weaves and totters since the thing he has missed out on and the thing he has become are too painful to acknowledge. As Verlaine writes in "Quatrain," "With neither joy nor penitence / In these lethargic times, the one / And only laugh that still makes sense / Comes from a grinning skeleton."[48] Stripped of both reason and desire, Jan constitutes a drained husk of a human, the perverse laughter of which heralds death and emptiness across a warped void of time and space.

---

[46] Fred Chappell, "The Rose and Afterward," *Southern Humanities Review* 28/1 (Winter 1994): 66.

[47] Martin Heidegger, *What Is Called Thinking?*, trans. J. Glenn Gray (New York: Harper & Row, 1968) 92 f.

[48] Verlaine, *One Hundred and One Poems*, 267.

Chapter 3

Appropriations of History, Gothicism, and Cthulhu: *Dagon*

The Nile flows north. A train runs north / From Roanoke to Chicago. The snow / Is like cold satin. There is a gibbous moon. / North to Chicago, towards Minnesota. / Where the Mississippi oozes from a frozen bank / And wanders south, to Wisconsin / Where August Derleth prints the books / Of Lovecraft, dreamer of The Book of Thoth, / The Necronomicon, *lost work of Abdul Alhazred, / Lovecraft who wrote of Nug and Dagon, / Old gods, Nÿogtha and Cthulhu, / And east of this train, south of Virginia, / In western North Carolina, Fred Chappell / Has written a novel,* Dagon, *and all these things / Come together, turn together, and will pass on / To come again. The Nile flows sluggish / And is thick with mud. It bears the news.* —R. H. W. Dillard, "News of the Nile," in *News of the Nile*, 27

That is not dead which can eternal lie, And with strange aeons even death may die. —Abdul Alhazred, *The Necronomicon*

At first glance, Fred Chappell's third book, *Dagon*, possesses a number of striking similarities with his first two novels. Once again, the reader is confronted with a rural western North Carolina milieu, an unhappy inward-looking male protagonist, an element of domestic unrest, and symbolic acts of violence. However, these seemingly significant commonalities ultimately melt away as the reader sinks progressively deeper into *Dagon*'s unique and even bizarre combination of history, horror, and wide-ranging intertextuality. With its myriad sources, multiple levels of meaning, and an aesthetic technique utilizing various conventions of intertextuality, gothicism, horror, Southern grotesque, and postmodernism, *Dagon* constitutes Chappell's most versatile novel, as well as his most ambitiously experimental.

Chappell's dark third book is singular in a number of disparately important respects, and I begin with an account of its composition—an anguished three-year process that stands out against the succinct development of his first two books, each written in less than two months. Using *Dagon*'s composition as a visceral foundation, I move into a discussion of the book's preliminary sources, those texts that fueled its initial conception. Turning to the novel's specific internal dynamics, I proceed to consider the relationship between its gender-conscious construction of character and its gothic qualities, demonstrating how each informs the other. I then examine the book's innovative appropriation of authentic and fictional historical sources: its unorthodox use of ancient theology, American Puritanism, and the constructed mythology of H. P. Lovecraft. Chappell's use of historical sources in the novel is not altogether serious, and I consider the parodic elements of his appropriations before illustrating how his satirical portrayal of Puritan history informs his serious observations on debilitating American materialism. Finally, I demonstrate how the book's transcendent resolution reiterates its gothic and fantastic qualities, arriving at a conclusion suggesting Randall Jarrell's critical estimation of Ivan Turgenev's *A Lear of the Steppes*—that *Dagon* is "one of the best and most unusual short novels that I know."[1]

"Great Agonies" and "Puzzlement": *Dagon*'s Composition and Early Reviews

More than thirty years after *Dagon*'s publication, Chappell appeared uneasy and slightly reluctant when asked about his third book, the composition of which he paints in unpleasant terms: "I recall sweating out that novel over here on Spring Garden Street and having great agonies with it" (INT).[2] In an autobiographical essay he elaborates, "*Dagon*, my third novel and the

---

[1] Randall Jarrell, "Six Russian Short Novels," in *The Third Book of Criticism* (New York: Farrar, Straus & Giroux, 1969) 248.

[2] "I wrote *Dagon* in a ratty student apartment on Spring Garden St. 2 blocks from campus" (letter to the author, 30 March 2002).

shortest of my books of fiction, gave me trouble from which I never quite recovered. Though I was willing to harrow readers with my books, I never expected one of my books to harrow me."[3] In addition to its psychologically trying subject matter, *Dagon* "harried" Chappell in terms of its largely irreconcilable themes and labyrinthine concepts, upon which he spent massive amounts of time and energy trying to resolve. He recalls, "Well, I put a lot into it. I put a lot of horrible feelings—all my fears and doubts and pride—into that novel. And I tried real hard. Of the novels I've written, I had the most ambition for that one. It was a difficult failure...but then I was trying for difficult things."[4] Chappell's struggles with the book are obvious in a number of respects. A fluid and prodigious writer who produces essays, reviews, poems, and stories with little revision and at a consistently rapid rate, he toiled over *Dagon* for three arduous years. By contrast, as a result of economic and publication pressures, Chappell had written both *It Is Time, Lord* and *The Inkling* in remarkable six-week intervals. Yet *Dagon* constantly evaded and exhausted him, driving him to bouts of heavy drinking and numerous fruitless efforts: "When I worked on it, I worked on it furiously. But then I kept throwing away large sections, great patches of it, so that it was a case of writing ten pages and throwing away 40."[5] After multiple drafts and months of turmoil, having reached a point where he felt he could go no further or achieve anything better, Chappell settled on a manuscript and arrived at the conclusion, "I'd given it my best shot and failed."[6] His editor at Harcourt, Brace, & World, Hiram Hadyn, had reservations about publishing *Dagon* and insisted on extensive changes. Yet, having nothing left to offer the book, Chappell simply put the rejected manuscript away for a year before sending it back to Hadyn unchanged—it was accepted.[7]

When Chappell labels *Dagon* a "failure," he points to his professed inability to carry out and reconcile the book's complex themes. He maintains, "I think it's the best of the novels, in that it's the most

---

[3] "Fred Chappell," box WM-1, writings by Chappell, miscellaneous subseries, 21.

[4] S. A. Stirnemann, "Fred Chappell: Poet with 'Ah! Bright Wings,'" *Poetry Review* (Winter 1990): 45.

[5] Tersh Palmer, "Fred Chappell," *Appalachian Journal* 19/4 (Summer 1992): 404.

[6] "Remarks on *Dagon* for Lovecraft Conference," box WF-1, writings by Chappell, fiction subseries, 5.

[7] "Fred Chappell," box WM-1, writings by Chappell, miscellaneous subseries, 23–24.

adventurous and most courageous. I think it's the worst in terms of execution. It simply just does not work."[8] Like some of the poems of Stefan George, the book possesses a kind of mesmerizing and suffocating aura that resists organization and is difficult to measure in terms of technical proficiency. As was the case with *The Inkling*, Chappell's intricate themes, obscured and buried beneath a dense, tenebrous narrative, confused and frustrated early reviewers. He recounts, "*Dagon* received puzzled, irritated, and even furious reviews and sold, I would guess, 4000 copies."[9] Confronted with another challenging and enigmatic Chappell novel, reviewers—as they had done with *The Inkling*—characterized *Dagon* in terms of its most superficial characteristics, hoping to arrive at convenient and conventional estimations of its literary value. Peter Buitenhuis, for example, made the oblique comment, "The style of the novel is of a very high order. Its precise, dry elegance contrasts piquantly with its sleazy material."[10] Another early reviewer, Allen Cohen, was just as opaque in describing Peter Leland's actions during the second half of the novel: "For the rest of the book he indulges in alcohol, and in sexual, physical, and mental degradation with the help of a farm girl."[11] Reducing Mina Morgan's dark, perverse, archetypal character to a simple "farm girl" underscores the half-hearted and superficial analysis with which the book initially was greeted. Furthermore, as with Chappell's first two novels, those readers who succeeded in noting *Dagon*'s considerable symbolic depth generally were confused and put off by it. As one reviewer complains, "Symbolism is scattered throughout with almost too heavy a hand."[12] Confronted with a text that conceded few ready meanings, puzzled early reviewers criticized its baffling depth and most literal qualities, readily dismissing the book without having successfully delved into it.

---

[8] David Paul Ragan, "Flying by Night: An Early Interview with Fred Chappell," *North Carolina Literary Review* 7 (1998): 110.

[9] "Remarks on *Dagon* for Lovecraft Conference," box WF-1, writings by Chappell, fiction subseries, 3.

[10] Peter Buitenhuis, "Desire Under the Magnolias: Review of *Dagon*," *New York Times Book Review* (29 September 1968): 58.

[11] Allen Cohen, Review of *Dagon*, *Library Journal* 93/17 (1 October 1968): 3576.

[12] Review of *Dagon*, *Virginia Quarterly Review* 45/1 (Winter 1969): viii.

Preliminary Literary Sources

The underlying themes of Chappell's third book that so evaded and confused early reviewers are revealed initially through the sources that supplied them, which are numerous and wide-ranging, making *Dagon* Chappell's most thoroughly researched and ambitious novel. He says of his intentions for the book: "I had erected too many ambitions for the story to fulfill: it was to be a thesis about American fecklessness and wastefulness; it was to be an exposé of a hidden American religion; it was to tell the Biblical story of Samson in modern terms; it was to employ the artificial mythology of the H. P. Lovecraft circle of writers, the Cthulhu mythos, in a sarcastic pop-art fashion...."[13] Disparate and even contradictory, Chappell's attempted reconciliations of *Dagon*'s general themes frustrated him, resulting in the book's arduous and prolonged composition process. However, Chappell had specific literary texts in mind while he labored on *Dagon*, which he hoped would serve as models for working out his numerous philosophical concerns. He relates:

> I had ambitions for it I could not bring off. I had hoped that it might be thought of somewhere along the level of Thomas Mann's *Death in Venice*. That's kind of what I had in mind. I had lots of things, models and such, which were very literary in mind, but if I wanted people to think of it, wanted them to react to it, I wanted *Death in Venice* to be the one, except much more believable and shocking. Now you can find it in stores as a horror novel—which is what it is—with covers that my mother would *not* like. I love them, though.[14]

Death in Venice anticipates *Dagon* in the way that the aesthete Aschenbach becomes a slave to pagan passions through his fascination with the sensual young boy, Tadzio. Aschenbach becomes irrationally attached to the boy, to the point that he does not leave Venice even when a deadly Asiatic cholera strikes the city. Similarly, the bookish Peter Leland remains inextricably bound to young Mina Morgan, even as his perverse dedication threatens to destroy him.

Chappell notes that his appropriation of *Death in Venice* did not keep the novel off the shelves of bookstores' horror sections. In fact, in addition

---

[13] "Fantasia: On the Theme of Theme and Fantasy," *Studies in Short Fiction* 27/2 (Spring 1990): 181–82.

[14] Stirnemann, "Fred Chappell," 45–46.

to his confessed use of Lovecraft, Chappell seems to have drawn on his extensive fantasy reading in assembling various aspects of *Dagon*. For example, Leland's investigation of his grandparents' cryptic letters in the big "dark secretary" (*DAG*, 9) suggests identical episodes from George MacDonald's novels *Lilith* and *Phantastes*. MacDonald was one of Chappell's favorite writers in a fantastic genre he labels "visionary fiction," and he cites *Lilith* and *Phantastes* as two of the best exemplars of this tradition.[15] A former Scottish clergyman, MacDonald often worked interesting theological concepts into his somewhat didactic plots, just as Chappell effectively uses Leland's theological scholarship and sermons to address some of his book's philosophical concerns.

Chappell also drew on his own western North Carolina background in establishing some of the novel's more literal characteristics. For example, he admits, "The house from *Dagon* is a variation on my grandfolks' house. The house I grew up in for the latter part of my adolescence. This is also the house of *I Am One of You Forever*."[16] As in May Swenson's poem "My Farm"[17] and various narratives by Lee Smith, Chappell compares the physical aspects of a farm to various aesthetic and symbolic components in his work, the literal geography of the Leland land projecting psychological and artistic qualities. Early in the book, the narrator remarks, "The big ugly house sat almost in the center of the wide farm, the four hundred acres shaped vaguely like an open hand" (*DAG*, 16). Resembling "an open hand" and surrounded by large hills, the physical nature of the farm symbolically suggests Leland's diminutive insignificance and imminent confinement. As Leland progressively succumbs to his family's gloomy past, the farm's fingers slowly close in on him.

In his summary of *Dagon*, John Lang likens the Leland house to that in Hawthorne's *The House of the Seven Gables*.[18] Although Chappell does not specifically mention Hawthorne's third novel, he readily admits to its author's influence on *Dagon*: "There is always Hawthorne in my work; after

---

[15] Fred Chappell, "Visionary Fiction," *Chronicles* 11/5 (May 1987): 19.

[16] Carmine Palumbo, "Folklore and Literature: The Poetry and Fiction of Fred Chappell" (diss., University of Southwestern Louisiana, 1997) 195.

[17] *Nature* (New York: Houghton Mifflin, 1994) 140–41.

[18] John Lang, *Understanding Fred Chappell* (Columbia: University of South Carolina Press, 2000) 35.

Poe, he's my principle author, almost, of American literature."[19] In fact, Chappell notes that *Dagon*'s initial conception was based on one of Hawthorne's more distinguished short stories: "*Dagon* started first in my mind as a sort of short story that would make a pendant to Hawthorne's story 'My Kinsman, Major Molineaux,' but then when I got to thinking about it a little more it would seem to be more fun as a short novel, because I could retell the story of Samson at the same time. And as a kind of dark joke I could use H. P. Lovecraft's Cthulhu mythology as background."[20] Putting aside, for the time being, the influential mythology of Lovecraft and the Bible, it is especially noteworthy and illuminating that Chappell's novel had its genesis in one of Hawthorne's dark *bildungsromane*. For *Dagon* is a kind of initiation narrative for Peter Leland, a youthful and naive Methodist preacher whose half-hearted, postured theological idealism blinds him to the presence of evil, both in others and himself. Lacking the moral and theological seriousness of Hawthorne's Hooper and Dimmesdale, Leland nonetheless shares with them a dimension of harsh self-analysis that borders on the perverse. Yet this dynamic is essential to his character, paving the way for his descent into self-abasement. In fact, Chappell maintains that he is drawn to ministerial characters "because they have a little more leisure-time than other folks, more time to explore their psyches than other folks."[21] Although "My Kinsman, Major Molineaux" lacks a ministerial protagonist, its similarities with *Dagon* are difficult to ignore. Both Leland and Hawthorne's young protagonist, Robin, journey eastward from western rural areas to seaport towns, where tenebrous epiphanies await them that are both violent and perverse in their implications. In addition, both young men are inhibited by their dark, Puritan *Umwelten*, or self-worlds, which inform their imperceptive misinterpretations and hesitant inabilities to act decisively. At the end of *Dagon*'s first chapter, the narrator reveals that Leland "had never before felt his will to be so ringed about, so much at bay" (*DAG*, 12). Moreover, in Hawthorne's story, Robin's cudgel, like Leland's water-pump handle (*DAG*, 119), is brandished but never used—an obvious corresponding symbol of physical and psychological impotence.

---

[19] Palumbo, "Folklore and Literature," 198.

[20] Palmer, "Fred Chappell," 404.

[21] Leila Easa, "A Conversation with Fred Chappell," *The Archive* 108/1 (Fall 1995): 53.

Considerations of Gender and Leland as Gothic Heroine

Hawthorne's story gave Chappell the idea for a young naive male character haunted by a Puritanical legacy and wholly predisposed to impotence. As he explains, "My protagonist, a misguided minister named Peter Leland, turned out to be the most gullible and spineless creature who ever haunted book paper."[22] Although Leland is weak and ineffective, his character is neither pointlessly shallow nor superficial. As Chappell notes, convincing the reader of Leland's flat passivity proved to be an extraordinarily difficult chore:

> The hardest character I've ever had to draw was the protagonist of *Dagon*, Peter Leland, because he was so bleeding passive. All he did was sit there, and I stuck pins into him, and it was very difficult to give him any character at all. I started out by making him a scholar—a research scholar going up to his homestead—but that gave him no character. So I made him into a minister which at least gave him some strand of character. After that I could point him up a little more by having his wife in particular make fun of his earnestness—and that helped a little bit. But I was never able to make him more than a sad puppet. That's because the events of the novel were so crushing that he could never get out from under it.[23]

Although Chappell views Leland's flatness as a shortcoming in the novel, it is perhaps an unavoidable one. After all, a strong, well-developed character likely would have resisted Mina's influence altogether, or at least held out against it for a much longer period of time. Leland's puny willpower and unsympathetic underdevelopment are necessary for him to function as a kind of symbol for both the deluded Puritan *Umwelt* and the American gothic tradition, his name calling to mind Charles Brockden Brown's novel *Wieland, or The Transformation*, generally considered the first successful gothic narrative written in America. Leland's impotence also balances the book's symbolic gendered narrative since Mina, his erotic puerile captor, embodies a potently dominant female authority, channeled through a cruel ancient fertility god with brutal gothic qualities. At the etymological root of "gothic" is "Goth," the term Roman writers employed in identifying the various wandering pagan tribes of northern Europe who swept down upon Rome in the early fifth century, raping and looting as they

---

[22] Chappell, "Fantasia," 187.

[23] Irv Broughton, "Fred Chappell," in *The Writer's Mind*, ed. Broughton, vol. 3 (Fayetteville: University of Arkansas Press, 1990) 117.

came. As Richard Davenport-Hines recounts, "Their love of plunder and revenge ushered in a dark age, and the word 'goth' is still associated with dark powers, the lust for domination and inveterate cruelty."[24]

Channeled through Mina's willful, sexualized character, the novel's gothic ruthlessness and authority take on a potently feminine hue. Not surprisingly, aspects of the text's dense symbolism are illuminated through a consideration of gender power relationships between the characters. In his extreme psychological sensitivity and inability to act, Leland demonstrates qualities of the traditional weak gothic female—the beleaguered and objectified damsel in distress. His incapacity for action and unlimited potential for victimization are made obvious from the book's beginning: "Never before had he realized so acutely the invalidity of his desires, how they could be so easily canceled, simply marked out, by the impersonal presence of something, a place, an object, anything vehemently and uncaringly itself..." (*DAG*, 12). Chappell repeatedly underscores Leland's reluctance for action, paving the way for his abdication to Mina's dark feminine authority. For example, like the irresolute speaker in D. H. Lawrence's poem "Snake," he hesitates to kill the serpent that frightens his wife (*DAG*, 76), becoming churlish after Sheila finally taunts him into destroying the hapless reptile. More indicative of his weak incapacity, he is unable to hold his liquor and, by the end of the novel, incapable of having sex, an impotent condition magnified by his traditionally asexual and emasculating vocation. As Cyndy Hendersot notes in *The Animal Within: Masculinity and the Gothic*, "The Gothic disrupts. It takes societal norms and invades them with an unassimilable force."[25] Fatigued, nervous, and alone, Leland is completely enervated of any normative masculine potency, taking on instead the feminine qualities of the traditional gothic heroine, and becoming victim to a powerfully irresistible and equally nontraditional feminine evil.

What little inkling of manhood Leland possesses at the beginning of the book is defused from him in the first few chapters. His lack of masculinity is also underscored and countered early in the novel by his seemingly traditional feminine wife Sheila, a "pretty little wife" (*DAG*, 26)

---

[24] Richard Davenport-Hines, *Gothic: 400 Years of Excess, Horror, Evil and Ruin* (London: Fourth Estate, 1998) 1.

[25] Cyndy Hendersot, *The Animal Within: Masculinity and the Gothic* (Ann Arbor: University of Michigan Press, 1998) 1.

who cooks, cleans, sews (*DAG*, 47), and wears "pink cotton slacks" (*DAG*, 17). However, for all her stereotypical ultra-feminine characteristics, Sheila is both smarter (*DAG*, 21) and physically stronger than Peter, mocking his dense theological doctrines (*DAG*, 41) and outmuscling him during their wrestling match/foreplay (*DAG*, 22). When he accidentally locks himself in the attic, she comes to his rescue and chides him, "Just like a child, can't stay out of trouble" (*DAG*, 54). Immediately after this episode the narrator muses, "How often it had seemed to Peter that she was a man, maybe more male in the way it counted than he..." (*DAG*, 66). However, Sheila's indefatigable patience and blind wet-nursing of Leland ultimately alienate her to the reader and compromise her safety. Like Ellen Trainer in E. F. Benson's rural thriller "At the Farmhouse," Sheila is made unsympathetic to the point that her murder goes unlamented and even unremarked. However, her general physical and mental superiority to Leland made Chappell worry that Leland's murder of her would seem impractical and unconvincing. Years after the book's publication he confessed, "The difficult thing was in getting the reader to accept a sudden violent event, the murder of the wife, which opened the doorway to the supernatural."[26] Having made Leland, like the traditional gothic heroine, a figure of passivity and mental and emotional instability, Chappell all but compromised his protagonist's ability to act. However, through Leland's dreams and irrational behavior, he drops enough hints along the way to suggest that the backsliding minister's deepening madness might conceivably drive him to murder. At one point, the narrator says of Leland, "Nor was he delighted to see his mind so often turning upon himself" (*DAG*, 8). Though stronger and more intelligent than her husband, Sheila, blinded by her ill-advised devotion, becomes a casualty of the degenerative homicidal madness that plagues him.

As Chappell remarks, Sheila's murder opens "the doorway to the supernatural," a tenebrous realm where the nature of evil is potently feminine. In one of their barely literate letters, Leland's grandparents remark that the members of the Morgan family are "the most high adepts" (*DAG*, 74) in the Dagon cult and, although her parents possess unusual qualities, Mina appears to be the dominant Morgan in administering the religion. Chappell uses archetypal feminine traits in describing both the Morgan women and the cult in order "to get the powerful female principle

---

[26] Broughton, "Fred Chappell," 101.

in there."[27] For example, he based Mina's mother, Mrs. Morgan, with her enormous breasts and belly (*DAG*, 29), on the Heidelberg Venus—an ancient depiction of a fertility goddess. Although she is large and potent, Mrs. Morgan never speaks in the novel, functioning instead as a symbol of primitive and powerful, though unthinking and inarticulate, female sexuality. Mina too, despite being "maybe fourteen or fifteen or sixteen" (*DAG*, 30), projects a vigorous sexuality, copulating incessantly with Leland, Coke Rymer, and several others. Leland imagines, "She had no nose, Mina, any more than a fish. She deeped in oceans of semen" (*DAG*, 51). Yet, there is much more to Mina than powerful perverse sexuality. Whereas Mrs. Morgan constitutes a stolid, large, dominant feminine sexuality, the spirit or intellect of the novel's dark femininity resides in her prodigious daughter, whose character suggests the seductive Philistine Dagon-worshiper Delilah in the well-known biblical narrative, as well as the pubescent tormentor Emmie in Nabokov's Russian novel *Invitation to a Beheading*.[28]

As Chappell notes, to an extent, Mina also grew out of the sensual character, Lora Bowen, in *The Inkling*: "It seemed to me that the kind of personality or force that Mina represents, is present to some degree in Lora."[29] Just as Lora unravels Jan Anderson's rationalistic will, wearing it down with maddening lust, so Mina seduces Leland into a state of debilitating psychological agitation that leads to the senseless murder of his wife. As Joseph Andriano remarks in *Our Ladies of Darkness: Feminine Daemonology in Male Gothic Fiction*, "The female demon in Gothic fiction, then, is often an image of the archetypal feminine, with which men must struggle in their attempts to define themselves and their relation to the female Other."[30] Having been weakened and perverted by his brooding, repressive Puritanical *Umwelt*, Leland is unable to resist the dark feminine archetypal urges manifested through Mina's supernatural enchantments, becoming instead a slave to his basest impulses, which is the same as becoming Mina's slave. In their literal form and function, Mina's demonic supernatural characteristics suggest those of the protagonist in Arthur

---

[27] Palumbo, "Folklore and Literature," 198.

[28] Vladimir Nabokov, *Invitation to a Beheading*, trans. Dmitri Nabokov (New York: G. P. Putnam's Sons, 1959).

[29] Ragan, "Flying by Night," 111.

[30] Joseph Andriano, *Our Ladies of Darkness: Feminine Daemonology in Male Gothic Fiction* (University Park: Pennsylvania State University Press, 1993) 146.

Machen's novel *The White People*, in which a young girl is taught the orgiastic rites of an ancient witch-cult.[31] Mina's role as priestess, or at least prime participant, in a cult ceremony that amounts to little more than a hillbilly gang-bang (*DAG*, 107–109) underscores her centrality both as a sexual object and prime authority figure in the worship of Dagon. Although, in the course of the ceremony, she has sex with several men, it is evident that she controls—in the same way she commands Leland and Coke Rymer—both the unfolding of the ritual and the men involved.

Historical Intertextuality

While gender functions as the underlying dynamic in power relationships between characters, the novel's use of history, both genuine and fictional, illuminates the universality of its themes and constitutes an important dimension of its experimental technique. In her book *Gothic America*, Teresa Goddu reads the gothic "as an integral part of a network of historical representation" and this is literally true of Chappell's novel.[32] For instance, Chappell summons local history in maintaining that his hometown of Canton, North Carolina, "was one of the strongholds of this particular cult which has been outlawed and many times prosecuted."[33] On a larger historical scale, over the course of the book, Chappell relates at length the history of the Dagon religion in well-known theological and literary texts. Although H. P. Lovecraft creatively appropriates a fictionalized Dagon in at least three of his stories,[34] the god did enjoy a legitimate following in ancient times as a Philistine deity whose name and worship were developed originally in Babylonia. Although the received text of the Septuagint hints that he may have possessed feet, subsequent descriptions characterize Dagon's lower body as fish-like. Dagon was a fish-god, a fact not in the least surprising, as he seems to have been the foremost deity of such ancient maritime cities as Azotus, Gaza (the early sites of which are supposed to be

---

[31] Incidentally, H. P. Lovecraft based aspects of his Cthulhu terminology on passages from *The White People*.

[32] Teresa A. Goddu, *Gothic America: Narrative, History, and Nation* (New York: Columbia University Press, 1997) 2.

[33] "Remarks on *Dagon* for Lovecraft Conference," box WF-1, writings by Chappell, fiction subseries, 6.

[34] "Dagon" (1919), "The Shadow Over Innsmouth" (1931), and "The Lurker at the Threshold" (1945).

buried under the sand mounds that run along the seashore), Ascalon, and Arvad. The Bible relates that Dagon had temples both in Gaza and Azotus, and from this it seems likely that shrines existed in other Philistine cities as well. The Philistines attributed their successes in war to Dagon, often praising him with lavish sacrifices. In his temple they celebrated and rejoiced over the capture of Samson, the ark, and the head of Saul. It has also been suggested that Dagon played a prominent part in doctrines concerning death and future life. As to the ritual of his worship, little can be gathered either from documents or Scripture, which afforded imaginative writers like Lovecraft and Chappell the freedom to create that facet of the religion themselves.

In addition to recounting the biblical Samson and Delilah legend, the culmination of which takes place in the temple of Dagon, in his book manuscript Leland summons Milton's allusion to Dagon in *Paradise Lost*: "Sea Monster, upward man / And downward fish" (*DAG*, 38). However, it is the title of Leland's projected book, *Remnant Pagan Forces in American Puritanism*, that suggests his most central historical concern: the lingering and incapacitating Puritan influence on decadent modern culture. Chappell subtly suggests Puritan history even outside of Leland's book. Early in the novel, he describes a pair of sofa pillows stitched with the image of a young woman and displaying the respective expressions: "I slept and dreamed that life was beauty" and "I woke and found that life was duty" (*DAG*, 5). The pillows, created by Leland's severe grandmother, both in their form and message, suggest the despairing and even perverse couplets of the New England primer Puritan children were forced to master.[35] In terms of the novel, they underscore the Puritanical tendencies of Leland's grandparents and their lingering influence on Peter. Furthermore, in his manuscript, Leland retells the familiar story—adapted by Hawthorne and William Carlos Williams, among others—of how William Bradford's Puritans combated the pagan festivities of Thomas Morton's free-loving community at Merrymount, drawing attention to the fact that Morton's foiled merry revelers later renamed their existential playground Mount Dagon. Both the pillows and the Merrymount adaptation constitute narratives in which

[35] "JOB feels the Rod,—/Yet blesses GOD" and "XERXES did die,/And so must I" are but two of the cheerless expressions young Puritans used in learning the alphabet.

Puritanism, ideally seeking to control and purify aspects of existence, corrupts the individuals involved, killing the spirit of the young woman on the pillows and converting the vigorous sexuality of Merrymount into the perverted rituals of Mount Dagon. When Leland becomes Mina's willing prisoner he founders in a rotgut-induced "clear acid delirium" (*DAG*, 88) and, amid his drunken reveries, comes "to recognize the necessity for a diseased temperament in the understanding of any religious code" (89). Despite his debauched condition, Leland perceptively discerns the close relationship between Puritanism and disease, although by then—having become a casualty of that correlation—it is too late for him to use the knowledge for any constructive purpose.

The Power of Fictional History: H. P. Lovecraft's Cthulhuism and Yog-Sothothery[36]

Chappell cleverly draws on actual historical and literary texts in constructing *Dagon*; however, not all of his sources are historically authentic, his dominant basis for the Dagon religion deriving from the fictional work of H. P. Lovecraft, perhaps the most important and influential writer of supernatural fiction in the twentieth century. In *The Weird Tale*, Lovecraft scholar S. T. Joshi explains his system of interpretation in terms of the practice of appropriation and variation among writers of the "weird": "Weird writers utilize the schemas I have outlined (or various permutations of them) precisely in accordance with their philosophical predispositions."[37] Possessing his own philosophical agenda, Chappell utilizes Lovecraft's original philosophical and mythological system and plays by its rules in order to achieve a specific supernatural effect in his novel. He comments significantly and at great length on his appropriation of Lovecraft's material:

> I was especially pleased with myself for appropriating and using in a contemporary fashion the fantasy materials of H. P. Lovecraft; my notion was that I could take inferior literary matter from the old pulp horror magazines and by including it in a distinctly modernist story, reinterpret it

[36] The term "Cthulhu Mythos" was invented after Lovecraft's death by his associate August Derleth in order to categorize those Lovecraft stories that function beneath his primary mythical system. Lovecraft biographer L. Sprague de Camp notes that Lovecraft referred to these narratives "as his 'Cthulhuism or Yog-Sothothery'" (*Lovecraft: A Biography* [Garden City: Doubleday, 1975] 270).

[37] S. T. Joshi, *The Weird Tale* (Austin: University of Texas Press, 1990) 10.

> and rework it into artistic respectability. I had in mind the use of such quotidian "inferior" materials as newspaper pages, matchbooks, bicycle wheels, and so forth by such renowned artists as Picasso, Kurt Schwitters, and Man Ray.
>
> Now I recognize how woefully I deceived myself. In the first place, Lovecraft in his best works is a good writer, and certainly much more expert in the art of the horror story than I was or am likely to become. His work did not need me to give it a literary legitimacy that was not in my power to give—a legitimacy already inherent. In the second place, any inclusion of such highly specific fantasy materials—the Cthulhu Mythos had already acquired a largish literary "cult" following—aroused certain expectations in readers who recognized the materials, expectations which *Dagon*, a little too self-important, a little too pretentious entirely, could not fulfill.[38]

Although few of Chappell's readers, excepting Lovecraft enthusiasts, have recognized *Dagon*'s Lovecraft motif,[39] the dynamic is essential to understanding both the internal nature of the Dagon cult and much of the novel's abstract language and imagery. Lovecraft's mythology is revealed in many of his stories through individuals, cults, and towns that worship the Old Ones, cosmic beings who ages ago journeyed from another part of the universe to rule the earth from the now submerged city of R'lyeh—a word that appears in one of the few widely translated passages of *The Necronomicon*, which Chappell uses as an epigraph for his book: "Ph'nglui mglw'nafh Cthulhu R'lyeh wgah'nagl fhtagn (In his house at R'lyeh dead Cthulhu lies dreaming)." In selecting a constructed fictional mythology as the dominant intertexual source for his book, Chappell made the conscious and decidedly postmodern decision to blur the fiction and reality of the real world in the one he had created.

In his little-known poem "H. P. Lovecraft," Chappell attempts to portray the disquieting atmosphere Lovecraft achieves in his work: "The worst of it, everything alive. / Had you thought to escape without dreaming? / The walls bulge with what you come to know. / Squamous. Obscene.

---

[38] Chappell, "Fantasia," 182.

[39] For an informative earlier account of Lovecraft's influence on *Dagon* see Amy Tipton Gray, "R'lyeh in Appalachia: Lovecraft's Influence on Fred Chappell's *Dagon*," in *Remembrance, Reunion, and Revival: Celebrating a Decade of Appalachian Studies* (Boone NC: Appalachian Consortium Press, 1988) 73–79.

Hybrid. Eldritch."[40] As the poem's last line demonstrates, a major component of Lovecraft's weird power is based on the compelling alien words he so convincingly adopted and created. This dynamic translates into *Dagon* through the enigmatic Lovecraftian terms Leland discovers in his grandparents' correspondence. As he seeks to open the secret tongue, one gets the impression that the ugly infectious phrases are fueling Leland's madness, crippling his ability to organize language and rational thought. The narrator remarks, "He felt that the letters were obscurely responsible for the bad dreams that came on him late in the mornings" (*DAG*, 47). As Leland degenerates further, he studies the letters more regularly and intently, as if the words and his madness are feeding off each other.

An examination of the various Cthulhu terms Chappell appropriated is helpful in explaining certain events and images in the novel. The most frequently occurring of these words, "Cthulhu" (*DAG*, epigraph, 47, 70, 90), in addition to suggesting Lovecraft's general mythological system, has a major function in that scheme. In "The Call of Cthulhu" Lovecraft identifies Cthulhu as the great slumbering priest of the submerged city R'lyeh, who—at an indeterminate time, when the stars are properly aligned—will rise and rule the earth again. However, although he sleeps, Cthulhu is not inactive, constantly transmitting his dark, mad, cosmic thoughts to the puny, vulnerable dreaming minds of humans. While sleeping Leland is made victim to Cthulhu's unconscious influence, his dreams of bizarre aquatic cities coupled with nightmares about murdering his wife (*DAG*, 69–70). As L. Sprague de Camp says of Cthulhu and the Old Ones, "They are absorbed in their own affairs and are no more interested in the petty concerns of men than men are with those of mice, and they have no more compunction about destroying men who get in their way than men have about slaying mice."[41] Like the aliens of Chris Carter's *X-Files* mythology, Lovecraft's extraterrestrials remain shadowy and remotely malevolent, manipulating human affairs only indirectly and torturing the psyches of those who actively seek them out. At one point in the novel, Chappell makes Leland dimly aware of the Old Ones: "[He] felt obscurely the presence of other systems, other universes, to which humanity—his humanity—was irrelevant. Mocking crowded points of corruscation, infinite

[40] Box WP-2, writings by Chappell Series, poetry subseries, 1960–1996.
[41] De Camp, *Lovecraft: A Biography*, 333.

coldness" (*DAG*, 127). In her essay on Chappell's use of the Cthulhu Mythos, Amy Tipton Gray accurately concludes, "In short, Lovecraft's lexicon does not include the concept of hope; there is no escape from Cthulhu."[42] Pervasive, corrupting, and controlling, Cthulhu functions in the novel as a shadowy symbolic harbinger of madness, imprisonment, and doom for Leland.

Other Lovecraft terms that appear in *Dagon* generally suggest names and places from the mythology, baffling and maddening Leland with their nonsensical, alien sounds. "Nyarlath—" (*DAG*, 74), for example, appears as the incomplete articulation of "Nyarlathotep," a story Lovecraft composed in 1920. In the narrative, Lovecraft portrays Nyarlathotep, or the "crawling chaos," as a thin, sinister Egyptian with ties to the Old Ones and an ability to generate awe and insane fear among the crowds he addresses. Although he terrifies his audiences, people still come to hear him speak, as if some imp-of-the-perverse invests them with an unquenchable lust to be horrified. This dynamic suggests Mina, who is both powerfully compelling and horrific, drawing Leland to her for the purpose of his chilling debasement and destruction. "Nephreu" (*DAG*, 47, 70, 90) also constitutes a partial articulation of a Cthulhu figure. In "The Haunter of the Dark" Lovecraft describes Nephreu-Ka, or Nephren-Ka, as the Egyptian pharaoh who acquired the "Shining Trapezohedron," a device created by the Old Ones to manipulate time and space. Nephren-Ka constructed a temple around the "Shining Trapezohedron" with a windowless crypt, and the passage "Ka nai Hadoth" (*DAG*, 47) is a reference to the valley of Hadoth, the geographical location of Nephren-Ka's temple. Not unlike Nephren-Ka's "Shining Trapezohedron," "Yog-Sothoth" (*DAG*, 47, 70, 90) appears in "The Case of Charles Dexter Ward" and "The Dunwich Horror" as an eternal portal to the realm of the Old Ones, which may be breached through the repetition of various cryptic incantations. Carrying connotations of time manipulation and space travel, "Nephreu" and "Yog-Sothoth" serve as subtle elements of foreshadowing for the transformation and galactic wandering Leland experiences at the conclusion of the novel.

In order to activate "Yog-Sothoth" various phrases must be uttered, and this condition serves as a microcosm of the importance Lovecraft placed on ritual in his mythology, which also carries over into *Dagon*. The

---

[42] Gray, "R'lyeh in Appalachia," 79.

expression, "Iä! iä!" (*DAG*, 70, 109) is a cryptic exclamation associated with Cthulhu rituals in a number of Lovecraft's stories. In addition, Chappell seems to have appropriated dynamics from specific Lovecraft narratives in describing his worshipers and the people with whom they interact. For example, in "The Shadow over Innsmouth" the Innsmouth people who venerate the Old Ones are, like the Morgans, odd-looking bootleggers. Furthermore, the inquisitive protagonist of the story journeys east to a dilapidated cult-infested village, just as Leland, Mina, and Coke Rymer drive east to the hookwormy coastal town of Gordon, North Carolina, where they encounter the lesbians Bella and Enid and establish a Dagon-sect/whorehouse. In an early four-page handwritten manuscript of *Dagon*, the Leland figure is diagnosed with a strange disease and wanders down to a waterside bar peopled with mysterious Innsmouth-like customers.[43] In more than one of Lovecraft's stories the protagonist is either afflicted by an aquatic disease traceable to the Old Ones or, more generally, suffers, as in Lovecraft's "Dagon," "under an appreciable mental strain."[44] The fragile mental constitutions of Lovecraft's protagonists, which suggest Leland's precarious condition, make them especially susceptible to the Cthulhu phenomena they encounter. In Lovecraft's "Dagon" the narrator recounts, "The odour of the fish was maddening," suggesting Mina's powerful fish odor in Chappell's book (*DAG*, 83).[45] In both texts, the smell functions as a kind of mind-numbing narcotic, blocking the rational thought processes of the compromised protagonists. However, the fish odor is not the only aquatic characteristic Chappell inherits from Lovecraft. In "The Shadow Over Innsmouth" the narrator encounters a citizen possessing "a flat nose" and proceeds to comment, "He was evidently given to working or lounging around the fish docks, and carried with him much of their characteristic smell."[46] Likewise, when Leland initially encounters Mina, "[H]e had thought she had no nose, it was so small and flat, stretched on her face as smooth as wax" (*DAG*, 30). Using characteristics of Lovecraft's worshipers

---

[43] "Dagon," box WF-1, writings by Chappell, fiction subseries.

[44] H. P. Lovecraft, *Dagon and Other Macabre Tales* (London: Panther, 1969) 7. In Lovecraft's "Dagon" the god appears as an aquatic monstrosity possessing ties to both Philistine theology and the Old Ones.

[45] Lovecraft, *Dagon*, 9.

[46] H. P. Lovecraft, *The Lurking Fear and Other Stories* (New York: Ballantine, 1971) 126.

in portraying the members of his own North Carolina cult, Chappell adds an element of disturbingly familiar fantastic legitimacy to his creations.

The protagonist of Lovecraft's "The Thing on the Doorstep" is a Mina-like co-ed student—small and dark, with a touch of the "Innsmouth look"—who seduces a hapless professor. In his review of L. Sprague de Camp's Lovecraft biography Chappell observes that Lovecraft's work often is made up of "scholars who pursue their psychological lives until they are utterly—and logically—destroyed by them."[47] Besides serving as an important critical comment on Lovecraft's work, Chappell's remark suggests the protagonists in two of his early attempts at composing *Dagon*. In an untitled early handwritten version of *Dagon*, the Leland figure, Vaughn Newcome, appears as a renaissance scholar preparing to go on sabbatical.[48] Although Mina does not appear as a tenant girl, she is almost identical to her namesake in the novel, "flat-nosed," with "wet and cold" hands.[49] Newcome encounters Mina at a college party and, like the weak academic in Lovecraft's "The Thing on the Doorstep," proceeds to fall under her debilitating influence. Also suggestive of *Dagon*, in *The Bad Luck*, a sixty-page novella, a young, delinquent outlaw couple kidnaps a spineless professor pretentiously yet aptly named Percival Norman.[50] Uneducated, apathetic, and amoral, the young couple, resembling Mina and Coke Rymer, contrast dramatically with the pompous, ineffective, and Leland-like Norman. Furthermore, Anna Long's voice hisses like Mina's and the highway abduction sequence mirrors the eastward trek of Mina, Rymer, and Leland in *Dagon*. When asked to comment on these interesting early versions of *Dagon*, Chappell humorously replies: "I don't even remember those [laughter]. Are those actual versions? I have no idea.... I'm sorry, I don't recall either of those versions.... I think I must have written other versions too and simply discarded them. I'm surprised to hear that there are any of those versions left. I think what I finally had published probably takes

---

[47] "Lovecraft: A Biography," box WR-1, writings by Chappell, reviews subseries, 1.

[48] "Untitled," box WF-1, writings by Chappell, fiction subseries. Chappell has no recollection of this version of *Dagon*, but maintains, "I can see why I might have chosen a Milton scholar because I wanted to bring the Dagon material into it" (INT).

[49] "Untitled," box WF-1, writings by Chappell, fiction subseries, 10.

[50] *The Bad Luck*, box WF-4, writings by Chappell, fiction subseries.

from a number of discarded versions, certainly a lot of discarded chapters and pages" (INT). Although Chappell does not recollect them, these early versions of *Dagon* are significant in the way they may be used to trace the development of specific characters and events, as well as Chappell's various compelling applications of Lovecraft's fictional techniques and extraordinary mythological world.

Parody

In his review of L. Sprague de Camp's Lovecraft biography Chappell summarizes Lovecraft's achievements: "He invented a mythology, confused and deliberately playful, which imposes a metaphysical justification for the horror story on the whole of human history. He forged logical and unbreakable links between personal fear and the physical cosmos. He perfectly analyzed an illogical state of consciousness, the American non-Christian Calvinism."[51] The peculiar blend of "playfulness" and America's Puritanical tendencies, which Chappell so admires in Lovecraft's fiction, forms an important philosophical component of *Dagon*. In addition to his tongue-in-cheek use of Lovecraft's mythology, Chappell employed humorous parodic representations of Puritan religious modes. He maintains, "A great deal of the book—this isn't too important—but a great deal of the book is a parody of books written about Puritanism. Some sections parody Hawthorne's *Scarlet Letter* and there are sections which parody *Moby Dick*."[52] Suggestive of the *The Scarlet Letter*, early in the novel Leland's and Sheila's bucolic picnic sequence, in which he combats his anxiety and laughs "at the hard core of stodginess in himself" (*DAG*, 20), resembles the conciliatory and liberating meeting between Hester Prynne and Arthur Dimmesdale in the woods. In both texts the relaxed pastoral scenes intensify the dark dramatic events that follow.

Also reminiscent of *The Scarlet Letter*, in the book's third chapter Chappell mocks the dramatic sermons of Hawthorne's Dimmesdale and his historical precursor Jonathon Edwards (*DAG*, 33) in having Leland deliver

---

[51] "Lovecraft: A Biography," box WR-1, writings by Chappell, reviews subseries, 1.

[52] John Sopko and John Carr, "Dealing with the Grotesque: Fred Chappell," in *Kite-Flying and Other Irrational Acts: Conversations with Twelve Southern Writers*, ed. John Carr (Baton Rouge: Louisiana State University Press, 1972) 217.

an academic treatise of almost overpowering "weighty boredom" (*DAG*, 41) on the history of Dagon and materialism in America to a contemporary Methodist congregation. Chappell maintains: "I just had to stop the book at one point and put a sermon in it. There's a sermon right in the third chapter, which sort of explains what the book is about. If you happened to skip the sermon, the book would make absolutely no sense whatsoever. Whatever sense it makes, it makes because of that chapter. And that's a technical fault, but I just couldn't find any other way in the world out of it."[53] Covering complex theological, historical, and cultural themes, the unconventional sermon, as Chappell points out, reveals several of the novel's symbolic concerns. Humorously, the congregation is neither bewildered nor outraged by Leland's intellectual harangue, but simply bored to death by it. Directing the tedious actions of a deliberate, plodding scholar and speaker, Leland's mind, like that of the speaker in Chappell's "The Peaceable Kingdom of Emerald Windows," "is about as sprightly as a shelf of Dreiser."[54] Skillfully, Chappell simultaneously mocks the Puritanical dreariness of Leland's rhetoric while also revealing both several of the novel's philosophical motifs and the intellectual atrophy of average contemporary protestant church-goers, largely unaware of the decadent consumer forces surrounding them. And Chappell was quite cognizant of the book's comic qualities, despite the tenebrous sadistic plot, characterizing *Dagon* as a rendition of "*Death in Venice* as filtered through *Miss Lonelyhearts*."[55] Chappell's Nathaniel West-influenced parodic absurdities, rendered with fine subtlety, add an occasional element of sharp humor to his otherwise dark, gothic, historical concerns.

"Detroit Pontiac": American Materialism and Decadence

Although Leland's sermon has comic and parodic qualities, it is central to the book in its pairing of the decadent Dagon cult with wasteful corporate America, both creations of and backlashes to a fanatical Puritan work ethic. As Chappell says, "The secret cult is a metaphor for the whole of Detroit,

---

[53] Ibid., 229.

[54] Fred Chappell, *Earthsleep* (Baton Rouge: Louisiana State University Press, 1980) 17.

[55] Fred Chappell, "Two Modes: A Plea for Tolerance," *Appalachian Journal* 5 (1978): 335.

Gleem toothpaste and that whole business."[56] Like the despairing and zealously frugal nineteenth-century Methodist congregation in Harold Frederic's *The Damnation of Theron Ware*, Leland's Puritanical Methodist ancestors were obsessed with money, their correspondence containing numerous references to property values and bills of sale (*DAG*, 10).[57] Like William Harmon's *Treasury Holiday*—a long poem of contemporary America focusing on the greed, evil, humor, and complexity of society, beginning with a reference to the "Gross National Product"—*Dagon* explores the relationship between capitalist materialism and depraved inhumanity.[58] For example, Mina's materialism—her seizure of Leland's checkbook and car, along with the manner in which she uses him up as an object—is inextricably bound with her perverse sexuality. In his unpublished poem "Detroit Pontiac," Chappell connects the Midwestern industrial hub with carnal lust, describing it as "Furiously decaying, bubbling / With red erotic dreams."[59] Confronting the perverse sexualized materialism of the Dagon cult with his naive esoteric intellect, Leland's senses are drowned and he becomes an object of consumption for the cult. As in Theophile Gautier's *The Evil Eye*, in which primitive Italian superstition foils and overcomes imperialistic British enlightenment, and several works by Kipling, Leland's feeble rationalistic constructs are no match for the pervasive, mindless power of the Dagon cult, using up objects and people for no apparent constructive purpose. At the end of his sermon, Leland traces the shadowy legacy of Dagon in contemporary America at great length:

> Didn't the Dagon notion of fertility dominate? Frenzied, incessant, unreasoning sexual activity was invited on all sides; every entertainment, even the serious entertainment, the arts, seemed to suppose this activity as basis. This blind sexual Bacchanalia was inevitably linked to money—one had only to think of the omnipresent advertisements, with all those girls who alarmed the eye. A mere single example. And wasn't the power of money finally dependent upon the continued proliferation of product after product, dead objects produced without any thought given to their uses? Weren't these mostly objects without any truly justifiable need? Didn't the

---

[56] Sopko and Carr, "Dealing with the Grotesque," 230.

[57] Harold Frederic, *The Damnation of Theron Ware* (Chicago: Stone & Kimball, 1896).

[58] William Harmon, *Treasury Holiday* (Middletown CT: Wesleyan University Press, 1969) 1.

[59] Box WP-2, writings by Chappell Series, poetry subseries, 1960–1996.

whole of American culture exhibit this endless irrational productivity, clear analogue to sexual orgy? And yet productivity without regard to eventual need was, Peter maintained, actually unproductivity, it was really a kind of impotence. This was the paradox which the figure of Dagon contained. (*DAG*, 39–40)

Fueled by the Puritan legacy of blind duty and work, American capitalism simultaneously produces useless products and the constructed and skillfully marketed, propagandistic lust for them, resulting in a fruitless masturbatory cycle of waste. Such also is the microcosmic purpose of Dagon and his decadent cult, breeding desire and lustfully using up everything in its path without thought or rationale.

At one point in the novel, Leland says of Mina, "No question about her purposes with his possessions; she would waste them totally and carefully" (*DAG*, 129). Leland's sermon turns out to be prophetic when he himself becomes the wasted material object of the mutated Puritan *Umwelt*. Just as the repressive Puritanical work ethic had created both the Dagon cult and corporate American waste, so Leland's Puritanical worldview eventually transforms him into the pathetic and deranged object he becomes—a being devoid of intellect, a figure of wasteful dissipation. As Leland enters the last stages of alcoholic dementia, he strangles a chicken to death (*DAG*, 151) and performs humiliating acts for Mina and her friends/followers in order to obtain his precious ration of moonshine—the primary object of his materialistic addiction. Chappell drew on a number of intriguing sources in portraying his broken-down protagonist as a senseless, used-up material commodity, basing the chicken-strangling aspect of Leland's character on a carnival geek he encountered who ate raw chickens and committed other strange acts in order to earn enough money for the next bottle. He also made use of Erskine Caldwell's novella, *Poor Fool*, in which the protagonist, Blondy, a punch-drunk boxer, falls under the influence of Mrs. Boxx, a woman who possesses a hypnotic power similar to Mina's and who, having already castrated her husband, plans to emasculate Blondy as well.[60] Like

[60] Erskine Caldwell, *Poor Fool* (New York: Rariora Press, 1930). Chappell underscores the book's influence, recounting: "Then I was wondering if I could write a whole book about some jerk who was a victim from page one, almost, to the end of the book and still make an interesting book out of it. I came across a small obscure novel by Caldwell—it was privately published, he paid for its publication before he got to be well known—called *Poor Fool*, about a broken-down boxer who falls in with

Leland, Blondy ultimately is measured in terms of his literal usefulness—an object to be appraised, devoured, and thrown away.

Transcendence

Although Chappell wanted to make a serious and powerful point about wasteful American materialism, he found Leland's ritualized death to be too hopeless and heartless a way to conclude his novel. Rather than leaving his protagonist drained and broken, literally an article of objectified trash, Chappell follows Leland's consciousness as it dwindles into infinity, a phantom afterlife in which he roams the universe contemplating its mysteries. One of the relatively early studies of contemporary gothicism, Linda Bayer-Berenbaum's *The Gothic Imagination* maintains, "The Gothic philosophy deals with the nature of transcendence."[61] This bears upon Chappell's novel in the manner that Leland, through his suffering, becomes more an object than a human being, until finally, with his death, he becomes a part of the universe. Chappell describes Leland's transformation in the following terms:

> It seems to me we define ourselves by suffering. That's what the human being is very good at; much of his existence is suffering in one form or another. In order to live with this suffering, in order to endure, we make myths of it; we make narratives and meaning of it. We tell ourselves it means something. Whether that's true or not doesn't make any difference to me; even if it weren't true, we wouldn't know any better. Even if we said, "We admit it," we wouldn't know if it was true or not. So what we do is live within mythology.
>
> In that chapter, I tried to imagine another kind of existence, an afterlife if you will, in which idea and physicality are co-terminals, co-equals. An existence in which the fact of idea can influence the shape and "punch" of the physical. That seemed to me very close to what I can imagine an ideal world must be like, a world in which sensual objects embody and show

---

some weird people who just victimize him completely, and that gave me the idea that it could be done. There was something very strange and surrealistic about that book. It's not well written, but even so it had a kind of power and vision that I wanted to get on my own" (Broughton, "Fred Chappell," 110–11).

[61] Linda Bayer-Berenbaum, *The Gothic Imagination: Expansion in Gothic Literature and Art* (Rutherford NJ: Fairleigh Dickinson University Press, 1982) 12.

forth their mathematical forms and relationships immediately to the senses.[62]

Giving Leland's extensive suffering a constructive and redeeming purpose, Chappell imagines an afterlife in which idea and physical form enjoy a symbiotic relationship. Like the figure in Chappell's poem "Message," Leland ascends: "a finer dimension of event, he feels with senses / newly evolved the wide horizons unknown till now. / He is transformed head to foot, taproot to polestar. / He breathes a new universe, the blinding whirlpool / galaxies drift round him and begin to converse."[63] Having become privy to the universal relationships of objects and ideas, Leland "contemplated with joy the unity of himself and what surrounded him" (*DAG*, 180), exploring both galactic space and the spaces between things and thoughts.

Leland's preparation for this final transformation is reflected in a parody of *Moby Dick*, in which Mina and the other Dagon initiates tattoo religious symbols on Leland's body before sacrificing him to their deity. The final section of the novel, concerning Leland's afterlife, extends the parodic *Moby Dick* motif when Peter assumes the form of a spiritual leviathan, a huge, inscrutable, and omniscient being. Furthermore, the final chapter owes its tone and form to Chaucer's *Troilus and Criseyde*, the conclusion of which constitutes a trivialization of a powerful succession of events. Finally, the meditative finale of *Dagon* is suggestive of William Hope Hodgson's conclusion to *The House on the Borderland*, in which the protagonist finds himself a naked explorer of outer space.[64] *Dagon*'s sudden and dramatic shift from Leland's literal sacrifice to his fantastic afterlife, which troubles some readers, is an obvious convention of Hodgson's work. In the second chapter of *The Nightland*, for example, Hodgson's milieu shifts suddenly from a quaint English countryside to a black nightmarish future.[65]

---

[62] Chris Redd, "A Man of Letters in the Modern World: An Interview with Fred Chappell," *The Arts Journal* 14/8 (May 1989): 99.

[63] Fred Chappell, *Source* (Baton Rouge: Louisiana State University Press, 1985) 55.

[64] William Hope Hodgson, *The House on the Borderland* (London: Chapman and Hall, 1908).

[65] William Hope Hodgson, *The Nightland* (Westport [Connecticut]: Hyperion, 1976).

More important than its intertexual antecedents, Leland's supernatural condition at the end of *Dagon* informs the structure of the text. Just as Leland's essence transcends the natural world, so the book transcends conventional gothic tropes to create something artistically authentic. Although the result of Chappell's appropriations is an often fragmented and confusing narrative, *Dagon* is ultimately protected from claims of organizational disintegration by what critics interpret as the gothic novel's inherent tendency to disrupt form. George Haggerty perhaps makes this point best in *Gothic Fiction/Gothic Form*: "What really takes place is a process of formal insurgency, a rejection of the conventional demands of novel form, first within the gloomy confines of Gothic novel, causing disruption and inconsistency, and later as a liberated and liberating alternative to the conventional novel."[66] Long before Haggerty's book existed, H. P. Lovecraft, in his important extended meditation "Supernatural Horror in Literature," had stated as much: "Naturally we cannot expect all weird tales to conform absolutely to any theoretical model.... Much of the choicest weird work is unconscious.... Atmosphere is the all-important thing, for the final criterion of authenticity is not the dove-tailing of a plot but the creation of a given sensation."[67] Just as Matthew Lewis's novel *The Monk* broke the Radcliffian gothic tradition of creating natural explanations for supernatural events,[68] and opened up a new world of fantastic imagination, so *Dagon* compromises conventional genre paradigms with its remarkable and unorthodox meshing of wide-ranging intertextuality, gender, history, humor, and horror. As Haggerty and Lovecraft likely would contend, its singular fragmented form is simply a continuation of what memorable gothic narratives and weird tales have always done: breaking and reinventing the rules of the genre and forcing it to evolve as an aesthetic form.[69] *Dagon*

---

[66] George E. Haggerty, *Gothic Fiction/Gothic Form* (University Park: Pennsylvania State University Press, 1989) 3. Robert K. Martin and Eric Savoy include the reader in this distinction, arguing that gothic texts "[situate] the reader at the border of symbolic dissolution" (Robert K. Martin and Eric Savoy, eds., *American Gothic: New Interventions in a National Narrative* [Iowa City: University of Iowa Press, 1998] vii).

[67] Lovecraft, *Dagon*, 144.

[68] Matthew Lewis, *The Monk* (London: Routledge, 1907).

[69] For an account of how the evolution of the gothic possesses similarities with cultural change see Aldine Clemens, *The Return of the Repressed: Gothic Horror from* The Castle of Otranto *to* Alien (Albany: State University of New York Press, 1999) 12–13.

participates in this tradition, or anti-tradition, skillfully and artfully, and it likely deserves greater recognition in the contemporary cannon of gothic narratives. In a genre overpopulated by superfluous clichéd texts, Chappell's novel shines as a rich and innovative work, genuinely embracing the tradition and shaping it into something new.

Chapter 4

Locale: *The Gaudy Place*

Place is that, which is the same in different moments to different existent things, when their relations of co-existence with certain other existents, which are supposed to continue fixed from one of those moments to the other, agree entirely together. —Bertrand Russell, *A Critical Exposition of the Philosophy of Leibniz*, 252.

The spirit of the place is poetic, as is the spirit of any place when you come closer to the heart of it. I can't think of any book of real worth, except maybe Dante's Inferno, *that says, underneath, "This is a horrible, lousy place, nobody should live here, and the people are dumb" [laughs]. On the other hand, every book that deals with place is also a criticism of place, but not simply a wholesale thrashing.* —Chappell, INT.

On the dust jacket of the first edition of Chappell's fourth novel, *The Gaudy Place*, is a room naked except for a table and two empty chairs. On the table sits a napkin dispenser, a bottle of whiskey, a tumbler (empty except for two large cubes of ice), and an ashtray containing two crushed-out fags and one burning low. A single door stands at the far wall, the light beyond the glass panes inked in the same rich golden hue as Chappell's name. Is this scene the Ace or Juanita's Place, Gimlet Street bars where Arkie works his two-bit cons? It is the Big Bunny, another seedy dive where Oxie informs Clemmie he no longer can afford to pimp her? The Brass Rail, a swank, new, carpeted downtown establishment where Ted Pape makes his upwardly mobile political maneuverings? The back room of some elitist country club where the aristocratic Zebulon Johns Mackie bullies city leaders into submitting to his crooked business schemes? Probably it is all of these places, for it is the collective scene of the book itself.

The Gaudy Place essentially is a meditation on place (the small fictional city of Braceboro, North Carolina), which separates it conceptually from Chappell's first three novels. To be sure, milieu is important when considering the earlier novels, especially since they share, with some varied and notable exceptions, similar rural western North Carolina settings. However, Chappell's interests during the compositions of those books lay more in working out the psycho-philosophical complexities of his young male protagonists than in relating an authentic sense of a specific culture and community. In *The Gaudy Place*, as is the case in novels such as Ivo Andric's *The Bridge on the Drina* and Sherwood Anderson's *Winesburg, Ohio*, the book's setting also serves as its dominant character, with the various personalities contributing distinct aspects and avenues of interpretation to the collective identity of Braceboro.[1] Like Mary Lee Settle's *Blood Tie*, the book frequently switches characters and perspectives, which, in turn, episodically construct the small municipality that serves as both the novel's backdrop and its central subject, defining and defined by the people and objects that exist in its space.[2]

Using locale or place as its guiding point of inquiry, this chapter reads Chappell's fourth novel as a historically significant social text that critiques its setting through cross-section and narrative-advancing representations of its socioeconomically disparate denizens. After presenting significant details of the novel's composition, early reviews, and structural qualities, I move into a largely theoretical meditation on place, underscoring its significance in Southern literature, how it is specifically portrayed in terms of urban milieus, and the way in which convincing characterization is essential to its construction. The consideration of characterization leads logically into an examination of the book's major characters in terms of the various sub-environments in which they function—how individuals operate in their immediate place, which in turn affects seemingly unrelated events and, in fact, the entire city itself. Finally, I argue that *The Gaudy Place*, with its interest in a small, closed society, marks Chappell's shift from an existential,

---

[1] Ivo Andric, *The Bridge on the Drina*, trans. Lovett F. Edwards (London, Allen & Unwin, 1959); Sherwood Anderson, *Winesburg, Ohio* (New York: B. W. Huebsch, 1919).

[2] Mary Lee Settle, *Blood Tie* (Boston: Houghton Mifflin, 1977).

philosophical, and intellectually disciplined mode of prose expression in his first three novels to a more humane, comic, and community-based style of writing—paving the way for the Kirkman stories he would begin writing in the 1970s and that would appear eventually as four novels in the 1980s and 1990s.

Composition, Early Reviews, and a Tenuous Structure

Chappell maintains that the original germ for *The Gaudy Place* arose in the late 1960s out of the most unlikely and disparate of elements, most notably satire, civil rights, and societal violence:

> My wife and I belonged to CORE, you remember that, the Congress of Racial Equality, one of the first civil rights groups? It was a corrupt group in the town we were active in [Durham, North Carolina]. It was a corrupt political group. It really didn't do that much. That's why it died, I'm sure. There's no CORE now, at least as far as I know. And I thought, I'm going to do a long satire about civil rights and how corrupt sometimes it is at the beginning, though the great organizations like SNCC, NAACP, those are fine. But then, Mr. King, Martin Luther King, was assassinated while we were in Italy. And you couldn't write any satire on civil rights anymore. It would break your heart to think about writing something like that. So I got taken with the notion of how a violent act occurs. And this new novel is about a guy getting shot through the collarbone—not a terribly violent act, you know, no death, but violent enough. I wanted to follow it from the very beginning, the full act itself. How it came about.[3]

Having originally intended to write a bitter fictional satire of Durham, North Carolina's fraudulent CORE chapter, Chappell felt compelled to alter his plans after the tragedy of King's death, which he believed effectively rendered any such critique politically inappropriate. King's passing, along with Robert Kennedy's killing and the general violence of the late 1960s, persuaded Chappell to redirect his attention from the corrupt nature of a supposedly idealistic organization to the societal essence and causes of individual violent acts. Interestingly, Chappell's shift in intellectual focus mirrored the general cultural movement of the 1960s from abstract youthful idealism to visceral violence—from Woodstock to Altamont, from genuine

---

[3] John Graham, "Fred Chappell," in *The Writer's Voice: Conversations with Contemporary Writers*, ed. John Graham and George Garrett (New York: William Morrow, 1973) 41.

drug experimentation to narcotic addiction and junkies, from nonviolent protest to the Black Panthers and outright insurrection. Witnessing the riots in Detroit and Watts and other forms of urban unrest, Chappell also became interested in the way violence could be produced, often unintentionally, by the various socioeconomic participants in an urban society. This society-based line of thinking led him into a new realm of aesthetic and philosophical possibilities that excited him:

> When I came to write *The Gaudy Place* I was tired of writing little novels that take place in one immediate family, with a limited cast of characters. I'd never had the opportunity to write at length because of the pressures, of work, school, and my other commitments. I wanted to try to draw the street society of Asheville as I knew it in the mid-1950s. I wanted to try to draw it from A to Z, from [the characters] Arkie to Zebulon, as somebody has pointed out. I just wanted to write that kind of novel and to show that all the classes are intertwined, that they affect one another's destinies. It's kind of a mechanical way to do it, but it was fun, both because I got to use a broader canvas, and I got to use some observations that I really hadn't had an opportunity to use before. And I got to employ some humor for the first time. It's the only one of my novels that doesn't take place on the farm.[4]

Taking as his model a small urban milieu (Asheville, North Carolina), utilizing the dynamics of its "street society," and generously employing levity and humor, Chappell found himself applying materials and methods radically different from the more meditative and overtly intellectual techniques that had informed the compositions of his first three books.

Ironically, Chappell wrote most of his comic and community-based Southern novel in Italy on the backs of the galley proofs for the largely despairing and solipsistic *Dagon*. When the book was published, Chappell's shift to a lighter, more readily accessible tone generally seemed to surprise and please critics, several of whom previously had appeared to suffer through *It Is Time, Lord*, *The Inkling*, and *Dagon*, ignoring, misreading, and/or condemning the dense intertextual and philosophical structures at the centers of those works. As opposed to the first three novels, reviewers seemed to grasp Chappell's moderate ambitions for *The Gaudy Place* and were generally laudatory of his attempt, praising the novel's clear, witty writing style and its convincingly accurate construction of a small urban

---

[4] Tersh Palmer, "Fred Chappell," *Appalachian Journal* 19/4 (Summer 1992): 405.

milieu. Critics literally applauded the book's tight readability with comments such as, "This delightful little novel is a series of character studies connected by an unpretentious plot."[5] However modest they may have regarded the book in terms of its conceptual aims, reviewers were generally complimentary in regard to the effectiveness with which Chappell fulfilled his intentions.

The only major problem early critics found in Chappell's fourth novel stemmed from its organization and point of view. As Jonathan Yardley notes, "If there is a serious problem to *The Gaudy Place*, it is structural."[6] Yardley's remark seems to have been extraordinarily perceptive since Chappell himself claims he was never comfortable with the book's organization: "Now the structure of the book—ponderous job that it is—is all mine, as far as I know. I'm not very satisfied with it" (INT). Chappell's shifting narratives and sudden transition to the first person in the book's final section seemed unnatural and contrived to some critics, several of whom believed the technique came across as a little too distracting or technically cute. Sammy Staggs, for example, laments that Chappell suffers from a "showy craftsmanship, which calls attention to itself so often that one finally wants to shout 'Plot! Point-of-view!'"[7] Staggs's concern, hyperbolic as it is, was shared by Chappell in slightly more deliberate and articulate terms:

> I feel ambivalent about that novel. I like some things about it. I like the first—I forget how many parts it has now—but I like all the parts except the last part. The last part does not quite work; it's not quite successful. But I was real proud of the first three or four parts.... But it needs—it only has one last chapter. It needs two more last chapters. And the last chapter switches over to first person; it all should have been in third person for the novel to work better. It's just that I discovered, as I was writing along, that if I shifted to first person in the last chapter, I wouldn't have to write one of

---

[5] Review of *The Gaudy Place*, *The New Republic* 168/22 (2 June 1973): 30.

[6] Jonathan Yardley, Review of *The Gaudy Place*, *New York Times Book Review* (13 May 1973): 36.

[7] Sammy Staggs, Review of *The Gaudy Place*, *Library Journal* 98 (15 February 1973): 563.

> the sections. I could cut it down. But it makes a sudden shift of point-of-view that is not really quite smooth or artistic, I'm afraid.[8]

Attempting to shorten the book, bringing about its conclusion without lengthening the narrative, Chappell moved to first person in the final section, which slightly disrupted the novel's structural rhythm. However, the book's overall formative composition remains a lively and original technique for developing largely mundane characters without allowing the text itself to become mundane. This observation was shared by at least one initial reviewer who praised Chappell for successfully rendering his periodically bland street people "without duplicating the despairing banality of their lives."[9] On a decidedly smaller scale, Chappell's task was not unlike John Dos Passos's in *Manhattan Transfer* and *USA*: to create a largely urban sense of place in compelling aesthetic terms through a convincing and realistic portrayal of less than ideal characters.[10] Attempting simultaneously to introduce and develop characters, advance a story, and construct a vivid sense of place, Chappell arrived at a promising structure that in the end he was required to bend, perhaps a little surreptitiously, in order to make it succeed.

The Importance of Place

Putting aside *The Gaudy Place*'s specific structural issues and how they interact with the book's setting, it is essential to establish how Chappell conceptualizes a purely general sense of place in art and writing. Speaking of portraying Appalachia, he maintains: "The spirit of the place is poetic, as is the spirit of any place when you come closer to the heart of it. I can't think of any book of real worth, except maybe Dante's *Inferno*, that says, underneath, 'This is a horrible, lousy place, nobody should live here, and the people are dumb' [laughs]. On the other hand, every book that deals with place is also a criticism of place, but not simply a wholesale thrashing" (INT). In composing his fourth novel, Chappell was more interested in the accurate representation of a place through interesting aesthetic means, as

---

[8] Carmine Palumbo, "Folklore and Literature: The Poetry and Fiction of Fred Chappell" (diss., University of Southwestern Louisiana, 1997) 168–69.

[9] Review of *The Gaudy Place*, *Kirkus Reviews* 41/1 (1 January 1973): 17.

[10] John Dos Passos, *Manhattan Transfer* (New York: Harper & Brothers, 1925); *USA* (New York: Harcourt, Brace, 1938).

opposed to polemical social criticism or the sentimental romanticizing of a specific community. With its focus on the street life of Braceboro and the corruption of its various leaders, *The Gaudy Place* is not unlike some of the more notable work of Hermann Broch, who in books such as *Die Schlafwandler* (*The Sleepwalkers*) and *Die Schuldlosen* (*The Guiltless*) chronicled the depravity and decadence of German life in the decades leading up to the Third Reich. Broch, gifted in demonstrating how noble impulses are almost always sullied and warped by unconscious depravity, often portrays corruption without changing a narrative's tone, which further enhances its power. Broch believed art that is not capable of reproducing the totality of a defined world is not really art, and such an aesthetic conceptualization is applicable to *The Gaudy Place* in which Chappell presents a nondiscriminatory, unifying vision of contradictory moral, economic, and social types, which results in a successful totalizing vision of a specific place. Just as A.'s and Zacharias's rambling conversation covers everything from A to Z in Broch's *Die Schuldlosen*, so *The Gaudy Place* offers a wide-ranging construction of place literally "from A(rkie) to Z(ebulon Johns Mackie)."[11]

Broch entertained the conviction, borrowed from Oswald Spengler, that history progresses in cycles of disintegrating and reintegrating value systems. Such a perspective is useful in considering the history of Appalachia as a place and the impact its development has had on its traditional cultural norms. As Ernest Lee notes in his introduction to an anthology of Appalachian writing, *Discovering Place*, "[The] struggle to feel a sense of place is a major one for writers who have lived or are living in the Appalachian region, an area of the country that has experienced profound changes...."[12] When Lee speaks of "profound changes" he suggests the presence, beginning in the mid- to late twentieth century, of interstate highways, large industries (such as the menacing Canton, North Carolina, paper mill that haunts several of Chappell's narratives), and the general economic hegemony that grasps the rest of the country in the form of corporate-owned drive-thrus, strip malls, and super chain stores. In *The Gaudy Place* Chappell moves from a more traditional, rural Appalachian background to an Appalachian city in the initial stages of being affected by

[11] R. H. W. Dillard, "Letters From a Distant Lover: The Novels of Fred Chappell," in *Hollins Critic* 10/2 (April 1973): 13.

[12] Ernest Lee, *Discovering Place: Readings from Appalachian Writers* (New York: McGraw-Hill, 1997) xi.

the transition of which Lee speaks—a place in which traditional values are disintegrating while new immigrant variables, such as Oxie/Theodorik Paparikis/Ted Pape, are in the process of being integrated.

In her essay "Place in Fiction," Eudora Welty explains, "For the artist to be unwilling to move, mentally or spiritually or physically, out of the familiar is a sign that spiritual timidity or poverty or decay has come upon him; for what is familiar will then have turned into all that is tyrannical."[13] Moving "out of the familiar" rural Appalachian landscape and into a more remote urban one, Chappell faced the challenge of conquering and portraying an entirely new sense of place. Furthermore, in choosing Asheville, North Carolina, as his model he was working with a setting that already had been etched memorably into the American literary imagination. As Frederick Turner asserts in his preface to *Spirit of Place*, "Thanks to our writers we also have a national literary landscape, places made special, if not sacred, because they have been the inspiration of literature."[14] Synonymous with Thomas Wolfe as much as Dublin is commensurate with Joyce, Asheville carries with it a "literary landscape" and legacy that Chappell had either to confront or ignore. Because Appalachia, rural and urban, had changed to the extent that it had since Wolfe's time, Chappell was able to choose the latter path. Furthermore, Wolfe's Asheville was constructed in relation to the Gant family and especially the youthful and dreamy Eugene of *Look Homeward, Angel*, which allowed Wolfe to write in the wistful, poetic, and occasionally sprawling prose he so admired.[15] Although Chappell's Lin Harper has certain naive and idealistic similarities with Eugene, the novel as a whole, both in its compact stylistic tone and street-based subject matter, is a vastly different work from Wolfe's, opening up previously neglected aspects of Asheville in a distinctly contemporary format. Anais Nin commented in the late 1960s, "It is a curious anomaly that we listen to jazz, we look at modern paintings, we live in modern houses of modern design, we travel in jet planes, yet we continue to read novels written in a tempo and style which is not of our time and not related to any

[13] Robert H. Brinkmeyer Jr., *Remapping Southern Literature: Contemporary Southern Writers and the West* (Athens: University of Georgia Press, 2000) vii.

[14] Frederick Turner, *Spirit of Place: The Making of an American Literary Landscape* (San Francisco: Sierra Club, 1989) x.

[15] Thomas Wolfe, *Look Homeward, Angel* (New York: Charles Scribner's Sons, 1929).

of these influences."[16] With its episodic, multiple narratives and use of street diction, *The Gaudy Place* brings Asheville up to date in a manner of which Nin would have approved. Although Wolfe and Chappell addressed the same geographical area, they were, in fact, describing, as a result of their respective times and divergent aesthetic intentions, two very distinct places.

In an early study of American city fiction, Blanch Gelfant makes the obvious but important generalization, "Behind the rise of the modern city novel has been the awareness—always growing stronger and more clearly articulated—that city life is distinctive and that it offers the writer peculiarly modern material and demands of him literary expression in a modern idiom."[17] Beneath Gelfant's focus on the city is the assertion that place in general shapes aesthetic technique, which is true of Chappell's novels. In the first three books, and especially the second and third, the isolated pastoral landscapes are conducive to meditation and reflection. Beyond associations between family members, human relationships are largely deemphasized in favor of the protagonists' interior psychological and philosophical monologues. In *The Gaudy Place* relationships and dialogue are constant and fundamental to the novel, especially as they begin to overlap and interact in unforeseen ways toward the book's conclusion. Chappell's fourth novel is also "faster" than the first three, the urban pace of life causing events and action to unfold at a quicker, sparser, more literal pace. Time is also important in the book in a different sense. In their introduction to *Literary Landscapes of the British Isles*, David Daiches and John Flower remark, "It would surely be a needless puritanism that would deny to readers the satisfactions and insights provided by topographical aids to reading and especially by linking place with time so as to understand more clearly the total ambience within which a writer's imagination moved."[18] With the exception of Andrew Harper's brief academic regional history (*GP*, 150–53) and Zebulon Johns Mackie's pompous amateur genealogical studies, less importance is placed on time-related aspects of place such as memory and history in *The Gaudy Place.* Unlike the reflective protagonists of Chappell's first three books, the characters in the fourth novel are generally forward-

---

[16] Anais Nin, *The Novel of the Future* (New York: Macmillan, 1968) 29.

[17] Blanch Housman Gelfant, *The American City Novel* (Norman: University of Oklahoma Press, 1954) 3.

[18] David Daiches and John Flower, *Literary Landscapes of the British Isles: A Narrative Atlas* (New York: Paddington, 1979) 1.

looking, searching for the right con, deal, or general course of action to improve their various stations in life. Even the self-proclaimed backward-looking Mackie boasts that he studies and likes history "even though there didn't seem much a feller could *do* with it" (*GP*, 155), subordinating his interest in the past in order to become a corrupt, real-estate developing civic leader instead.

As Robert Brinkmeyer maintains, the movement away from memory and historical introspection is a postmodern quality of contemporary Southern literature: "In part because of the influence of developments in postmodern literature—a literature, broadly speaking, celebrating imaginative free play rather than memory—Southern writers have more and more been striking out on their own, moving away from the 'imaginative' shape of 'classic' Southern literature that is so secure in regional place, history, and memory."[19] Although Chappell does not forsake "regional place," in his case North Carolina, in any of his novels, *The Gaudy Place* does portray a different western North Carolina environment, an urban one, and does so without invoking history and memory as major themes. Instead of employing the meditative and often traumatic histories and memories of what Brinkmeyer calls "'classic' Southern literature," Chappell reveals place through the largely spontaneous and visceral manner in which his characters function in their environment. In listing his key elements for considering place, Leonard Lutwack includes "place in its literalness, a character's response to this place in both its concreteness and its symbolical relation to his life, and an important action transpiring in this place. This is a proper use of place in a measure not too meager to do justice to the importance of place in narrative not so concrete as to overwhelm with fact the imaginative power in the art of fiction."[20] In pointing out the significance of "a character's response" to place, Lutwack underscores the defining importance of the independent variables existing in the same space that constitutes a place. Along similar lines, Bertrand Russell paraphrases Leibniz when he puts forth the definition, "*Place* is that, which is the same in different moments to different existent things, when their relations of co-existence with certain other existents, which are supposed to continue fixed from one

---

[19] Brinkmeyer, *Remapping Southern Literature*, 26.

[20] Leonard Lutwack, *The Role of Place in Literature* (Syracuse: Syracuse University Press, 1984) 26.

of those moments to the other, agree entirely together."[21] Throwing different "existent things," in this case different characters, into an environment that is the same for all of them, Chappell, drawing on the roots of the naturalistic novel, constructs a drama in which place and its variables/characters mutually work together in order to define each other.

Although characters in the book both shape place and are defined by it, Braceboro constitutes a setting in which people are unable to map clearly in their minds either their own positions or the urban totality in which they find themselves. Yet the novel bases much of its literary drama and humor upon this very tension and ambiguity. Concentrating on urban aspects with literary potentialities, James Machor describes his book *Pastoral Cities* as "a study of a conception of America's urban environment that has played an important role in our culture and literature. I have called this conception urban pastoralism."[22] In the interesting way in which its environment is conceptualized as revealing and being revealed by truths about its characters and human nature, *The Gaudy Place* would seem to constitute one of Machor's works of "urban pastoralism." However, any substantial conclusions regarding the relationships between characters and place remain speculative and elusive since, ultimately, at least in terms of perception, Braceboro constitutes a different place for every character. As Gerd Hurm argues in *Fragmented Urban Images: The American City in Modern Fiction from Stephen Crane to Thomas Pynchon*, "The social and literary modes emerging in the modern city cannot be reduced to single causes and deterministic relationships."[23] In *The Gaudy Place* a static set of environmental conditions has varying effects on characters, while characters construct and define the same place in erratically different terms. Out of this complex matrix emerges a place producing divergent characters, characters perceiving different places, and a novel of varied and conflicting perspectives and faces.

---

[21] Bertrand Russell, *A Critical Exposition of the Philosophy of Leibniz* (London: George Allen & Unwin, 1900) 252.

[22] James Machor, *Pastoral Cities: Urban Ideals and the Symbolic Landscape of America* (Madison: University of Wisconsin Press, 1987) xi.

[23] Gerd Hurm, *Fragmented Urban Images: The American City in Modern Fiction from Stephen Crane to Thomas Pynchon* (New York: Peter Lang, 1991) 326.

Hustlers and Whores

Richard Gray begins his book *Southern Aberrations: Writers of the American South and the Problems of Regionalism* with the blunt yet accurate observation, "All relationships with place are difficult, but some are more difficult than others."[24] The most difficult and satisfying aspect of *The Gaudy Place* for Chappell was the successful and convincing construction of Gimlet Street and its seedy inhabitants as an original urban environment. He remarks:

> I drew, I think I was the first person to draw, the street people of the New South. The whole first three chapters are about street people, the people who live and make their living by their wits on the street. One's just a two-bit hustler, a kid that I knew and admired—this really takes place on Lexington Avenue in Asheville in the late fifties—and a prostitute. I used to see bunches of them and interviewed them in a couple of bars on Lexington Avenue. And I knew a bail bondsman who had made his way off the street and had landed a little bit of a semi-legitimate business. I just kind of went up the ladder of society in that novel.[25]

Chappell's interest in multi-/cross-class relationships is genuine and evident in other works such as his unpublished and undated short story "The Little Wedding," which involves a wealthy man's temporary marriage to a prostitute.[26] *The Gaudy Place* embraces this class theme on a much larger scale, introducing a cast of characters, each generally higher in social standing than the previous individual, and providing a number of conflicting narratives that eventually merge into a single story.[27]

At the bottom of Chappell's social and narrative ladders are the hustlers and whores of Gimlet Street, and he begins the novel with a character so far down the ladder that he hardly exists in society's eyes: Arkie (James Parker McClellan). Chappell underscores Arkie's lack of societal presence on the book's first page by having the omnipresent barfly Teach mock his lack of public documentation: "You got a driver's license? ...You

---

[24] Richard Gray, *Southern Aberrations: Writers of the American South and the Problems of Regionalism* (Baton Rouge: Louisiana State University Press, 2000) ix.

[25] Palumbo, "Folklore and Literature," 168–69.

[26] Box WN-2, writings by Chappell, notebooks subseries.

[27] The possible exception to this pattern would be the introduction of Linn Harper (*GP*, 61) before Oxie (*GP*, 101). Although Oxie is a wealthy, mature adult, Linn is the product of a higher socioeconomic circle. One assumes that Oxie would have appeared before Linn had Linn been an adult instead of a naive boy.

got a social security number? ...Birth certificate? ...And no school records and no vaccination scars and no doctor's records and no dentist's records. I guess you don't even have a mailing address" (*GP*, 3). By all societal measures Arkie is not a real person, utterly invisible to the organized governments administering his city and state. However, in response to Teach's premise that he does not exist, Arkie stubbornly maintains, "I do though" (*GP*, 4), and in the context of Gimlet Street's loose, undocumented society he does function as a kind of plankton or parasite, scurrying about at the bottom of the economic food chain, living off other people's crumbs—a dime here, a quarter there. His grand life's ambition, to replace Oxie as Clemmie's pimp, serves as a humorous point of transition between his own paltry socioeconomic status and Oxie's, the successful Gimlet Street mover and shaker having passed on to more lucrative and socially acceptable downtown cons and manipulations.

Arkie's street-hustling characteristics align him with memorable impoverished fictional juveniles such as Dickens's Oliver Twist and Horatio Alger's Ragged Dick, and his name suggests the word "archetype." In fact, Chappell maintains that Arkie grew out of a specific literary source:

> Sometimes you can't tell what's a literary inspiration and what comes from what you observe, because sometimes those two are very similar. There's a wonderful novel called *Don Sequndo Sombra* about a street hustler and how he makes his way in the world.[28] I must have read that when we were visiting Italy, I'm not quite sure. At any rate, that novel seemed to me to have a lot of energy and a lot of affection for its waif, and I admired the ingenuity of the poor characters, how they made a living in the city in the novel. I had some knowledge of how that worked in Asheville, North Carolina and so that novel kind of gave me the idea for how to do it. (INT)

Chappell based Arkie on Ricardo Guiraldes's memorable fourteen-year-old *guacho* Fabio Cáceres, and just as Fabio leaves his trivial, streetwise existence behind him to become a nomadic *gaucho*, so Arkie constantly looks for ways to improve his condition and, at the novel's conclusion, implies that he is fleeing Braceboro ("Fuck the law, I'm going down to ARKANSAS!" [*GP*, 177]), presumably to lead a wandering life resembling Fabio's.

[28] Ricardo Guiraldes, *Don Sequndo Sombra* (Buenos Aires: "El Ateneo," 1929).

Despite the fact that he lacks any substantial knowledge of the way larger business and society function, Arkie possesses a sleazy cleverness that enables him to make a living and even accumulate a small savings from working the streets. Furthermore, although uneducated he has an extraordinarily quick mind and excellent memory. For instance, the narrator reveals that he "could jabber it [the gambling odds] off like a radio announcer, faster than they could take it down, and never a mistake. He could carry policy numbers too, all in his head like that" (*GP*, 7–8). In addition to his intelligence, Arkie is uncommonly perceptive, astonishing Oxie with his prophetic prediction that Oxie will stop pimping Clemmie, and constantly keeping his ears open in the bars and on the streets, hungrily digesting any information that might be useful to him. Arkie might well boast, like the narrator of Chappell's poem "Page," "But I'm no featherwit, as soon you'd see, / Were you my master. For I have a clever / Way with secrets, how to weasel them out."[29] When he "weasels out" the fact that Oxie is likely to cut Clemmie loose he surprises the hardened hustler and earns Clemmie's respect.

Although he lacks any formal education, Arkie succeeds in making money and predicting events because he is so thoroughly a product of the place in which he functions. Like the cockroach or the rat, he thrives at the bottom of the food chain while the larger animals work each other over and wear each other down. The name of his environment, "gimlet," is defined as both a small tool with a crew tip for boring holes and a cocktail. It is a perfect moniker for Arkie's section of Braceboro, where alcohol flows freely and one is constantly either screwing others or being screwed in a ceaseless struggle to survive. Chappell emphasizes Arkie's suitability for this urban jungle in a number of ways. For instance, he records Arkie's seemingly unnatural hatred of sunlight and the smells of vegetables and earth at the farmer's market: "Arkie rubbed his nose with his wrist, not caring for the smells of vegetables and jonquils and fresh earth. The sunlight seemed worse. When he cut the corner of Rance Avenue he was in the shadow of the buildings and he felt a lot better" (*GP*, 13–14). Chappell effectively couples Arkie's dislike for the life-giving sun and traditionally pleasing organic matter with his love of cool, hard concrete—when he ducks out of

---

[29] Fred Chappell, *Castle Tzingal* (Baton Rouge: Louisiana State University Press, 1984) 10.

the sunlight he is not only thankful for the dark coolness but also the reassuring nearness of the synthetic buildings themselves. Chappell extends this condition as the day comes to an end: "He began to feel better as the sun got lower" (*GP*, 25), underscoring Arkie's nocturnal predisposition. While most boys his age are preparing for bed, Arkie is licking his lips and making his rounds, hunting for inebriated johns to hustle.

Young and still developing, Arkie is formed by the place in which he functions, which allows him to recognize patterns in his environment, enabling him, in turn, to make accurate predictions regarding future events. Chappell effectively uses Arkie's prophetic capacity in order to foreshadow various incidents in the novel. In addition to his aforementioned prediction of Clemmie's rejection by Oxie, Arkie believes that Oxie does not know Gimlet anymore: "[H]e don't know this territory near as good as I do. Got too many other things on his mind" (*GP*, 29). Arkie intuitively senses Oxie's borderline existence between Gimlet Street and downtown politics, between the hulking pimp Oxie and the suave bondsman Ted Pape, and believes that Oxie's juggling of these two spheres has lessened his knowledge of the former. Chappell also has Arkie foreshadow the introduction of Linn Harper when he describes Arkie playing Space Patrol pinball (*GP*, 30). Arkie's ability to win money at Space Patrol sets him off against his youthful opposite, Linn, who reads *Galactic Patrol* and contemplates cosmic ideals. Whereas Arkie plays the game for the literal and practical purpose of winning money from opponents, Linn reads a book with an almost identical title in order to revel in abstractions and later purposefully performs a materialistic act of theft for something he does not want or need (chicken feed) as a humorously absurd philosophical exercise.

Arkie also foreshadows his own criminal actions at the end of the novel and suggests an earlier version of the book when he performs his endearing dance while singing, "I'm going down to Arkansas!" (*GP*, 26, 30). At the book's conclusion the song implies that Arkie will be fleeing Braceboro, yet he has been singing it throughout the novel, insinuating that his unplanned departure has been inevitable all along. In fact, in an earlier version of *The Gaudy Place* Chappell had arranged for Arkie to leave Braceboro much sooner:

> I wanted to write a picaresque novel and it was the one I was working on that became *The Gaudy Place*. I think I had written the first chapter of *The Gaudy Place* and I thought it would be great for Arkie to take off and get

> out of there, bum around the country. Then, as I was pondering this, the design of *The Gaudy Place*—how it really could be a very tight story and a very wry one—came to me, so I went in that direction. I really would like to write a picaresque novel. I enjoy reading them, but I guess I'll never have much chance to do it. Two of my favorite novels are *Don Quixote* and a novel by Thornton Wilder called *Heaven's My Destination* and, of course, *Huckleberry Finn*. I love the spirit of the picaresque. (INT)

Resisting the temptation to transform Arkie into a picaresque waif, Chappell kept him scurrying around the cage that is Braceboro rather than turning him loose on the rest of the country. However, if Arkie is a rat, he is an uncommonly adept one, knowing his way around the maze and how to work both it and its other inhabitants to his own, albeit small, advantage.

As the speaker summarizes in Chappell's poem, "The Peaceable Kingdom of Emerald Windows," "But then we-all is a primitive sort / Of animule," and this effectively describes the instinct- and material-based existences of the people who live and work on Gimlet Street.[30] If Arkie is a kind of parasitic predatory rodent living off others, his slow-witted love interest, Clemmie, resembles an exploited herd animal. A victim of and slave to her environment, she lacks the proper skills to survive on her own. By turns naive, paranoid, and feeble-minded, Clemmie, both humorously and poignantly, demonstrates—through her own darkly ironic, ignorant actions—that she really does need a pimp to look after her. Nowhere is her ineptitude more in evidence than when she hands over one hundred dollars to Teach for safekeeping (*GP*, 34, 55). A weak-willed alcoholic, Teach promptly spends all but a few dollars on drinks. Although she is generally unhappy and unsatisfied with her life on Gimlet Street, Clemmie cannot conceive of any alternative. When Arkie tells her that Oxie is climbing out of Gimlet Street, she wonders, "What did you climb *to*, though, if you left Gimlet?" (*GP*, 33). Like Arkie, Clemmie is a product of the environment in which she functions; yet, unlike her diminutive admirer, she lacks the ability to manipulate her environment to her own ends, helplessly allowing it to shape her destiny instead.

Relatively early in the book Teach is reading the futuristic science-fiction novel *Galactic Patrol* (*GP*, 35–36), in which the protagonist Kim

---

[30] Fred Chappell, *Earthsleep* (Baton Rouge: Louisiana State University Press, 1980) 15.

Kinnison tries to survive inside a hostile alien base.[31] The plot of *Galactic Patrol* comments on *The Gaudy Place* in general in the way it follows an individual's attempt to survive in a closed unfamiliar system. Although this theme is applicable to several of the novel's characters, it seems to have particular resonance for Oxie/Ted Pape who is trying to move into the exclusive alien system of downtown politics from his familiar roots on Gimlet Street. Pape is fearful of going back to Gimlet ("A man could work his way up from Gimlet Street once in his life but he could never do it twice" [*GP*, 102]), fearful of becoming Oxie again. He has escaped the cage or been granted a furlough and does not want to be thrown back into it. Ironically, his semi-legitimate job involves getting people out of jail.

Pape's fear of returning to Gimlet Street humanizes his character but also results in several humorous incidents. For instance, in the nouveau-rich tradition, he equates outward image with success: "His carefully resplendent appearance, for example, was for him no luxury but grinding necessity" (*GP*, 102). The theme reappears a couple of pages later when the woman he sleeps with corrects his grammar (*GP*, 104). In the tradition of William Gay's *The Beggar's Opera*, *The Gaudy Place* uses Oxie/Pape to portray, often comically, trashy people imitating their supposed socioeconomic betters while, as we shall see, their so-called betters dabble in trash themselves. The humorous quality of Pape's attempted ascension of the class ladder is intensified by the utter seriousness with which he toils up it. Practical and methodical, he plods through the best-selling *How to Win Friends and Influence People* (*GP*, 41) despite the fact that he can barely read, and perhaps the funniest scene in the book involves the nearly illiterate Pape searching in vain for a newspaper at the city library (*GP*, 124).[32] Yet for all of Pape's comic superficiality and illiteracy, he is neither shallow nor ignorant. In fact, his inability to read aids him in recalling Linn Harper's face from an obscure newspaper article—not having words to distract him, he remembers the picture. Pape also measures his practical knowledge favorably against Freene Sluder, a college-educated local of decent social standing who lacks common sense (*GP*, 107).

---

[31] E. E. Smith, Ph.D., *Galactic Patrol* (New York: Fantasy Press, 1950).

[32] Dale Carnegie, *How to Win Friends and Influence People* (New York: Simon and Schuster, 1936).

If Pape is unsure of himself in his downtown dealings and in the Harper home on Wedgewood Drive (*GP*, 140), he is precisely the reverse when he returns to Gimlet Street as Oxie, a place where people respect his accomplishments and influence. Clemmie underscores his high status when she muses, "Any dumb john could work hard. Luck was part of Oxie's class" (*GP*, 38). Oxie's success is based on his ability to know his environment; like Arkie he is a product of Gimlet Street and knows it the way Zebulon Johns Mackie understands downtown politics: "He knew every inch of it, every wall, corner and door.... He knew the graffiti painted on the bricks and the weeds that sprang up in the gravel strewn alleys. And he knew the faces; especially he knew the faces. He knew everything" (*GP*, 108). Like Arkie, Oxie uses his perceptive wits in order to prosper, and Chappell unites the two hustlers in a number of ways. In addition to the obvious similarity of their names, when Clemmie mentions Arkie to Oxie, Oxie visualizes him nostalgically: "The picture of him stayed in Oxie's head because when he saw him he couldn't help but remembering the way he himself had come along" (*GP*, 116). The narrator also juxtaposes descriptions of the hustlers, especially "everybody knows Arkie" (*GP*, 24) and "everybody knows Oxie" (*GP*, 126). Oxie evokes the novel's title when he thinks of Gimlet as a "feverish gaudy place" (*GP*, 134), yet it is a place that reflects and is reflected by him, a place that has produced him and of which he is master.

Academics and Aristocrats

After recounting the everyday existences of Arkie and Clemmie, the novel undergoes a dramatic shift in terms of tone and subject. With the chapter titled "Ignominy of a Skylark," the book segues from the visceral hustling themes of Gimlet to the formless adolescent and academic idealism of Linn Harper's nerdy, adolescent boys club (*GP*, 61). In contrast to the uncensored reality of the first two chapters, the Skylark section portrays a failed attempt to apply a "code of behavior" (*GP*, 61) to practical conditions, namely as a result of the organization's humorous virgin naiveté with regard to genuine adult experience. Since the group's founding, membership has shrunk from nine to three as the boys have matured hormonally and developed strong interests in sports, girls, and James Bond. Yet, the club toils on led by its idealistic leader and aspiring intellectual, Linn Harper, who, like Wolfe's Eugene Gant in *Look Homeward, Angel*, seeks dreamy solace from the mundane reality of Asheville, North Carolina, in books and ideas. Unlike Eugene, however, Linn's interest in literature is a result of his heavy science-fiction reading (*GP*, 62–65), which allows him to make a connection between physical science and the universe as being "a gaudy place in which we live" (*GP*, 64). Linn's conception of a "gaudy place," with its focus on science, space, universality, and abstract thought, stands in direct opposition to Oxie's, which absorbs only the literal characteristics of life on Gimlet.

Despite his fascination with idealism, Linn's days of pure abstraction are numbered. As the narrator relates, "For ours is an age in which, even among the innocents, idealism cannot long endure" (*GP*, 66). Ironically, it is the Skylarks' very idealization of philosophy that leads to their ridiculous attempt to apply it practically and results in its inevitable rejection. Just as the reader chuckles while Ted Pape illiterately stumbles about the local library, so Chappell pokes fun at Linn as he tries to reason his way toward a practical theory of existence without the benefit of any real life experiences. In the mountain cabin of Terry Burge's father—an isolated, pastoral setting where, as in William Golding's *Lord of the Flies*, the juveniles make their own immature and unrealistic rules—the Skylarks challenge Linn to apply Camus's fictional representation of a gratuitous criminal act (*GP*, 75–76).[33] The absurdity of the idea's conception is matched by the humor with which Chappell renders the act as the square, clean-cut boy awkwardly attempts to pilfer a bag of chicken feed. The comedy reaches its height when one of the arresting officers accuses Linn of being a dope-fiend, completely shocking him since he is ignorant of the fact that such people exist (*GP*, 82). As opposed to Arkie's effective street smarts, Linn's intelligence is abstract and ultimately useless in the practical sense: "Yet for all his reputation for brains he'd been unable to steal twenty-five pounds of chicken feed" (*GP*, 84). Like George Brush in one of Chappell's favorite picaresque novels, Thornton Wilder's *Heaven's My Destination*, Linn applies his idealism and naiveté to everyday people only to have them end up either misunderstanding or disliking him.[34]

The inability of Linn's background and worldview to handle practical situations dawns on him while in jail: "[H]e didn't live like this, he had never even imagined the possibility of living like this" (*GP*, 91–92). Like the aliens

---

[33] William Golding, *Lord of the Flies* (New York: Coward-McCann, 1955).

[34] Thornton Wilder, *Heaven's My Destination* (New York: Longmans, 1934).

in one of his science-fiction books, who "believe in an ancient legend which says that their race arose as a result of immigrants from another galaxy" (*GP*, 145–46), Linn constitutes an immigrant in unknown territory. Interestingly, his father Andrew Harper finds himself in similar immigrant circumstances when he moves his family to western North Carolina and learns about the history of his wife's family, the Mackies. Figuring out on his own the involvement of Zebulon Johns Mackie in local political corruption, Andrew initially is resistant when Katherine suggests that they let Mackie get Linn out of jail. Yet Andrew is forced to compromise his idealism when he realizes he lacks the ability to function effectively in the downtown Braceboro environment. As Katherine says, "You don't know any of those people down there" (*GP*, 149).

Although Linn and Andrew are united by their common idealism ("an abstract double allegiance to an idea of justice" [*GP*, 139]), Andrew has no practical choice but to submit to Mackie's authority. A product of class and privilege, Mackie has the inherent ability to manipulate the events of downtown Braceboro to his advantage. Furthermore, as a successful politician, he also is capable of swaying people purely as a result of his formidable charisma and powerful personality. For example, he coerces a less-than-enthusiastic Andrew into undertaking a history of Bunker County, a purely narcissistic exercise since, as Mackie maintains, "A lot of it I don't even have to look up. Part of our family history, you know" (*GP*, 156). Mackie's historical browbeating of Andrew foreshadows the political bullying he employs in illegally making money from the city (*GP*, 159), and when he finally encounters Pape he speaks down to him "with a distant, almost cold, reserve" (*GP*, 176)—the same manner in which Oxie condescendingly addresses his Gimlet Street acquaintances. Chappell makes this connection purposefully since he is trying to demonstrate that, rather than being morally or socially superior, Mackie constitutes only a larger, older, more powerful, and socially acceptable thug, opportunistically pimping and conning his way about city hall. Even the appearance and sound of his name associates him with the tactics of the Gimlet Street crowd (Mackie, Arkie, Clemmie, Oxie). With grim irony, Chappell illustrates how little difference there is after all between people from seemingly distant points on Braceboro's socioeconomic ladder.

Toward the Kirkman Novels

At the conclusion of *The Gaudy Place* nearly everyone is displaced from the environments in which they best function: Arkie is jumping town, the seemingly invulnerable Mackie lies bleeding in a parking lot, Oxie perhaps has overreached his ambitions, and Andrew Harper laughs at it all while his son sits in a jail cell. The rich golden light of freedom and possibility shining just outside the door on the book's dust jacket seems an almost laughably distant thing for everyone except perhaps the highway-bound Arkie—an ironic twist since he is the perpetrator of the book's central violent act. Yet it is crucial to acknowledge that the reader *can* laugh along with Andrew at the book's ugly company and their comedy of errors. Mackie's wound is superficial, Oxie will keep striving upward, and Linn will walk out of his cell a more mature young man. Chappell's first three novels have debilitating traumas and body counts, flirting with madness and destroying lives; *The Gaudy Place* also interrogates existence but does so with humor and forgiveness—the characters have futures and life will go on. In this way one recognizes the transitional importance of the book between the first three novels and the Kirkman narratives Chappell began writing in the 1970s—a relationship he unknowingly underscores himself when describing the composition of *I Am One of You Forever*:

> I had been engaged for many years in writing a very dark, experimental kind of fiction, which everybody else called Southern Gothic. Except for a novel called *The Gaudy Place*, in which I tried to write a very detailed, realistic novel, these were kind of symbolic novels of heavy philosophical import, and then when I switched over to poetry I didn't need to write things quite so heavy as that any more, it seemed to me. I wanted to lighten up a little bit, and write a book that people might enjoy reading, a book that might sell some copies for a change.[35]

Between *Dagon* (1968) and *The Gaudy Place* (1973) Chappell published his first book of poetry, *The World Between the Eyes* (1971), which he felt allowed him to "lighten up a little bit" in his fiction. Seen in this manner, the golden light on the novel's cover might have more to do with the book's author than its characters. Forsaking the brooding existentialism of the first three books and escaping, opening a door, into another way of writing novels—emphasizing such elements as place, humor, and

[35] Palumbo, "Folklore and Literature," 167.

storytelling—Chappell passed into a new stage of novel-writing that would light the way for his output in the ensuing decades.

Part 2

Short Fiction

Chapter 5

Projecting the Inner Life: Initiation, Appalachian, and Academic Narratives

> *I guess because I'm always working on some manuscript, I feel like...it's almost as if my inner life is the manuscript I'm working on—whatever kind of manuscript that is. And I use that to project my characters' inner lives on the page too. It's a rather old device but it's one I feel comfortable with.* —Chappell, INT.

In his foreword to the dark collection of fiction *The Nightshade Nightstand Reader*, Chappell says of short stories, "In the best, the most original stories, there is a sense of fresh discovery in almost every line. This is what makes a short story lifelike. Without this sense of discovery the novel would put the short story out of business forever because of the greater power of verisimilitude possible to the longer form."[1] Many of Chappell's short stories portray their "sense of discovery" through the life-changing epiphanies of their respective protagonists, who confront various dilemmas and are significantly altered by them. Not surprisingly, most of Chappell's stories that reflect such changes are, as opposed to many of his historical and fantastic tales, works of contemporary realism, often summoning distinct settings and dynamics from Chappell's own life. In this way—like most

[1] Fred Chappell, foreword, in *The Nightshade Nightstand Reader*, ed. Roy Zarucchi and Carolyn Page (Troy ME: Nightshade, 1995) vi.

writers—Chappell energizes the discoveries of his fictional protagonists with the authentic intensity and knowledge of his own experiences and background.

This chapter investigates incidents from Chappell's extensive short fiction, published and unpublished, in which central discoveries are effected against primarily autobiographical backdrops. Since a disproportionately large number of these narratives were written early in Chappell's career, I contend that many of the texts constitute attempts by Chappell to discover his own fictional themes and voice while portraying the familiar tensions and challenges of both his Appalachian youth and his more immediate academic surroundings as an aspiring student writer and professor. As Bakhtin asserts in his consideration of the *bildungsroman* form, "The hero himself, his character, becomes a variable in the formula.... Changes in the hero himself acquire *plot* significance, and thus the entire plot of the novel is reinterpreted and reconstructed."[2] The central discoveries of many of Chappell's protagonists follow Bakhtin's pattern in the sense that they are not only life-changing but narrative-changing—disrupting and reconstructing the fictional world of the developing protagonist for the reader. Furthermore, on occasion the sense of discovery and development goes beyond the characteristics of individual narratives to exhibit collective dynamics of Chappell's general approach to short fiction. For example, his first collection of short stories, *Moments of Light* (1980), follows an initiating and developmental framework in conveying an episodic history of humanity. As Chappell relates, although he intended for the general pattern to be veiled, he was pleased when Annie Dillard identified it: "I chose the stories and arranged them according to a secret design that I was confident would never be discovered. But when Annie Dillard sent her introduction to the book, I found that she understood and outlined in cold print my every best intention. I was exhilarated but a little dismayed too."[3] Central to specific stories as well as groupings of them, Chappell's discovery narratives reveal his evolving exploration of fictional voice through his treatment of primarily autobiographical subjects.

---

[2] M. M. Bakhtin, "The *Bildungsroman* and Its Significance in the History of Realism (Toward a Historical Typology of the Novel)," in *Speech Genres and Other Late Essays*, trans. Vern W. McGee, ed. Caryl Emerson and Michael Holquist (Austin: University of Texas Press, 1986) 21.

[3] "Fred Chappell," box WM-1, writings by Chappell, miscellaneous subseries, 37.

Many of Chappell's initial discovery narratives involve the introduction of young boys into adult experience. His early prose contributions to *Under Twenty-five: Duke Narrative and Verse, 1945–1962* (1963) ("Inheritance" and "January") and two issues of the *Red Clay Reader* ("Band of Brothers" [1964] and "Gothic Perplexities" [1966]) all center on the lives of juvenile male protagonists. Of these stories, "Band of Brothers"—its title, a reference to Shakespeare's *Henry V*, originally was "Invasions"—is singular as a kind of prequel to initiation for the unusual way in which it conceptualizes developmental events that never occur.[4] Dave and Kurt, two restless high school males, fantasize about fleeing home and, like Huckleberry Finn, contemplate "floating a raft down the Mississippi."[5] However, resembling Tom Sawyer more than Huck, the boys are too firmly anchored to their sheltered childhoods to undertake such a drastic initiation experience. Instead, they ironically return to the school "playground" where they join other boys in making realistic, empty juvenile remarks and threats and smoking cigarettes. The immaturity and triviality of the boys' lives and stresses are perhaps most evident at the story's conclusion when Dave freezes up pathetically while giving a book report on *Madame Bovary* in front of his English class. In the early unpublished version of "Band of Brothers," "Invasions," Dave's character is named James Christopher, directly linking him to the sensitive, sheltered protagonist of *It Is Time, Lord*. Like the central figure in Chappell's first novel, Dave and James are compromised by minor events because their range of experience is so small. As a result, potential initiation episodes—fights, sex, flights down the Mississippi—are constantly deferred, and an exciting alternative life remains always just barely not quite out of reach.

Chappell progresses from an insular high school setting to a college milieu in "Gothic Perplexities"—an excerpt from an unpublished, untitled novel manuscript—in which two young undergraduates, John Sharp and Wayne Walker, travel to a remote lake to fish.[6] As in "Band of Brothers," Chappell emphasizes the immature triviality of the young men's lives at school, introducing Wayne's roommate Ray Courtney, a stereotypical undergraduate male, who habitually stays out into the early morning hours

---

[4] "Invasions" appears as a handwritten manuscript in one of Chappell's notebooks (box WN-1, writings by Chappell, notebooks subseries).

[5] Fred Chappell, "Band of Brothers," *Red Clay Reader* 1 (1964): 34.

[6] Box WN-3, writings by Chappell, notebooks subseries.

partying and womanizing. Ray's petty, desultory existence contrasts with that of John Burnette, the perceptive elderly man from whom Wayne and John rent their fishing boat. Although he lacks a formal education, Burnette is exceedingly wise in the ways of life, prompting John to remark in admiration, "[T]here's all kinds of education."[7] The young men's experience with the old man gives them a new perspective on their own lives, and the story concludes with the epiphanic passage: "When they arrived at the college, the parking lot was loud with racing motors and shouts from adolescent throats. The students were scurrying off to beer halls and to Friday night dates. Tomorrow there was an important home football game.... Sharp drummed the heel of his open hand four times on the steering wheel. 'Jesus Christ, Walker,' he said, 'what are we *doing* here?'"[8] Having temporarily escaped to a hard, vivid reality away from college, Walker and Sharp return to realize the ridiculous, plastic decadence of their existence on campus. Having participated in another life, one much more genuine and real than their own, they are initiated into the pain, beauty, and "perplexity" of the adult world.

The rich, eventful life of John Burnette, portrayed against the superficial backdrop of Winton College, serves as a catalyst for change in "Gothic Perplexities." Tensions and choices involving two distinct worlds fuel several others of Chappell's early narratives. For example, in the unpublished short story "The Two Ministries" a sixteen-year-old hitchhiker, Paul, witnesses a violent encounter between an evangelist and an agnostic hitchhiking wanderer.[9] As in "Gothic Perplexities," conflicting worlds and worldviews are used in order to define realistic and superficial aspects of existence for a young protagonist. The fervent evangelist Sam, drunk on scripture, is callously oblivious to the tenuous pregnant condition of his wife Martha and the dangers of confronting strangers. On the other hand, the agnostic wanderer Ray Morris is a pure literalist—not wanting to be bothered by the preacher's useless abstractions, he wrestles away the fanatic's gun and pistol-whips him with it after he is forced to pray at gunpoint. Morris tells the preacher's wife, "I feel plumb sorry for you," and walks off in the direction of his predetermined destination, unaffected either

---

[7] Fred Chappell, "Gothic Perplexities," *Red Clay Reader* 3 (1966): 49.

[8] Ibid.

[9] Box WF-4, writings by Chappell, fiction subseries. Included in the appendix ().

by the preacher's shaky theology or their visceral struggle.[10] Witnessing this exchange casts the boy into a wilderness of existential doubt, although at the end of the story it appears his own views more closely approach those of the wanderer. His literal reply to the question "What if Jesus came tonight?" ("Not tonight.... I'm tired") and his practical response to the news of his uncle's death associate him with the pragmatic outlook of Ray Morris—an allegorical irony since Paul's roadside epiphany is the diametric opposite of his biblical namesake's.[11]

Chappell again constructs realistic and superficial worlds, this time along cultural lines, as a stimulus for initiation in his unpublished story "The Ambush."[12] The narrative's epigraph from John Donne's "Meditation VII," "Age is a sickness, and youth is an ambush," suggests the sixteen-year-old rural protagonist's sudden coming of age and realization of responsibility through the stoic actions of a Native American tenant farmer.[13] After the tenant farmer, Johnny, loses his four-year-old daughter to an undisclosed illness and expresses no outward remorse, the boy's bigoted father speaks of him as a merciless heathen and "Goddam savage."[14] Yet the boy, Cass, recognizes something in Johnny's Native American worldview that makes him resolve to take his own life more seriously. As in Guy Owen's *Journey for Joedel*—a North Carolina *bildungsroman* involving a poor, tobacco-farming, part Native American boy who struggles with his bicultural identity—the tensions between white and Native American cultures alternately plague and enrich the protagonist.[15]

In addition to philosophical ("The Two Ministries") and cultural ("The Ambush") development narratives, in stories such as "The Prisoner" and "The Weather" Chappell portrays the imminent, inevitable, and largely inarticulate sexual yearnings of unsure young male protagonists. In the unpublished story "The Prisoner," he introduces a pubescent thirteen-year-old boy, Hugh, who is both in love with and jealous of a slightly older girl, Joan Caldwell, who used to be his childhood playmate.[16] Flirting with Hugh

---

[10] Ibid., 16.
[11] Ibid., 18.
[12] Box WN-2, writings by Chappell, notebooks subseries.
[13] Ibid., 1.
[14] Ibid.
[15] Guy Owen, *Journey for Joedel* (New York: Crown, 1970).
[16] Box WF-4, writings by Chappell, fiction subseries.

and dating an older boy who can drive, Joan manipulates Hugh's emotions, tantalizing and infuriating him in ways he does not understand. At the conclusion of the story the narrator remarks that Hugh "looked for all the world like a prisoner, already convicted of his innocence and sentenced to an indefinite term."[17] Plagued by yearning, yet still trapped in his childhood world, Hugh is a typical suffering adolescent on the threshold of sexual awareness. "The Weather" (1980) picks up where "The Prisoner" leaves off, portraying the first sexual experience of an adolescent boy. The story's title serves as a reference to the boy's confused feelings and perceptions: "I cannot even say what the weather was.... I shall say that it was the weather of late summer, variable, uncertain" (*MOL*, 106). Over the course of the tale, the protagonist progresses from immaturity and uncertainty to the sober, life-changing realization of physical passion. Although the experience is mostly positive, it also results in a perceived irrecoverable loss of innocence that unites the protagonist forever with "the rest of the stricken world" (*MOL*, 110).

In *Moments of Light*, "The Weather" functions as a kind of transitional link between "January" (1963) and "Broken Blossoms" (1976), between varying childhood and early adolescent traumas. The pairing of "The Weather" and "Broken Blossoms" associates the sexual curiosity of the former with a more general, awkward, and destructive adolescent inquisitiveness in the latter, the boy breaking open a locked chest and discovering his father's highly explosive blasting caps. Chappell speaks of "Broken Blossoms" as one of his finest tales: "The three stories in *Moments of Light* I most often recommend to prospective readers are the title story and 'Broken Blossoms' and 'Blue Dive.' I certainly cannot describe them as classics of the form, but they are the closest I have ever come to satisfying the imperious demands this discipline imposes."[18] "Broken Blossoms" succeeds as an initiation narrative centered on the simultaneous loss of innocence and arrival of adult responsibility. Having discovered that he had nearly blown his house to bits, the dreamy young protagonist is jarred into the realization that even his most "innocent" actions have the immediate potential for death and destruction. Evoking not only the story's exploding

---

[17] Ibid., 19.

[18] "Fred Chappell," box WM-1, writings by Chappell, miscellaneous subseries, 39.

cap and disfigured, budding apple tree, "Broken Blossoms" signifies the speaker's crushed naiveté as the reality of "the world about suddenly rushes in upon [him]" (*MOL*, 133).

In the unpublished notebook fragment "Dead Soldiers," an adolescent boy impulsively runs across an unstable bridge in danger of being swept away by a flood.[19] As he reaches the other side, a man grabs him roughly and chastises him for his reckless behavior, the boy having failed to consider the destructive (or, in this case, self-destructive) possibilities of his visceral actions. Like "Broken Blossoms" and "Dead Soldiers," another notebook fragment, "An Allegory of Victory," centers on young male characters' inability to recognize the life-threatening dangers and responsibilities of the adult world.[20] The story's action involves a group of boys arriving at a local jail in an attempt to free their friend James Montag, who has assaulted another boy with a knife. Discovering that the police will not simply release Montag into their custody, the boys struggle with the harsh realities of the adult world as they realize their imprisoned friend will be facing real consequences for his impulsive, violent crime.

The violence of James Montag's transgression in "An Allegory of Victory" distinguishes the tale from Chappell's better known, more bucolic initiation narratives, including Jess Kirkman's growth over the course of the four Kirkman novels. Yet, as evinced in his first three novels, Chappell does not retreat from investigating violent and abusive domestic milieus. In fact, such settings, with their strong emotions and natural tensions, often prove to be rich fields for investigating psychological and artistic phenomena. Although they may not reflect aspects of Chappell's own upbringing, which the Kirkman novels clearly do, Chappell's abusive domestic narratives are no less vivid or engaging, reflecting his general belief that "there is no use in the writer's undertaking a story project with which he does not feel temperamentally compatible, a narrative whose trials he is not willing to undergo. Because that sort of necessary sympathetic participation cannot be faked, nor can it be forced. When it is, the discerning reader will find an unconvincing hollowness in the story, which shall have become for the writer an academic exercise."[21] Although it takes place, as the title indicates,

---

[19] Box WN-3, writings by Chappell, notebooks subseries.

[20] Ibid.

[21] Fred Chappell, "Visible Allegiances," *Abatis One* (1983): 59.

against a contrived philosophical, academic backdrop, Chappell's "Homage to Plato" (1969) convincingly presents an explicit episode of domestic violence. The twenty-nine-year-old protagonist, John Archer, performs "the most important deeds of his life," destroying his material possessions one by one as his horrified wife and four-year-old daughter look on.[22] Chappell captures Archer's instinctive, "deep sexual elation" while also offering an interesting application of Plato's belief that only the world of forms is completely real. Archer feels he has "discovered a secret which everyone had been carefully keeping from him," namely that the world of ordinary things, consisting as it does of imperfect copies of forms, is an imitation world, hence of a lesser degree of reality.[23] Yet the viable application of Plato's abstract philosophy—the annihilation of Archer's imperfect, copied possessions—results in the accompanying literal destruction of Archer's family and his probable institutionalization. When he erratically shouts to his wife that everything will turn out fine, she placatingly "smiled and nodded as the howling of the sirens got louder, closer."[24]

A similar degree of familial unrest appears, minus the philosophical symbolism, in the unusual vignette "Say It Was Me" (1987), in which a couple has sex after the male partner returns home from killing someone—presumably the woman's lover. The story's title captures the woman's response to the murder and her accompanying perverse sexual arousal. As in "Homage to Plato," a child—in this case, a baby—witnesses the traumatic action. The couple never hears the baby crying until they finish having sex. In the last line, the narrator remarks, "It may have been awake a long time, they didn't know," increasing the story's dramatic power by exposing its violent, sexual events to a young, neglected (the baby is described merely as an ignored "it") child.[25] Such also is the case in "Children of Strikers" (1978), in which two poor, young, derelict mill siblings reflect the anxiety and violence manifested in their suffering parents and community. The narrator reveals, "They [the striking mill workers] had all turned into strangers, and among them at night in the houses were real strangers from far-off places saying hard wild sentences and often shouting and banging tabletops. In the overheated rooms both the light and the

---

[22] Fred Chappell, "Homage to Plato," *Brown Bag* (1969): 1.

[23] Ibid.

[24] Ibid., 3.

[25] Fred Chappell, "Say It Was Me," *Balcones* 1/3 (Fall 1987): 23.

shadows loomed with an unguessable violence" (*MOL*, 137). The children echo the turbulent feelings of their parents through their imaginative interpretation of the dismembered doll leg the girl discovers. Rather than attributing the lone leg to some random mishap, the children conclude that someone has purposefully cut off the leg as a practice exercise for carving up real children. In fact, at one point the boy roughly slaps the girl in disappointment because she had hidden the leg from him initially, claiming it was a genuine infant appendage. The boy's violent blow and the grisly tale the children invent both reflect the tension and violence to which they are subjected at home as a result of larger socioeconomic forces.

The theme of imaginative violence against a backdrop of domestic discord continues in "The Encyclopedia Daniel" (1996), in which the boy protagonist, Daniel, attempts to work through the insinuated traumatic violence of his institutionalized father by composing his own encyclopedia. Like the young characters in "Homage to Plato," "Say It Was Me," and "Children of Strikers," Daniel has witnessed his parents' disturbing actions. When, for instance, he describes to his mother a bit of dialogue he has in his mind about a man and woman threatening to kill each other, she responds, "Oh Danny, ...I didn't know you heard us that time. I didn't realize you knew."[26] What distinguishes this story from the earlier domestic dispute narratives is the dark foreshadowing with which it concludes. After Daniel's mother encourages him to put down what is troubling him, he confidently writes, "Then in August the father got away and came back to the house. It was late at night and real dark. He didn't come to the front door. He went around back. He was carrying something red in his hand."[27] Providing a powerful and disturbing conclusion to his story, Chappell hints at both the father's possible violent return and the evolving and deepening influence of the traumatic violence to which Daniel was subjected.

Not all of Chappell's dysfunctional family narratives resemble books like Richard Yates's *Revolutionary Road* in their alternately brooding and illuminating violence and perversity.[28] In some stories Chappell portrays domestic friction with levity and wit. For example, in the unpublished story "In Hospital," a nurse agrees to help a mental patient get discharged so long

---

[26] Fred Chappell, "The Encyclopedia Daniel," *Janus* 2 (Winter 1996): 45.
[27] Ibid., 46.
[28] Richard Yates, *Revolutionary Road* (Boston: Little, Brown, 1961).

as he promises to marry her.[29] Although there is an element of perversity in the couple's agreement, the story's tone is mostly comic and ironic. At the conclusion, the reader chuckles at the patient's nuptial anxiety when the narrator explains, "He began to realize what had been said now, and he began to discover that he was frightened—in fact, scared stiff."[30] Like "In Hospital," the two unpublished notebook short stories "The Little Wedding" (1967) and "An English Story" are comic tales organized around problematic intimate relationships.[31] However, both stories take place in England and resemble, both in their style and brand of humor, the work of P. G. Wodehouse. Throughout much of the first half of the twentieth century, Wodehouse excelled in producing tightly written, clever narratives that captured the contradictions and ridiculousness of everyday British life. In both of his stories, Chappell, like Wodehouse, uses the rigidity of English society to create tensions in interpersonal relationships. In "An English Story" an older couple decides to get married despite their relatively advanced ages. When the woman is not surprised by the man's socially unusual proposal, he exclaims, "Well, you take it damn calmly, I must say,"[32] underscoring the humorously light drama of their predicament. "The Little Wedding" flies considerably more into the face of social convention when George, a wealthy Englishman, strides into Signora Mathilda's brothel and boldly purchases a prostitute named Rosanna to be his wife. A naive materialist, George's abstract valuing of Rosanna is fueled by the simple fact that he *can* buy her. Once his fortune is ruined, he suddenly sees her as simply a whore, to which she unconcernedly replies, "Why yes.... Of course, yes."[33]

Appalachian Narratives

Although several of them contain epiphanic experiences, Chappell's dysfunctional family narratives generally led him away from his autobiographical initiation exercises as he experimented with new themes and styles. Chappell asserts that short stories come either from "off the wall"

---

[29] Box WN-3, writings by Chappell, notebooks subseries.
[30] Ibid., 10.
[31] Box WN-2, writings by Chappell, notebooks subseries.
[32] Ibid.
[33] Ibid., 20.

or "from other writers," and while most of his initiation narratives involving youths seem independently derived from the former, his tales of domestic strife more generally are apt to evoke the work of writers he admires such as Yates and Wodehouse.[34] Constituting a subcategory of their own, Chappell's purely Appalachian stories seem to spring mostly from "off the wall" of autobiographical experience, although they also participate with the work of other writers in a distinct pastoral tradition. Demonstrating the influence of authors such as James Still and William Goyen, while also anticipating notable Appalachian works such as Jeff Daniel Marion's *Out in the Country, Back Home*, Jim Wayne Miller's *Newfound*, and Wil Hickson's *Grab You a Handful*, Chappell's Appalachian short fiction contributes original ideas and material to an established genre.[35]

While Chappell is perhaps best known for the Appalachia-based writing that appears in *Midquest* and the Kirkman novels of the 1980s and 1990s, he had produced regional, pastoral narratives from the beginning of his career. As Chappell maintains, many of the chapters in the first Kirkman book, *I Am One of You Forever*, were written individually long before the novel was published or even conceived: "I have mentioned that in writing *Midquest* I made many missteps; many of the attempted poems had to be discarded, and there was other material that never quite fit into the design. Some of these aborted poems had been fashioned into short stories, and now when I looked at them I saw that they could be linked together, if a lot of new material were added, into a deliberately episodic novel something like *Winesburg, Ohio*."[36] In fact, the conception of at least one of the chapters in *I Am One of You Forever* actually predates the composition of *Midquest*. The setting and symbolic plot for "Helen," the concluding and perhaps defining piece of *I Am One of You Forever*, originally appeared in another extended form in 1963 as "Inheritance." Like Jess Kirkman in "Helen," the protagonist of "Inheritance," Locke, travels to a remote cabin as a member of a hunting party. Although he is considerably older than Jess, Locke is still in search of his masculine identity. Whereas Jess experiences a puberty-

[34] Chappell, "Visible Allegiances," 52.

[35] Jeff Daniel Marion, *Out in the Country, Back Home* (Winston-Salem NC: Jackpine Press, 1976); Jim Wayne Miller, *Newfound* (New York: Orchard Books, 1989); Wil Hickson, *Grab You a Handful* (Chapel Hill: O'Possum Books, 1997).

[36] "Fred Chappell," box WM-1, writings by Chappell, miscellaneous subseries, 41.

driven dream involving the female archetype Helen and contemplates what it means to be an Appalachian male (Johnson Gibbs asks, "Well, Jess, are you one of us or not?"), Locke, having recently graduated from college, contemplates his job and the prospect of marriage, telling himself that on the trip, "[I]t was a man you were after."[37] Significantly, Jess and Locke are both accompanied by their fathers on their hunting excursions and, like Daphne Athas in her memoir *Greece by Prejudice*, undergo a process of discovering their fathers' culture and places in it through their respective trips.[38]

Wil Hickson evokes Chappell in arguing, "Sentimentality has been the curse of Appalachian writing ever since the beginning. Back in the 1970s and '80s they thought they were getting rid of it, but it's easy to see now that the work of Fred Chappell, for instance, is just as sentimental in its own way as that of John Fox, Jr."[39] Reducing Chappell's output to Appalachian nostalgia, Hickson unceremoniously shovels his work onto the ever-rising refuse heap of clichéd monuments to the mountain past. However, just as many of Chappell's early narratives alternate between bucolic and dysfunctional settings, so his Appalachian fiction contains both gentle, pastoral or "sentimental" epiphanies and darker, more violent forms of initiation. While the plots of "Helen" and "Inheritance" unfold in natural settings amid the company of friends and family, the companion prose piece for "Inheritance" in *Under Twenty-five*, "January," hints at the possible rape of a young boy by convicts and the boy's anguished alienation from his family. The catalyst for Chappell's first novel, *It Is Time, Lord*, "January" summons the ambiguous turbulence that appears in many Appalachian narratives. Violent events, such as the suicide of Miss Cassie in Elizabeth Madox Roberts's *The Time of Man*, often appear random and ambivalent, and this is true of the troubling episode in "January," which—after it appears near the beginning of *It Is Time, Lord*—haunts the reader throughout the rest of the novel.

---

[37] Fred Chappell, *I Am One of You Forever* (Baton Rouge: Louisiana State University Press, 1985) 184; *Under Twenty-five: Duke Narrative and Verse, 1945–1962*, ed. William Blackburn (Durham: Duke University Press, 1963) 190.

[38] Daphne Athas, *Greece by Prejudice* (New York: J. B. Lippincott, 1962).

[39] Fred Chappell, "The Shape of Appalachian to Come: An Interview with Wil Hickson," in *The Future of Southern Letters*, ed. Jefferson Humphries and John Lowe (New York: Oxford University Press, 1996) 56.

Although it is not an overtly violent story, "A Property of Hope" (1964) undermines sentimental constructions of rural, Appalachian life with its account of a struggling tenant couples' attempt to become economically independent. Like Sylvia Wilkinson's *Moss on the North Side*, the story intimately captures the tenant's alternating feelings of poverty, stress, and hope, while also taking part in the Appalachian tradition, romanticized in books such as John Ehle's *The Land Breakers*, of strong, frugal people attempting to tame the land.[40] Furthermore, the story anticipates the relationship between Jess Kirkman and Johnson Gibbs in the Kirkman novels through the characters of Johnny—the talented, athletic tenant farmer—and Ernie Ballantine—the young son of the land-owning family. Just as Jess looks up to Johnson, so Ernie admires Johnny, plying him with complimentary questions like "When are you going to show me how to throw a curve?"[41] However, over the course of the story, Johnny uses Ernie in order to get information about his father's business actions, illustrating that his interest in the boy is not simply philanthropic. Ernie, spoiled and thoughtless, loosely throws about financial and real estate information in a careless manner that bothers Johnny's sensitive wife.

In Chappell's unpublished story "Thou Shalt Not," a prosperous and conceited feed-store owner, Brown, offends his hard-up employee Clifton when he buys a Bible from a sleazy evangelical salesman for twenty dollars.[42] After Clifton mocks the purchase, Brown realizes, "Twenty dollars was two-thirds of a week's salary for Clifton. And though his voice was flat and level, Brown felt very well the edge of derision in it."[43] An almost identical relationship exists in "A Property of Hope," in which Johnny hungrily catches all of Ernie's economic hints while the latter appears oblivious to their importance. In this way—and as he also does in *It Is Time, Lord* and the Kirkman novels—Chappell investigates the tenuous, bitter relationship between tenants and their employers.

"A Property of Hope" and "Thou Shalt Not" might be best be characterized as initiation narratives with persistent economic undertones.

---

[40] Sylvia Wilkinson, *Moss on the North Side* (Boston: Houghton Mifflin, 1966); John Ehle, *The Land Breakers* (New York: Harper & Row, 1964).

[41] Fred Chappell, "A Property of Hope," *Saturday Evening Post* 234/18 (9 May 1964): 64.

[42] Box WN-2, writings by Chappell, notebooks subseries.

[43] Ibid., 23.

Informing each is a preoccupation with the harsh financial realities of a poverty-stricken Appalachian region, which result in unfortunate scenarios of exploitation. However, in "Simples" (2003) Chappell turns the economic tables when a seemingly harmless and benign elderly mountain woman hustles a young traveling salesman. As the door-to-door peddler Richard Grives remarks near the end of his encounter with Granny Harper, "So far, my success as a salesman amounts to a personal outlay of one hundred sixty-five dollars and the threat of a lawsuit. Not to mention a bottle of silver polish. If I keep on going at this rate, I'll be a bankrupt charged with larceny."[44] Whereas Appalachian communities often have been the victims of outside corporate exploitation, in "Simples" Granny Harper gets the best of the young salesman, a local man who hopes someday to write a novel called *Cold Mountain*, while also subtly nudging him to call into question his assumptions about life.

As "Simples" demonstrates, not all of Chappell's Appalachian tales are as thematically serious or realistic as "Inheritance," "January," and "A Property of Hope." "Elmer and Buford" (1970), for example, functions as a kind of humorous allegorical rendering of Odysseus's time on the island of Ogygia with the Titan Atlas's entrancing sea-nymph daughter, Calypso. Inverting aspects of the Greek myth, Chappell shapes his heroic protagonist into a bumbling, slow-witted, coon-hunter, and his seductress into a horrifyingly ugly Native American woman. Like Odysseus, Buford is a warrior, albeit an inept one; during his tour of duty in World War II he earns the Purple Heart after falling into a Japanese steam bath and severely burning his bottom. Unlike Odysseus, who attempts to journey home, Buford leaves his house in search of his prized coon dog, Elmer. Becoming lost in the woods, Buford is rescued by the hideous Native American woman who, like Calypso, takes her new man back to her cave and spoils him with food and servility. Whereas Odysseus stayed with Calypso seven years, Buford leaves the cave after two, serving in World War II and then "training hound dogs again and going hunting all night long."[45]

Although "Elmer and Buford" shows Chappell having fun with the Appalachian pastime of hunting at the allegorical expense of Homer, nearly all of his other Appalachian narratives investigate and relate mountain

---

[44] Fred Chappell, "Simples," *Appalachian Heritage* 31/3 (Summer 2003): 23.

[45] "Elmer and Buford." *North Carolina Folklore* 18/2 (May 1970): 83.

culture with seriousness and occasionally concern. For instance, in "The Overspill" (1976), an early version of the section that would come to constitute the opening sequence of *I Am One of You Forever*, Chappell criticizes the negative presence of the Challenger Paper Mill by demonstrating the damaging effects of "those bastards" on the hard work of a local family.[46] When the mill releases its excess water, it floods all the nearby waterways, annihilating the beautiful bridge the protagonist and his father have built over their small brook. In rage, the father calls the mill workers "criminals" and exclaims, "It's against the *law* for them to do that."[47] As Chappell has written elsewhere, "He [the Appalachian] realizes, more sharply than the outsider does, that a sleazy and savage global history is overtaking his local one. But he does not have to like this state of affairs, and he can now and then find a bit of comfort in fighting against it."[48] Having witnessed a literal attack on his provincial way of life by a hostile, industrial, "outside" force, Jess—Chappell's autobiographical projection—forms a memorable, negative impression of industry's place in his community: a hostile view of regional industrialization that Chappell repeatedly reiterates in his fiction.

Academic Narratives

An extraordinarily versatile writer, switching genres and styles with ease, Chappell occasionally radically changes the settings and characters involved in a given story or poem—a poem about paper mill pollution might become a story about galactic contamination involving alien races, or a tale about an old professor who fishes could become an Appalachian yarn about fly-fishing. The latter example serves as a point of transition between Chappell's Appalachian and academic stories. "A Mountain Ghost" (1981) functions as a kind of character sketch of and memorial to Mr. Cole, a fly-fishing mountaineer with whom the younger protagonist, George, had been fishing many times. In one of his earliest essays, "Trout Fishing" (1964), Chappell reveals Mr. Cole's likely biographical identity: "I used to fish—when he would permit it—with an old fellow named Boone Osborne. A stocky little man with a square face, an enormous energy and a physical

---

[46] Fred Chappell, "The Overspill," *Long Pond Review* 3 (Winter 1976): 32.
[47] Ibid., 33.
[48] Fred Chappell, "Skepticism," *Hemlocks and Balsams* 7 (1986–1987): 8.

condition much stronger and more agile than mine although it was over half a century older, he has fished the western North Carolina streams for over forty years."[49] In "A Mountain Ghost," what the narrator admires most about Mr. Cole is his total sense of reconciliation with his mountain environment: "I had the impression that he was not merely observing but absorbing, in the way that his dry hair absorbed the cigarette smoke, all that was taking place in this spot."[50] In the earlier, unpublished version of "A Mountain Ghost," "The Good Things," the aged fisherman, retired professor Walter Stone, enjoys a similar sense of belonging in his environment, although as an academic the relationship is stated in slightly more intellectual terms.[51] He asks his younger friend, Fleming, "Do we fish the stream or does the stream fish us?"[52]—identifying the river environment as an entity capable of influencing those who enter its space. Stone's benevolence and respect for the stream and the fish are obvious at the end of the story when Fleming inspects Stone's pole and discovers that he "had fixed the hook so that it was impossible to catch a fish."[53] Portraying nearly identical ideas through both an unschooled mountaineer and a retired professor, Chappell exhibits his skill in integrating and applying material from his two dominant, life-shaping worlds: the environments of Appalachia and academia.

When asked about the preponderance of academic figures in his fiction—especially his early work—Chappell admits that they were attractive because "I could set them in settings that I was familiar with and felt comfortable writing about" (INT). Many of Chappell's early academic protagonists reflect his own anxieties about life and art, struggling with their voices and identities just as the young Chappell, already a capable fantasy writer and aspiring artist, constantly experimented with his materials and methods. One of the best examples of this autobiographical relationship appears in the unpublished short novel "The Thousand Ways" (1967), the

---

[49] Fred Chappell, "Trout Fishing: Ritual, Not Rapture," *Holiday* 36/1 (July 1964): 125.

[50] "A Mountain Ghost," *Long Pond Review* 7 (1981): 85.

[51] Box WF-4, writings by Chappell, fiction subseries. Chappell seems to have adapted the original story in a different way in "The Fisherwoman"—a chapter in the third Kirkman novel, *Farewell, I'm Bound to Leave You*—in which old man Worley, another incarnation of Boone Osborne, trains young Earlene Lewis to catch trout.

[52] Ibid., 13.

[53] Ibid., 18.

first forty-four pages of which were eventually published under the same title in *Moments of Light*.[54] Chappell's struggling young writer-protagonist, Mark Vance, is attempting to become an artist, constantly interpreting experience and his interpersonal relationships. His troubled older lover, Norma Lang, recalls that the most important aspects of their bond were based on his need "to tell her stories of new people he had met or to ask naive—but never stupid, never that—questions about poems he had read."[55] Although Vance has many superficial similarities with Chappell—for example, Vance's town of Winton resembles Durham, North Carolina, and Vance and Chappell both identify *A Midsummer Night's Dream* as their favorite Shakespearean play—his account is really an archetypal *bildungsroman* for all writers. Like the handsome but naive Lucien in Balzac's monument to young writers, *Lost Illusions*—who is patronized by the *beau monde* as represented by Madame de Bargeton and her cousin, the formidable Marquise d'Espard, only to be duped by them—Vance has an older, adoring benefactress in the form of Norma. Vance and Lucien are both young, poor, anguished, aspiring artists. However, whereas Lucien discards his poetic aspirations and turns to hack journalism, descending into Parisian low life until it finally kills him, Vance appears to benefit from his meeting with the wealthy Jim Tumperling, who literally throws his daughter Edwina at Vance. At the narrative's hopeful conclusion, the implication is that Mark Vance will marry Edwina and enjoy unlimited leisure time and economic resources for his writing.

Serving as a kind of chronological prequel to Vance's story is Chappell's untitled, ninety-six-page novel manuscript involving the aspiring undergraduate poet Blake Steward.[56] Whereas Mark Vance is in his late twenties, out of college and attempting to become a professional writer, Steward is a college freshman, and although he is exceedingly well read, he displays much of the immaturity and insecurity of the typical first-year undergraduate. Through autobiographical characters like Vance and Blake Steward, Chappell dramatizes the trials young men experience on the way to developing their artistic sensibilities. Unfortunately, their aesthetic

---

[54] Box WF-3, writings by Chappell, fiction subseries. Chappell's agent, Peter H. Matson, sent "The Thousand Ways" to editor Hiram Haydn on 8 December 1967, but it was never accepted for publication.

[55] Box WF-3, writings by Chappell, fiction subseries, 115.

[56] Ibid.

experiences often come at a literal price, as witnessed in Chappell's untitled, unpublished, incomplete notebook story involving Conrad Vermer, an alienated graduate student writer.[57] While attending a graduate student party, Vermer witnesses a fight and laughs uncontrollably as one young man severely beats the other. Vermer maintains, "It was probably just nerves,"[58] but he is confronted by one of the combatants just before the story trails off. Vermer's laughter—stemming from his nervous, artistic proclivity to perceive things differently than other people—aligns him with Chappell's other young intellectuals, who are all in the process of learning poetically to interpret and reinvent the world of experience. Perhaps the most fully realized of these young protagonists is Bader Thorne in "Prodigious Words" (1966), whose description might generally characterize Chappell's other undeveloped artists: "[O]f middle height, too slight, hypochondriac and in fact unhealthy, nervous, wracked, dreamy and violent by turns, and he drank secretly, hiding away the bottles behind an awkward bookshelf stuffed with books of verse and Western fiction."[59] Bader's grand ambition, "singlehandedly to poison the whole of American culture," underscores both his adolescent angst and his intellectual predisposition for subversive thought.[60] Kept in an attic by his gigantic, abusive mother and suffocating beneath the bland, Bible-thumping complacency of Withers, North Carolina, Bader's only outlet for his frustrations rests in his rebellious writing, a humorous sample of which constitutes the last half of the story.

Not all of Chappell's developing writers are literal youths; his unpublished vignette "Poets" portrays versifiers of all ages as "merely boys at [the] verge of adolescence."[61] Chappell's point is that, regardless of their age, poets "shriek mindlessly, tremble with unmentionable fears, and weep profusely over minor bloodlettings."[62] He literally applies this principle in "The Memorial Poem" (1977) through his middle-aged protagonist John Everhart, who loses his beloved wife and resolves to immortalize her with a

---

[57] Box WN-3, writings by Chappell, notebooks subseries.

[58] Ibid., 6.

[59] Fred Chappell, "Prodigious Words," *Southern Writing in the Sixties*, ed. John William Corrigan and Miller Williams (Baton Rouge: Louisiana State University Press, 1966) 66.

[60] Ibid.

[61] Box WF-4, writings by Chappell, fiction subseries, 1.

[62] Ibid.

poem. Possessing no background in the arts, he provocatively selects poetry over sculpting and other expressive mediums because of its longevity: "There are poems in tongues which the world has forgotten how to read, so that in one sense there are poems which have outlasted even themselves."[63] When Everhart plunges himself into poetry, the narrator compares him to a dreamy adolescent: "He began to hang around the outskirts of poetry, picking up gossip, pondering the immensely sordid shapes of poets' lives, wondering. He was rather like a teenager who thinks continually of movie stars."[64] In the end, Everhart's experience with poetry is more positive than he could have imagined, not only allowing him to honor his wife, but enabling him to experience everyday life at its deepest and richest levels.

In "Better Things" (1994), Noralee tells her friend Betty of her plans to desert her prosaic American family and domestic routine in order to become a singer on the island of Madeira. Furthermore, like John Everhart, Noralee has stopped watching television in favor of pursuing her artistic dream of becoming a singer. In several of Chappell's academic stories, the decision to be an artist or intellectual severely alters the protagonist's lifestyle. For example, "Dangers of the First Floor" records the trials of graduate life for a young married couple who are repeatedly accosted and annoyed by their upstairs academic neighbors.[65] In an untitled story fragment in one of his notebooks, Chappell describes the friendship of two academic bachelors, Franklin Dawson and his colleague Bogard. A good-looking artist, Dawson surrounds himself with attractive women only to feel lonely and unfulfilled—coming to favor instead the high-brow conversation of his ascetic friend. Professor Rodney Hegen's development moves in the opposite direction in "Alien Worlds" (1989), his extensive knowledge of "the ideas of wise men as they are revealed in books"[66] giving way to his attraction to his fun-loving, pickup truck-driving philosophy student Raylene Thomason. Yet their courtship is slow and ponderous, owing to Raylene's spare, mountain aphorisms and the New York-bred Hegen's inept social prowess. Indeed, Chappell humorously describes Hegen as "an academic of the ancient type: worn carpet slippers and no word processor, a devoted believer in careful thinking with a mercifully short list of

---

[63] Fred Chappell, "The Memorial Poem," *The Small Farm* 6 (Fall 1977): 38.

[64] Ibid.

[65] Box WN-3, writings by Chappell, notebooks subseries.

[66] Fred Chappell, "Alien Worlds," *Chronicles* 13/5 (May 1989): 22.

publications. He could not have recognized a jogging shoe."[67] When they decide to get married, Hegen says that he understands her, but the narrator concludes the story with the remark, "[B]ut he didn't. Not yet."[68] Having lived an insular, academic life—"sipping his dopey red wine and reading books that only wimps like himself had ever heard of, books that made no difference to the real business of the world"—Hegen, for the first time, has begun to engage in genuine human experience: a transition that will change his life forever.[69]

In "Things Beyond Us" (1982) Chappell partially shifts his narrative perspective from the challenged academic to a nonintellectual who, nonetheless, makes his living in the world of writers. Charles Musgrave, attractive and charismatic, functions as a kind of professional companion for successful female authors, attending parties, receiving money, and enjoying a modest celebrity lifestyle. At a party with his acclaimed feminist lover Andrea Ordway, he attracts the attention of Juliet Greene, a graduate student in history. Greene falls under Musgrave's spell and they have an affair. The rest of the story records their two other chance meetings and the changes they undergo. The tale's title is a reference to Musgrave's lack of interest in books and academics—when confronted with bookish questions he replies, "That kind of thing is beyond me."[70] Like the earlier Chappell protagonist upon whom Musgrave is based—the confidante William in "The Admirer" (1980)—Musgrave would maintain, "[I]ntellectual conversation is simply not in my line."[71] However, although Musgrave and William are not intellectuals they are, nonetheless, students of a sort. As William explains, "Many people spend their lives looking at paintings or watching birds or reading books. I read women, maybe, the way some people read books."[72] A reader of women, Musgrave moves from author to author, temporarily assuaging his emptiness with the presence of each new companion.

---

[67] Ibid., 23.

[68] Ibid., 24.

[69] Ibid.

[70] Fred Chappell, "Things Beyond Us," *Quarterly West* 13 (Fall/Winter 1981–1982): 6, 8.

[71] "The Admirer," *Black Warrior Review* 6/2 (Spring 1980): 29.

[72] Ibid., 31.

Just as Musgrave moves from woman to woman, reading and studying each one, so Chappell explored and continues to explore his life-shaping environments of Appalachia and academia; over time this has evolved into a prolonged investigation of the self. As Chappell maintains, "I guess because I'm always working on some manuscript, I feel like...it's almost as if my inner life is the manuscript I'm working on—whatever kind of manuscript that is. And I use that to project my characters' inner lives on the page too" (INT). Forged by the initiation experiences of his Appalachian and academic environments, Chappell, in turn, recalls and shapes them through his art, and—owing to his stylistic and thematic versatility—the overall result is, as the title of one of his short story collections implies, "more shapes than one." In this way, the discoveries of Chappell's protagonists often appear interwoven with the discoveries of their artistic maker who, periodically revisiting familiar materials, experiments with new ways of utilizing them. The result then is not only a collection of development narratives but the story of one writer's development.

Chapter 6

"Great" Men and "Weird" Events: Historical and Fantastic Narratives

> *So I tried to write science fiction and still do, but it's not normal science fiction because I like to place the stories in historical context, stories about scientists like Linneaus and Herschel and Ben Franklin.* —Chappell in Palmer, "Fred Chappell," 405

Discussing the reception of his fictional output, Chappell remarks, "My short stories have usually been divided into two types by critics and reviewers—the realistic ones like 'Children of Strikers,' say and the fantasies like 'Weird Tales.'"[1] Although this dichotomy constitutes a rough, useful pattern for classifying Chappell's short fiction, it does not do justice to the variation and versatility within his multiple and distinct "realistic" and "fantastic" narratives. The categorization of Chappell's "realistic" stories is perhaps more generally accurate and convenient, since nearly all of his largely autobiographical narratives involving youth, Appalachia, and academic life may be placed together—all of them concerned with accurately portraying discoveries within specific types of genuine subcultures from Chappell's own experience. However, the "fantastic" narratives are significantly more slippery, meshing together elements such as science, literature, traditional fantasy, and—perhaps most importantly—history, often in unconventional ways. Although they employ traditional practices of the fantasy genre, Chappell's "fantastic" narratives

---

[1] Tersh Palmer, "Fred Chappell," *Appalachian Journal* 19/4 (Summer 1992): 405.

are hardly ever just fantasies, frequently mixing disparate literary forms in a playful and experimental manner.

When Chappell mentions that critics have explained "Weird Tales" as a fantasy, he underscores the shortcomings of the realistic/fantastic binarism for interpreting his fiction. For "Weird Tales," with its use of authentic primary sources involving Hart Crane, H. P. Lovecraft, and Samuel Loveman, is as much a work of historically-based fiction as it is fantasy. Shifting his focus slightly from fantasy to science fiction, Chappell maintains he does not produce "normal science fiction because I like to place the stories in historical context, stories about scientists like Linneaus and Herschel and Ben Franklin."[2] As a result, his use of fantasy/science fiction and history are related and often intertwined, distinguishing themselves from his more autobiographical, realistic work. After a discussion of the ways in which Chappell conceptualizes his purely historical short fiction, this chapter considers his use of historical figures as catalysts for fantastic philosophical events. Although it maintains a connection between history and fantasy, this assessment eventually leads away from Chappell's historical fiction and into his more overtly fantastic tales, which I break down into subcategories such as allegorical fantasy, psychological/supernatural fantasy, and moral fable—demonstrating Chappell's scope and creativity within the fantastic genre.

Historical Narratives

Chappell's interest in historical fiction is genuine and enduring, his first published academic essay having examined Shakespeare's use of Plutarch's *Life of Cato* in composing *Coriolanus*.[3] Although his second novel, *The Inkling*, contains a hidden historical allegory, Chappell generally did not experiment with the form early in his career, and even in later years—after having written several historically-based stories—he remains cautious of the form: "I've thought now and again about historical fiction, but the more I look at it the tougher it looks to be. You just have to know everything in order to write it and I don't know enough" (INT). Beginning in the mid-1970s with the compositions of "Judas" and his stories involving scientists,

[2] Ibid.

[3] Fred Chappell, "Shakespeare's *Coriolanus* and Plutarch's *Life of Cato*," *Renaissance Papers 1962*, ed. George Williams (Japan: Charles Tuttle, 1963) 9–16.

Chappell began to explore historical themes in earnest. His theory of understanding historical fiction perhaps is best articulated in an introduction to the historical novels of George Garrett, in which he puts forth the proposition: "That almost all historical fiction is reductive in nature, whittling the giants of history down to size, showing that even the greatest movements and events must march on feet of clay, making the humble and even the flawed character equal with the most luminous, and casting a cold skeptical eye upon its own purview, whether this is a vast panorama or an intimate fictional diary."[4] Conceptualizing a historical vision that emphasizes humanity, equality of representation, and a skeptical portrayal of milieu, Chappell paints historical fiction as a challenging form charged with the important though difficult imaginative task of transforming mythical abstract figures into visceral human beings.

Chappell's contention that "historical fiction is reductive," that it "whittles down" figures, is especially true of his stories "Judas" (1974) and "Thatch Retaliates" (1979), which humorously demythologize legendary figures. In the former narrative, the much dramatized epic relationship between Judas Iscariot and Jesus Christ is reduced to convenient government bribery and petty jealousy. Judas's portrayal of Jesus as "goofy," a "nut" (*MOL*, 17), and an "ideological weasel" (*MOL*, 15), and his own bitter colloquialisms—"[Jesus] was never quite right in the head" (*MOL*, 15)—inject the story with humor and demythologize its characters on one level, while also delivering serious philosophical commentary on the tension between idealism and materialism. Judas interprets Jesus' idealism as a kind of debilitating, infectious madness, since he has justified his betrayal according to materialistic logic. However, in the end, he still feels guilty, underscoring the peculiar lingering power of Christ's "mad," romantic principles.

Chappell also employs comic historical revisionism in order to make a serious point in "Thatch Retaliates," in which two stiff, etiquette-adhering, Enlightenment-drunk Englishmen, Prescott and Toby, encounter Blackbeard the pirate in the small colonial North Carolina village of Bath. Allen Tate once summoned another famous sea dog in invoking Southern history: "The key to unlock the Southern mind is, fortunately, like

[4] Fred Chappell, introduction, in *George Garrett: The Elizabethan Trilogy*, ed. Brooke Horvath and Irving Malin (Huntsville: Texas Review Press, 1998) xiv.

Bluebeard's, bloody and perilous."[5] A mythical symbol of New World and Southern colonial violence, Blackbeard terrorizes the small town of Bath, which is struggling, not very successfully, to become civilized. A towering figure in pirate legends, the uncouth Edward Thatch appears in Chappell's tale as a sour, diminutive, soiled madman: "He was a shortish swarthy man who, when he had glanced at them, had shown a countenance almost obliterated by a long heavy black beard, a beard done up in filthy curls and ringlets which stuck out from his face in every direction.... Such strange fierce disordered eyes they had never seen before, and they concluded that the man was either mad or much under the influence of strong drink" (*MOL*, 36–37). When Blackbeard attacks the polite Englishmen, the effete pair cling to the impotent norms of civilization, which results in Prescott's brutal pistol-whipping and Toby's death. Toby's last words—"I remain a friend to Reason in this place" (*MOL*, 48)—sum up his inadequacy for existing in a land all but deprived of law or logic. In addition to offering a provocative historical revision of Thatch, Chappell captures the historical struggle between barbarism and civilization in the colonial South, dramatizing both the tragic beauty and inadequacy of the Enlightenment spirit.

If "Thatch Retaliates" "whittles down" Blackbeard, making the great figure unromantic and despicable, "Blue Dive" (1975) does the opposite with its memorably appealing protagonist, Stovebolt Johnson—lionizing a historically underrepresented figure: the wandering African American blues guitarist. Recently paroled and looking for work, Johnson heads for the Blue Dive, a club whose owner once had offered him a job. However, when he arrives he discovers that a different proprietor, Locklear Hawkins, now runs the bar. Hawkins, surly and cruel, insults Johnson, attempting to instigate a confrontation. However, Johnson, in defiance of his stereotypical blues-laced criminal past, ignores Hawkins's taunts and moves on. Over the course of the story it becomes apparent that Johnson is an uncommonly good and gifted man, the attributes of whom are catalogued by Dabney Stuart: "Decency, delicacy, balance, dignity, a sense of proportion and humor and perspective."[6] After initially introducing Johnson as a possible wandering

[5] Allen Tate, "The Profession of Letters in the South," in *On the Limits of Poetry: Selected Essays, 1928–1948* (New York: Morrow, 1948) 269.

[6] Dabney Stuart, "'Blue Pee': Fred Chappell's Mythical Kingdom," *Iron Mountain Review* 2/2 (1985): 19.

vagrant, Chappell steadily shapes and crafts him into a decent, unique, and memorable human being.

Chappell continues to imagine and describe the everyday aspects of historical figures, famous and obscure, in his stories concerning scientists. He relates that his grasp of history "is not very confident, but I am interested in odd corners of history—things people don't often write about. I wanted to write a whole series of short stories about scientists. For some reason they've been largely neglected in short fiction, but they make very interesting characters and the things they do are interesting" (INT). Chappell makes his scientific characters intriguing by relating their important discoveries to the peculiarities of their personalities and the defining events of their lives. In speaking about the interaction between science and literature, Italo Calvino mentions two ideological "poles": "On the one side is Barthes with his followers, 'enemies' of science, who think and talk with scientific precision; on the other is Queneau with his, friends of science, who think and talk in terms of caprice and somersaults of language and thought."[7] Concentrating on the personal and whimsical aspects of his scientists' lives, Chappell sides with Calvino and Queneau in recording the creative interplay between the unfettered imagination and disciplined thought.

In "The Snow That Is Nothing in the Triangle" (1981), Chappell intertwines the beauty of Karl Feuerbach's mathematical theorem and the anguish of his personal life, providing a striking portrait of a whimsical professor akin to that of the memorable academic figure in Gladys Swan's "Getting an Education."[8] Born in Jena, Germany, in 1800, Feuerbach, at the tender age of twenty-two, published the important theorem that now bears his name. The Feuerbach theorem concerns itself with five important circles related to a triangle. These five circles are the incircle (or circle inscribed in the triangle), the three encircles (or circles touching one side of the triangle and the other two produced), and the nine-point circle (or circle passing through the three midpoints of the sides of the triangle). A few years after his theorem was published, Feuerbach and several of his friends were arrested by the government for their supposedly subversive political views.

---

[7] Italo Calvino, "Two Interviews on Science and Literature," in *The Uses of Literature*, trans. Patrick Creagh (New York: Harcourt Brace Jovanovich, 1982) 31.

[8] Gladys Swan, "Getting an Education," *Of Memory and Desire* (Baton Rouge: Louisiana State University Press, 1989) 16-30.

During their incarceration, Feuerbach became obsessed with the idea that only his death could free his companions. One day he slashed the veins in his feet but was discovered and removed to a hospital before bleeding to death. During his recovery period, he managed to bolt down a corridor and leap out of a window, plummeting into a deep snow bank. Although the fall failed to take his life, Feuerbach emerged permanently crippled, his body shaped in the form of a question mark. Chappell's story takes place after Feuerbach's release, when—physically disfigured and mentally infirm—he returned briefly to teaching before suffering a nervous breakdown. When Chappell has Feuerbach ask his students, "Suppose a man were to plunge into a snow bank up to his neck, or even over his head. Will we then say that he has fallen into nothing?" (*MSTO*, 32), he demonstrates the jumbled condition of the mathematician's brain, unable to separate quantifiable abstraction from personal experience. Feuerbach's guilt over the death of his friend Klaus Hörnli and his inability to reconcile or solve the events of the past torture him. Having begun his life a mathematical prodigy in love with rational abstractions, Feuerbach ends it a broken victim of chaotic and elusive human history. He implores his students, "You must help me to recall the topic under discussion" (*MSTO*, 42), but still the hallucinatory snow falls in the classroom—a vision recalling his traumatic attempted suicide and Hörnli's death.

Like Zeno, the sixteenth-century, free-thinking scientist who must toe the line between innovation and heresy in Marguerite Yourcenar's *The Abyss*, Chappell's scientists often waver between madness and discipline, and deviance and convention—thinking and acting in unconventional ways while working through problems with formulaic precision.[9] In "Ladies from Lapland" (1981) Chappell introduces a character simultaneously possessing scientific exactitude and moral lassitude in Pierre-Louis Moreau de Maupertuis. As a geneticist, Maupertuis produced the first scientifically accurate record of the transmission of a dominant hereditary trait in humans. However, he is best known as the physicist who formulated the—aptly and ironically named, as we shall see—"principle of least action," which states that nature chooses the most economical path for moving bodies. However, for all Maupertuis's scientific accomplishments, he was

[9] Marguerite Yourcenar, *The Abyss*, trans. Grace Frick (New York: Farrar, Straus and Giroux, 1976).

lazy, lustful, and sleazy. Like Elizabeth Socolow's portrayal of Newton in *Laughing at Gravity: Conversations with Isaac Newton*, Chappell's representation of Maupertuis mingles his scientific ideas with his less-than-exemplary personal life.[10] When Maupertuis journeys to Lapland on an expedition to verify Newton's theory of gravitation, he lets his colleagues do all the work while he hosts grand orgies with the local women in his "pleasure tent" (*MSTO*, 26). As the time for Maupertuis's departure draws near, his mock humility is humorously pathetic: "The philosopher explained over and over again that his work here was ended, that he had a duty to science, that generations unborn would share his gratitude toward the Laplanders for their gracious hospitality" (*MSTO*, 27). Through Maupertuis, Chappell dramatizes how significant historical events—in this case, a notable scientific discovery—may be accompanied by the most primitive and exploitive human instincts and acts.

In "Barcarole" (1984) Chappell shifts his attention from distinguished scientists to the composer of *The Tales of Hoffman*, Jacques Offenbach. Just as Chappell relates the accomplishments of his scientists to their personal lives, so he describes the relationship between Offenbach's music and a simple melody that poignantly haunts him from his childhood. As in one of Chappell's favorite novels, *Doctor Faustus*, music is used as a metaphor for revealing the complexities of character.[11] In Offenbach's case, the waltz he heard as a boy serves as a kind of catalyst for discovering an unrealized dimension of both his music and himself. Chappell revised "Barcarole" for inclusion in *More Shapes than One*; however, the original published version contains a passage from Schopenhauer that comments on Offenbach's personal discovery: "First of all, no man is happy; he strives his whole life long after an imaginary happiness, which he seldom attains, and if he does, then it is only to be disillusioned; and as a rule he is shipwrecked in the end and enters the harbor dismasted."[12] Although Offenbach discovers the bawdy source of the waltz that gave him so much happiness as a boy, he does not become disillusioned. On the contrary, he is able to accept its role in his art and fall asleep again to its melody, at peace with it and himself.

---

[10] Elizabeth Socolow, *Laughing at Gravity: Conversations with Isaac Newton* (Boston: Beacon, 1988).

[11] Thomas Mann, *Doctor Faustus*, trans. Richard and Clara Winston (New York: Knopf, 1961).

[12] Fred Chappell, "Barcarole," *Chattahoochee Review* (Spring 1984): 61.

Historical Narratives with Fantastic Events

In his short essay on music and science in *Doctor Faustus*, "What Did Adrian Leverkuhn Create?" (1985), Chappell puts forth the thesis "that Mann employs the development of serial music as analogy to, and criticism of, the history and character of romantic science."[13] Imagining the historical meeting of Franz Josef Haydn and William Herschel, Chappell investigates the relationship between music and science himself in "Moments of Light" (1979). Initially wary of Herschel's telescope, Haydn becomes fascinated once he looks through it, his reaction evoking a passage from a later German artist, Gottfried Benn: "One may doubt and ridicule science...but the sciences are telescopes; now and then we put our eyes to them, and then we see that there have been infinities of human and extra-human development and formation before us, without us, far from us."[14] Haydn's fantastic out-of-body telescope experience introduces him to the inestimable size of the universe and the possibility of alien cultures. In fact, his imagined galactic journey, with its weird geometry and other Lovecraftian imagery, was drawn from an earlier story titled "Darkened Light" (1969). Just as Offenbach's knowledge of Zimmer's waltz results in a new appreciation of his music in "Baracole," so Haydn's experience with Herschel likely shaped his composition of *The Creation*, which appears to contain references both to the nebular hypothesis and the chaos that may have prefigured the known universe.

Haydn's space travel sequence gives "Moments of Light" a fantastic aspect that takes it beyond the historically-based meeting of the two famous German intellectuals. In his poem "Ballade of the Skeptic Donald Hall," Chappell hints at the artistic limitations of formulaic social writing: "Consider, though, what literature would be / If only Emile Zola and George Crabbe / Held frosty sway and no hyperbole / Ever brightened landscapes of olive drab."[15] In addition to linguistic play, Chappell often creatively injects fantastic and/or science fiction elements into otherwise realistic historical narratives. Using fantasy as a tool for artistic liberation,

---

[13] Fred Chappell, "What Did Adrian Leverkuhn Create?" *Postscript* 2 (1985): 11.

[14] Gottfried Benn, "Future and Present," in *Prose, Essays, andPoems*, trans. E. B. Ashton, ed. Volkmar Sander (New York: Continuum, 1987) 155.

[15] Fred Chappell, *Spring Garden: New and Selected Poems* (Baton Rouge: Louisiana State University Press, 1995) 88.

Chappell's conceptualization of the term appears to resemble that of Eric Rabkin, who asserts, "The fantastic is a quality of astonishment that we feel when the ground rules of a narrative world are suddenly made to turn about 180°."[16] When "Moments of Light" shifts suddenly from eighteenth-century propriety to space travel and alien cultures, Chappell introduces an element of fantasy or science fiction that breaks or changes the rules for his narrative. Making distinction difficult, fantasy and science fiction are slippery, interrelated terms. As Karl Kroeber maintains, "The genres of science fiction and fantasy overlap and interpenetrate. All literary genres are impure, each partaking of diverse formal modalities, but fantasy and science fiction are especially intertwined because they have a common origin."[17] To be sure, Chappell rarely drifts into "hard science fiction," a subgenre in which "both setting and dramatic situation must derive strictly from the rigorous postulation and working out of a concrete physical problem. The method then of the hard SF story is logical, the means technological, and the result—the feel and texture of the fiction itself—objective and cold."[18] Regardless of the scientific data and historical sources he often utilizes, Chappell remains interested in these materials as tools for exploring artistic and human truths, not as ends in themselves.

In "Mrs. Franklin Ascends" (1978) and "Linnaeus Forgets" (1978) Chappell presents overly zealous scientific classification as a debilitating, restrictive force in the respective lives of Benjamin Franklin and Carl Linnaeus. Chappell recounts that the former tale originally was conceived as a work of extended fiction: "I had planned to write a novel once I finished [*Midquest*]. I wanted to write a historical novel, eighteenth century, about colonial America, specifically about Benjamin Franklin."[19] An exemplar of eighteenth-century Enlightenment thought, Franklin comes home from England at the beginning of Chappell's story and immediately records his arrival in the family journal, noting with some annoyance his wife's random,

---

[16] Eric S. Rabkin, *The Fantastic in Literature* (Princeton: Princeton University Press, 1976) 41.

[17] Karl Kroeber, *Romantic Fantasy and Science Fiction* (New Haven: Yale University Press, 1988) 9.

[18] George E. Slusser and Eric S. Rabkin, *Hard Science Fiction* (Carbondale: Southern Illinois University Press, 1986) vii.

[19] William Walsh, "Fred Chappell," in *Speak So I Shall Know Thee: Interviews with Southern Writers* (Asheboro NC: Down Home, 1987) 72.

"disordered" entries. Franklin's wife, for her own part, is irritated with Franklin as well. Overwhelmed by his sudden return, her anxieties in regard to his personal habits reveal themselves at the conclusion of her fantastic dream: "Oh, this was too much! Must Dr. Franklin always be arranging everything? Even the musical entertainment of their afterlife? Deborah bit her lip. She was *exasperated*" (*MOL*, 28). Not having seen her husband in years, Deborah attempts to readjust herself to Franklin's irritating anal-retentive habits. From her perspective, we perceive the shortcomings of Franklin's celebrated system: in the process of recording and micro-organizing his life, Franklin runs the risk of not fully living it—neglecting his wife in favor of what he conceives of as "productive" pursuits.

Whereas Franklin remains oblivious to his domestic philosophical deficiencies, Carl Linnaeus discovers a new dimension for interpreting experience in "Linnaeus Forgets." Haunted by the criticism of rival botanist Johann Siegesbeck—who argued that Linnaeus's sexuality-based plant classification was degenerate and immoral—Linnaeus achieves peace through a fantastic experience involving an unusual plant he is unable to classify. Harold Bloom observes, "Literary fantasy, creative or critical, is the mode where pleasure/pain principle and reality principle become most inextricably blended, even as the mode appears to proclaim a negation of the reality principle."[20] His rational scientific faculties proving inadequate for solving his dilemma, the "Father of Taxonomy" undergoes a fantastic, hallucinatory psychological experience that enables him to "feel," rather than hypothesize, "that the plants of this earth carry on their love affairs in uncaring merry freedom, making whatever sexual arrangements best suit them, and that they go to replenish the globe guiltlessly, in high and winsome delight" (*MSTO*, 18). That Linnaeus's change in perspective is essentially artistic is revealed in the sense that "his love for metaphor sharpened" (*MSTO*, 18). Unable to explain the strange plant or even read his scientific journal entries on it, Linnaeus is momentarily dejected before realizing that the experience has enriched his method of observation, infusing his rigorous nomenclature with the artistic beauty of the world.

[20] Harold Bloom, "*Clinamen*: Towards a Theory of Fantasy," *Bridges to Fantasy*, ed. George E. Slusser, Eric S. Rabkin, and Robert Scholes (Carbondale: Southern Illinois University Press, 1982) 19.

In addition to notable composers and scientists, Chappell also draws on literary history in reconstructing documented events with an element of fantasy. For example, "Weird Tales" (1984) makes use of literary history, published and unpublished, regarding an unusual and diverse group of writers and artists who congregated around Cleveland, Ohio, in the 1920s. Chappell explains the story's unique source:

> One of my dearest friends in the early '70s was the great Southern poet Allen Tate, who, as it happened, was a close friend of [H. P.] Lovecraft's associate, Samuel Loveman, in those years. Well, not a close friend, I shouldn't say that, because he did not *like* Samuel Loveman, but he gave me all sorts of personal information about Loveman—who is really an obscure figure in American literature—and so I was able to use that as background. I felt I had access to a kind of information not many people would have. All the quotations that are in documents in the story are real. Those came from Hart Crane's letters or from H. P. Lovecraft's letters.[21]

Incorporating Tate's account of Loveman and the letters of Lovecraft and Crane, Chappell constructs a convincing historical structure into which he injects elements of fantasy, most notably Loveman's extraordinary mathematical teleportation to Antarctica. Furthermore, as becomes apparent at the story's conclusion, the account's anonymous narrator is writing sometime in the future, after the alien beings recorded by Lovecraft and his associates have returned to dominate the planet: "[I]t is unlikely that any human effort would have changed the course of events. There still would have come about the reawakening of Dzhaimbú and the other worse gods, under whose charnel dominion we now suffer and despair" (*MSTO*, 70). Through this ingenious, additional layer of narration, Chappell offers a playful interpretation of the Cthulhu Mythos stories as historical documents, cataloguing the imminent return of the malevolent aliens: "It seemed to me that if I could end the story correctly, it would treat all the Mythos stories of Long and Derleth as well as Lovecraft as being reportage rather than fiction—disguised reportage in order to save their lives."[22] Chappell's unusual mingling of literary history and Lovecraftian fantasy also produces some unexpected humorous events, such as the unlikely historical meeting between the manically reserved Lovecraft and debauched Crane,

---

[21] Darrell Schweitzer, "A Talk with Fred Chappell," *Weird Tales* 1 (Summer 1994): 42.

[22] Ibid.

and Dzhaimbú's voracious consumption of Crane's body after the beleaguered poet leaps into the ocean. Combining history, fantasy, and humor, Chappell constructs a "weird" tale that goes well beyond the traditional fantastic characteristics of the genre.

Chappell also couples literary history, albeit fictional, with fantasy and humor in "The Adder" (1989), which recounts a book dealer's desperate struggle with *The Necronomicon*, a fictional evil book named and created by H. P. Lovecraft that exists today in numerous bogus editions penned by various writers.[23] "The Adder," then, in taking *The Necronomicon* as its subject, uses fictional literary history as its base. In fact, Chappell subtly hints at the fraudulence of his source in naming his protagonist's book dealer's shop "Alternate Histories" (*MSTO*, 100). The story's central dilemma springs from the *The Necronomicon*'s ability to pervert and consume the contents of any text with which it comes into contact, affecting all editions of that text, everywhere. As the narrator explains, "[It] poisoned the actual content of the work itself, so that in whatever edition it appeared, in whatever book, magazine, published lecture, scholarly essay, commonplace book, personal diary—in whatever written form—a polluted text showed up" (*MSTO*, 110). Much of the story's humor stems from *The Necronomicon*'s corruption and destruction of *Paradise Lost*, perverting the stately verse into vulgar lines such as, "When I consider how my loot is spent / On Happy Daze, a fifth of darling wine..." (*MSTO*, 108). In its ability to affect texts and even the narrative that contains it, *The Necronomicon* exhibits a kind of literal magic realism in Wendy Faris's sense of the term: "Many magic realist fictions (like their nineteenth-century Gothic predecessors) carefully delineate sacred enclosures...and then allow these sacred spaces to leak their

---

[23] Lovecraft never penned an edition of Abdul Alhazred's *The Necronomicon* himself. Instead, he mentions the book in several of his works and quotes invented passages from it. In the years after Lovecraft published "The History of the *Necronomicon*" (1938), the volume's title began appearing in various places as readers initially believed in its existence and later took pleasure in perpetuating the diabolical literary legend, deliberately listing it in bibliographies, in bookseller's catalogues, and on phony library index cards (including one in the Yale library). As L. Sprague de Camp summarizes, "Lovecraft's scholarly quotations and references convinced many that the work existed, and they plagued librarians and booksellers by asking for it" (*Lovecraft: A Biography* [Garden City: Doubleday, 1975] 410). Probably the best-known (and also the most humorous) of the book's many fraudulent adaptations appears in Sam Raimi's *Evil Dead* film trilogy.

magical narrative waters over the rest of the text and the world it describes."[24] Functioning as a kind of ungainly and sinister "sacred enclosure," *The Necronomicon* floods its surroundings with its squamous, eldritch malignancy, thwarting and hypnotizing would-be readers and molesting neighboring texts.

Fantasy Narratives

Although Chappell's numerous Appalachian and academic stories are usually realistic works, exploring the everyday complexities of Chappell's most immediate and familiar environments, they are infiltrated occasionally by fantastic themes, which—like *The Necronomicon* infecting its adjoining works—enter the story and aid it in bursting forth from its otherwise restrictive genre constraints. For example, in the unpublished Appalachian story "Crow Knows," Chappell invests Burning Rock's Native American tales involving animal transformations with implied truths, the black snake the narrator encounters having once been Burning Rock's abusive wife.[25] Similarly, in several of Chappell's stories involving fantasy authors, the writers undergo unlikely genuine fantastic experiences. For instance, Myles Landon, the erotic fantasy scribbler in the unpublished story "Witchcraft," finds himself subject to the sort of fantastic forces he otherwise might attempt to dramatize in the form of Minnie, a country store clerk versed in the black arts.[26] The father of suggestive volumes such as *Hull Planet Virgins*, Landon becomes the erotic thrall of Minnie, who uses her incantatory perception to infect him with irresistible desire through an obligatory combination of witch implements—candles, parchment, pentagrams, and so on.

Although "Witchcraft" possesses an element of humor—the author of erotic, galactic fantasy becoming the object/victim of supernatural love—Chappell's fantastic tales involving writers are not academic comedies in the tradition of works like Don DeLillo's *White Noise*.[27] Instead of mocking dynamics of the writer's vocation, they experiment with the

---

[24] Wendy H. Faris, "Scheherazade's Children: Magic Realism and Postmodern Fiction," in *Magic Realism: Theory, History, Community*, ed. Faris and Lois Parkinson Zamora (Durham: Duke University Press, 1995) 174.

[25] Box WF-4, writings by Chappell, fiction subseries.

[26] Ibid.

[27] Don DeLillo, *White Noise* (New York: Viking, 1985).

concept of turning authors' creative abstractions into realities. Perhaps Chappell's best examples of this kind of writing are "The Dreaming Orchid" (1982) and "The Somewhere Doors" (1991), two substantially different versions of the same story. Both narratives center on the fantastic writings of R. K. Strakl, a lonely café worker in remote Cherry Cove, North Carolina, whose alien tales unconsciously are intertwined with the concerns of a genuine extraterrestrial culture. Whereas in the later version, "The Somewhere Doors," the value of Strakl's stories remains ambiguous, in "The Dreaming Orchid" the alien representative T. P. Coines reveals that Strakl's narrative ideas "are actually the memories and dreams of a being on another planet, a rather elderly female who has traveled about quite a bit and gathered a lot of experience."[28] In "The Somewhere Doors" Francesca/Sheila Weddell functions as Strakl's alien liaison, informing him of the strange doors he will receive and drawing the suspicion of Ugly Dick, the sleazy and possibly alien detective who harries Strakl. In both stories the writers' works have real consequences for their futures—in the earlier version Strakl meets the alien being whose dreams he records, while in the later narrative he eventually receives a pair of alien-constructed doors.

Fantastic Allegory and Visionary Fiction

At the conclusion of "Darkened Light" (1969), a much earlier brief tale involving an alien culture, the star-trekking narrator remarks, "It seemed to me that things, that everything I knew, was more nearly comprehensible to me now than formerly. Although I could not articulate what I understood, I felt that I did understand."[29] The stories involving R. K. Strakl end in almost the same manner as "Darkened Light"—in "The Somewhere Doors" Strakl bursts into tears in confronting the painful realities of the world, while in "The Dreaming Orchid" his meeting with the alien is "made a sharp difference, not only in the way he regarded the visions, but in the way he looked at the things about him.... He was forever now more carefully alert, more alive."[30] In addition to functioning as fantasies, "Darkened Light" and the Strakl stories are also allegorical, demonstrating symbolic changes in

---

[28] Fred Chappell, "The Dreaming Orchid," *New Mexico Humanities Review* 5 (Spring 1982): 71.

[29] Fred Chappell, "Darkened Light," *Brown Bag* (1969): 44.

[30] Chappell, "The Dreaming Orchid," 76.

their protagonists through fantastic means—each protagonist coming to appreciate the world more vividly and artistically as a result of their fantastic experiences. Chappell's term for this kind of allegorical fantasy is "visionary fiction": "Visionary fiction, as I conceive of it, cuts across several genres but totally includes, or is included by, none of them. It is fantasy, of course, but is not heroic fantasy of the sword-and-sorcery type in which leather-clad heroes with leatherbound brains do battle with evil magicians.... It may occasionally appear as science fiction, as with C. S. Lewis' *Perelandra*, but generally it does not do so.... Visionary fiction is always allegorical."[31] Going beyond literal fantasy, visionary fiction contains symbolic ideas that make the narrative important beyond its immediate fantastic action.

Chappell's practice of visionary fiction takes on many forms. For example, in the futuristic story "Hooyoo Love" (2003), Bronwell Lofton emulates an ambivalent nihilistic alien creed in order to express human love, an unresolved microcosm of the precarious human balance "between free will and destiny."[32] Another futuristic philosophical exercise, the unpublished play "Within and Without" uses narrative action and the Socratic dialogue between characters to function as allegorical commentary on the theological distinction that unity exists in a lack of opposites.[33] A more humorous and less learned application appears in "Mankind Journeys Through Forests of Symbols" (1981), in which an immense symbolist poem manifests itself on a rural North Carolina highway, pestering a cast of hapless local law enforcement officials straight out of Andy Griffith's Mayberry.[34] The guilty poet/culprit—actually one of Sheriff Balsam's good-ol'-boy deputies, Bill—strains to express the poem plaguing both his subconscious and the citizens he has sworn to protect, while his law enforcement colleagues offer words of encouragement. Inverting the symbolic endeavor—making an idea a visceral object, instead of the reverse—Chappell produces an unusual story in which everyday, literal-

---

[31] Chappell, "Visionary Fiction," *Chronicles* 11/5 (May 1987): 19.

[32] Fred Chappell, *Fantasy and Science Fiction* 105/4 & 5 (October/November 2003): 100.

[33] Box WN-3, writings by Chappell, notebooks subseries.

[34] Before its appearance in *Madison Review* (Winter 1988) and *The Sewanee Review* (Summer 1991), and its inclusion in *More Shapes Than One*, the story initially was published with only minor variations as "Detour on 51," *Writers' Choice: Selected Poetry and Fiction by 58 North Carolina Writers*, ed. The Greensboro Group (Greensboro: TransVerse, 1981) 123–35.

minded characters are forced to confront a bothersome abstract manifestation.

Chappell's allegorical shadings are much darker in "Blood Shadow" (1983), which—in the tradition of Olaf Stapledon's tragic, vivid accounts of doomed civilizations—traces the symbolic impact of a single evil act, the evisceration and burning of the witch Axla, on the history of the universe. Like David Lindsay's *A Voyage to Arcturus*, "Blood Shadow" is a work of fantasy that also functions as a search for meaning in the cosmos. When humans are extinct from the earth and the crimson shadow remains, it reveals itself to the solar system's dying sun as inverted, dark Logos: "The blood of Axla had taken the form of a hieroglyphic word.... Now this small and hungry sun looked at the word and laughed a bitter laugh and spoke the word, a curse; and then it gathered its elements into an angry swarm and exploded; and that titanic convulsion unleashed such naked evil in the cosmos that unnamed stars thousands of light years distant cried out in anguish and wept and fled away to hide."[35] Whereas John's biblical Gospel equates Logos with God, eternal life, and order, in "Blood Shadow" Axla's obscene "hieroglyphic" is a cosmic force of death, chaos, and destruction, polluting life on the earth and unleashing evil upon the universe.[36]

Noteworthy in "Blood Shadow" is the fact that Axla's debilitating stain is a *human* creation that has the capacity to affect the entire universe adversely. Chappell examines the opposite side of the coin in another civilization allegory, "After Revelation" (1985), in which—rather than altering the cosmos through its evil acts—humanity is reduced to dependent servility upon the arrival of the "Owners," alien beings who mesmerize humans with their attentiveness, even causing some to die of happiness. The narrator George reveals both the function of the Owners and the significance of the story's title when he states, "A great deal has been revealed to us, but it is revelation so pure that our minds and senses cannot interpret it" (*MSTO*, 197). Having been exposed to immense, pleasurable quantities of knowledge, humanity is still struck with the challenge of how

---

[35] Fred Chappell, "Blood Shadow," *Memphis State Review* 4 (Fall 1983): 9.

[36] "That which was from the beginning, which we have heard, which we have seen with our eyes, which we have looked upon, and our hands have handled, of the Word of life; (For the life was manifested, and we have seen it, and bear witness, and shew unto you that eternal life, which was with the Father, and was manifested unto us;)..." (John 1:1–2).

best to digest and apply it "after revelation"—will it ultimately lead to a new kind of human consciousness or forever pervade and pollute humanity like Axla's accursed blood?

In addition to constructing general fantastic allegories of human civilization, Chappell also employs fantasy in offering symbolic commentaries on specific political topics such as gender and race. For example, in "A Woman One Time" (1983) and "Alma" (1991)—two versions of the same narrative—Chappell creates an alternative world in which women are handled like animals and herded along by male "shoat drovers"—hybrid cowboy/pimp/slave owners who steal, sell, and trade women. When the narrator, Fretlaw, encounters a "shoat line" (a group of captive women) while on the trail, he feels the injustice of women's treatment but remains entirely ignorant of them. That changes when Alma/Heena frees herself at night and seduces him into binding her cruel jailer and setting all the women free. In the later version of the story, "Alma," Fretlaw and Alma live happily for a time until she departs for an island inhabited only by women in order to give birth. However, the more interesting conclusion belongs to the original version, in which Heena (Alma's original name) dies and Fretlaw follows Tiresias in switching sexes: "During the Years I became a woman, a lot of us switched sex, I'm still a woman but don't feel like one. Anyway not a woman like Heena, she was the best. I don't feel like the only woman I ever knew."[37] Moved by Heena's exemplary example of womanhood, Fretlaw becomes interested in the essence of feminine identity, admiring it to the point that he decides to become a woman.

In "The Three Boxes" (1977) Chappell paints the ordeal of people of color in equally oppressive and hopeful allegorical terms. Like Lydia Obukhova's *Daughter of Night: A Tale of Three Worlds*—which takes place during the dawn of humanity and serves as a poetic allegory for how civilization was formed—"The Three Boxes" symbolically explains the history of race through God's gift of three boxes to three early humans.[38] Whereas the first two boxes contain elements such as reason, law, and civil order, the third possesses cruelty and misery but also the potential for

---

[37] Fred Chappell, "A Woman One Time," *Crescent Review* 2 (Fall 1983): 26.

[38] Lydia Obukhova, *Daughter of Night: A Tale of Three Worlds*, trans. Mirra Ginsburg (New York: Macmillan, 1974).

justice. As God explains to the third, darker-skinned human, "Out of these justice shall be created. For it cannot come into being in the abstract, by fiat. It can inhabit only the human soul and the human body. You shall create justice in the ravaging of your spirit and in the torture of your blood" (*MOL*, 12). Despite the pain and oppression of their existence, it will be the earth's suffering people of color who hold the key to its deliverance from evil and the establishment of justice.

Shifting from social to international politics, Chappell's unpublished, fantastic play "Moonjox" allegorizes the cataclysmic potential of the Cold War with its science fiction-laced portrayal of the earth's imminent destruction.[39] In the tradition of books like Ruthven Todd's *The Lost Traveller*—a fantastic, futuristic political allegory of fascism—"Moonjox" criticizes a contemporary historical problem, the annihilatory capacities of the Soviet Union and United States, through a science fiction drama, in this case one involving rude aliens and foul-mouthed angels and taking place on the moon.[40] Chappell's imaginative interest in the moon both in nonfictional and fictional terms is apparent in his essay on space exploration after the first moon-landing and the fantastic moon voyage sequence in *Look Back All the Green Valley* (1999).[41] Like the space cycle from the last Kirkman novel, "Moonjox" appears significantly influenced by fantastic works such as Italo Calvino's *Cosmicomics* and *t zero*—surrealistic and often trite literary applications of various scientific principles, written in a purposefully pedestrian and comic style.[42] "Moonjox" also suggests Amon Liner's epic poem *The Far Journey and Final End of Dr. Faustwitz, Spaceman* in its characterization of Papa Professor, the brilliant human scientist whose actions may result in the earth's destruction.[43] In Liner's long poetic allegory a Jewish scientist, Dr. Faustwitz, escapes Auschwitz to become an important space pioneer only to discover that evil and nihilism do not die with Nazism, or the earth for that matter. As the immortal Faustwitz ventures through the

---

[39] Box WM-1, writings by Chappell, miscellaneous subseries.

[40] Ruthven Todd, *The Lost Traveller* (London: Grey Walls, 1943).

[41] Fred Chappell, "The Moon...Why Pay More?," *UNCG Alumni News* 85/3 (Spring 1970) 16–18.

[42] Italo Calvino, *Cosmicomics*, trans. William Weaver (New York: Harcourt, Brace & World, 1968); *t zero*, trans. William Weaver (New York: Harcourt, Brace & World, 1969).

[43] Liner, *The Far Journey and Final End of Dr. Faustwitz, Spaceman* (Chapel Hill: Carolina Wren Press, 1983).

future, he is confronted with new fantastic challenges that also reflect his struggles with aspects of himself. Like Dr. Faustwitz, Papa Professor is confronted with the dilemma of doing or not doing the right thing for humanity, and he searches for the solution within both himself and the essence of humans—an endeavor for which his scientific genius is useless. Yet history ultimately foiled the cultural immediacy of Papa Professor's decision and the play itself. As Chappell explains, once the real possibility of global human extinction became dramatically lessened, "Moonjox" lost much of its power: "The play unfortunately fell victim to the end of the Cold War by the time I really got it into any kind of shape. The worry that Russia and the U.S. were going to blow everything up had disappeared, which kind of invalidates the conclusion of the play. I had not realized, as a matter of fact, that it was such a Cold War play, because I had no conception of how a world without that frame of mind would be" (INT). A product of his time, Chappell inevitably failed to see the historical/allegorical dimension of his play until the historical conditions of existence changed suddenly and radically with the fall of the Soviet Union—a global transition that opened his eyes to the essence of what he unconsciously had been attempting to comment upon.

Psychological/Supernatural Fantasy and Moral Fables

Unconscious impulses in writers need not be allegorical and certainly not rational. Carl Jung observed, "The disturbing vision of monstrous and meaningless happenings that in every way exceed the grasp of human feeling and comprehension makes quite other demands upon the powers of the artist than do the experiences of the foreground of life."[44] Incomprehensible and "monstrous" happenings inform more than one of Chappell's tales, constituting yet another separate subcategory of his fantastic fiction. When asked about the compositions of *The Lodger* and "Free Hand," Chappell contends, "I think of this kind of fiction in a different way than I ordinarily think about a more realistic sort of short story. I'm very heavily influenced by Poe. I admire his work very much and I like the mode he sets his stories in, which is often not a realistic atmosphere at all, but a heavily symbolic and fantastic one. The advantage in supernatural fiction is the element of moral

[44] Carl Jung, "Psychology and Literature," in *Modern Man in Search of a Soul* (New York: Harcourt, Brace, 1933) 157.

fable, that's really what it is at bottom" (INT). More than general symbolic or allegorical fantasies, Chappell's distinctly supernatural narratives contain symbolic structures with ethical parables.

Although it is not "monstrous" in the Jungian sense, "Miss Prue" (1981) functions literally as a supernatural story while symbolically constituting a morality tale. The narrative's vaguely ghoulish dimension arises from the fact that Mr. M. May has physically returned from the dead to confess his love for Miss Prue, who coolly rebukes his advances. The tale's original version contains an epigraph from William Blake's *The Marriage of Heaven and Hell* that does not appear in *More Shapes than One* and without which the narrative's symbolic structure remains buried: "Prudence is a rich ugly old maid courted by Incapacity."[45] Blake's line essentially reveals the story's parable, perhaps too readily since Chappell omitted it from his second volume of short stories—that prudence and incapacity are well matched but also despairing and impotent. When Mr. M May, or Incapacity, departs, Miss Prue, alone and unwanted, is made to appear more prudish than prudent, mocked by the "big crow" that gives "her one cool and careless regard" (*MSTO*, 154) before flying away.

Prudence and incapacity do not cripple the protagonist of "Free Hand"(1990), who revenges himself upon his romantic rival Tate Keylor by employing the supernatural services of an old man who uses his hand to manipulate dreams, making them agonizing harbingers of madness and death for targeted individuals. Like Sadegh Hedayat's *The Blind Owl*, "Free Hand" is a dark and tangled, dreamy story, mingling and confusing supernatural fantasy with psychological trauma.[46] As in Italo Svevo's *Confessions of Zeno*, the narrator is insane—in this case, deranged with an unquenchable thirst for revenge—which forces the reader to examine carefully all of his claims, the paranormal intensity of which increase as the story progresses. The narrator alleges that the dream-shaping old man can "affect what [a] person dreams of and how he dreams," which places the story in the tradition of occult fiction in which characters utilize disciplines like witchcraft and voodoo in order to destroy or control their victims.[47] As one of Chappell's favorite supernatural writers, E. F. Benson, writes in "The

---

[45] Fred Chappell, "Miss Prue," *Cold Mountain Review* 9 (Spring 1981): 72.
[46] Sadegh Hedayat, *The Blind Owl* (London: John Calder, 1957).
[47] Fred Chappell, "Free Hand," *Death Realm* 11 (Spring 1990): 43.

Terror by Night," "The transference of emotion is a phenomenon so common, so constantly witnessed that mankind in general have long ceased to be conscious of its existence...."[48] In "Free Hand" the "transference" of dreams or unconscious emotion has both literal and abstract functions in the story, the symbolic moral being that the dream world and real world are irrevocably connected and that, as the old man says, "We are all of us dreaming small parts of one enormous dream."[49] In the process of infiltrating and destroying the dreams of his rival, the narrator psychologically destroys himself, and the complex, shadowy tale leaves open the possibility that the narrator and his rival may be one and the same—a suicidal lunatic who possibly has murdered his love interest. Investigating and mixing dreams, aberrant psychology, and the supernatural, "Free Hand" constitutes a grim and powerful work of dark fiction.

Chappell couples the psychological and supernatural elements of "Free Hand" with the partly-comic, historically-based fiction of "Weird Tales" and "The Adder" in *The Lodger* (1993), a light, supernatural drama in which the unassuming, contemplative librarian Robert Ackley undergoes a struggle—"not epic in proportion, nor cosmic in its philosophic terms"—with the spirit of the pompous, diabolical versifier Lyman Scoresby for possession of his body.[50] Like "Weird Tales," *The Lodger* makes use of literary history in summoning the 1920s Cleveland circle of writers that included Samuel Loveman, H. P. Lovecraft, and Hart Crane. As in his other fictional portrayals of literary history, Chappell employs humor—for example, he dramatizes Crane's review of Scorseby's ephemeral sonnet sequence *Spindrift Twilight*: "[P]retty unusual after all—at least not the usual wagonload of horseshit."[51] *The Lodger* also contains dark humor in the tradition of stories such as E. F. Benson's "Mr. Tilly's Séance," which concerns the afterlife of an Englishman flattened by a trolley while in route to a séance. Rather than dark and desperate, Ackley's battle against Scoresby's possession is riddled with hilarity as the bland librarian attempts to drive away the decadent poet by reading page after page of obtuse contemporary poetry and postmodern literary theory. Chappell also fleshes

---

[48] E. F. Benson, "The Terror by Night," in *The Collected Ghost Stories*, ed. Richard Dalby (New York: Carroll and Graf, 1992) 139.

[49] Chappell, "Free Hand," 43.

[50] Fred Chappell, *The Lodger* (West Warwick RI: Necronomicon, 1993) 14.

[51] Ibid., 8.

out Ackley and the story by including Scoresby's sarcastic reactions to late twentieth-century everyday items such as Budweiser and tennis shoes. Chappell explains that writers must include enough ephemera so that the story's main character is believable: "In other words, they can focus on the problem that confronts them, which is your theme, generally. I'm very conscious when I write a story of the supernatural that I've got to keep the character focused on theme and I've got to give the story a lot of suspense if it's possible, because otherwise it will be very flimsy and unreadable, as too much fantasy is, I think. Fantasy is very difficult but I enjoy it. I'd like to write more" (INT). Ackley's everyday materialism is related to the story's theme of supernatural possession in that both contribute to Ackley's eventual doom. Although he succeeds in driving out Scorseby, the struggle damns him to a fate worse than death: "[H]e had become the leading literary critic of the postmodernist generation."[52] In "exorcising the poet," Ackley abdicates from himself both the benevolent beauty and dark, destructive passions that fuel most artistic endeavors, becoming instead a soulless categorizer of art—the cheerless author of monotonous scholarly works such as *The Spirit Killeth: The Lost Signifier in the "Forgotten Poems" of Lyman Scoresby*.[53]

Having attempted to categorize and discuss Chappell's historical and fantastic short fiction, this chapter may well toil beneath the very curse—the bane that pervades all literary criticism and critics—Robert Ackley brought upon himself when he expunged Lyman Scoresby's poetic spirit. In the process of endeavoring to make new connections between Chappell's stories, it may fall victim to the *The Lodger*'s moral fable: that the technical classification of art can be mundanely reductive and even possesses the capacity to kill the spirit of the classifier. Yet this is a pox upon the critic and not the artist. For however their work is interpreted by scholars, the writings of Scoresby and Chappell, and all serious artists—good and not so good—remain genuine attempts at aesthetic expression: an endeavor to which Chappell remains dedicated. Experimenting with multiple genres and styles, Chappell's ambitious aesthetic attempts constitute unique and versatile forms of expression through which he provides new perspectives on

---

[52] Ibid., 28.

[53] Ibid.

human experience and goes about the poetic business of reinventing the world.

Part 3

Appendix:

A Story and an Interview

“The Two Ministries”:

A Previously Unpublished Short Story

“The Two Ministries” was written sometime in the early 1960s. Chappell never completed the story to his liking or attempted to publish it. In some respects it is raw and contrived and should not be evaluated as a finished work of fiction. I include it here as an example of what I term Chappell’s early “initiation fiction,” most of which was written when he was very young and resides now only among his unpublished papers and in obscure regional publications such as *Red Clay Reader*. Its shortcomings notwithstanding, the story—as a representative work—is important for the way in which its young protagonist, Paul Warner, wavers between conflicting philosophies while attempting to find his own way of interpreting the world: a theme Chappell periodically revisits in his work, perhaps most notably through Jess Kirkman in *I Am One of You Forever*.

The Two Ministries

It was during the long mid-spring that comes to the western North Carolina mountains. The air was sweetish and warm, although it was now past midnight, and big yellow stars were strewn in the sky like dandelions. Few cars passed Paul Warner, leaning stiffly forward with his begging thumb cocked back tensely like the hammer of a revolver, his body gangly, his head confused with the warm night, with first love. Behind him, beneath the high hill the little town lay mostly dark and somnolent except for the bright gray steamy patch where the paper mill boiled. He was trying to thumb a ride home—seven miles away—after a date with his girl, but he had stayed too late at her home, and the traffic was sparse and fast. He was sixteen years old.

When no cars were in sight he wandered about in a little circle, sometimes stepping into the highway, humming songs to himself, occasionally tossing pebbles at the billboard across the street; he kept trying to plug the blue eye of the lady ecstatic over her Red Dot coffee. When the broad swathe of headlights splashed on the side of the warehouse halfway down the hill, he straightened and hitched at his trousers and smoothed down the front of his tan windbreaker. When a car passed him by he stood still, gazing regretfully but not bitterly at the receding taillights. Sometimes huge trailer trucks groaned and shuddered the way up the steep hill; they had never stopped for him because here at the top the drivers were always busy changing gear.

At last a car stopped for him. He had watched it coming slowly up the hill. Wondering if the old coupe would be able to pull the grade. It was a '38 or '39 model, black but with large patches of rust on the hood and fenders.

"How far are you going?"

"About seven miles," Paul said.

On Paul's side a woman sat, about twenty-five years old. When she opened the door he saw that she was pregnant. Her hair was dark, short, tangled, and in the yellow light of the billboard sign she looked sallow and unhealthy. It was the driver who had spoken, but Paul couldn't see him and he hadn't asked him to get in yet. Evidently he wanted to look Paul over.

"All right, brother, get in," said the man. The woman leaned heavily forward, pulling up the back of the seat so that Paul could squeeze in behind.

The interior of the car held the nostalgic smell of felt upholstery and warm rubber matting that Paul associated with his early childhood, with the high, rackety model-T Ford his father used to drive about the farm. Now his father had gone into discount hardware business, and shuttled about the neat suburbs in a smooth blue Buick. Paul had forgot how low the top was in these old cars; when he sat tall his head brushed the ribbed felt under the car roof. The narrow back seat was scattered over with folded leaflets and printed papers which he slid carefully aside in order to give himself sitting space.

Still the car had not moved on. The driver twisted about in the seat, still looking him over. He seemed to be a small man—although it was hard to tell with the seat between them—with a pale complexion and dark hair. His face was thin and bony with shadows scooping hollows under his cheekbones. The whites of his eyes were lemon-colored in the light from the billboard, the pupils were ink black like bullet holes; fierce hot eyes they were, unwavering, unblinking. When he spoke his voice was high-pitched, but resonant, crackling in the close air like electricity:

"I hope you aint got a gun or a knife there, that you'll murder us."

Paul smiled, trying to exude friendliness, and held his arms arched away from his body. "I'm clean," he said. He giggled.

"Let me ask you one more thing, brother." He hadn't moved an inch, hadn't blinked. "Are you a Christian?"

"Yes," said Paul.

The man jerked around in his seat, turning to the steering wheel as readily as if he had received a military command. He set the car in motion with a raucous scraping of gears, so that Paul almost gave aloud the automatic response, *Grind me off a handful*, which was customary among the boys his age. He leaned back warily; he had expected more. Often with one of these fellows you had to go through a lengthy catechism, and you had to be letter-perfect on all points. He glanced down at one of the leaflets on the seat, trying to read the title in the darkness. In the oblique light of an oncoming car he saw, WHAT IF JESUS CAME TONIGHT? He closed his eyes, counting himself lucky. What he really wanted to do was to draw into himself, the warm windstream pouring through the window over his face, and to think of Helen, of how she looked only an hour ago after the long bidding good night.

The car went along slowly and painfully. Paul, thinking of the girl, reached into his shirt pocket for a cigarette, but remembered in time his situation. Even a cigarette would probably set off a long lecture, tearing the lovely image from the tight embrace of his memory. And what if Jesus came tonight? That too would be a pain in the neck. He felt desperately determined to protect his comfort; a kind of joyful lassitude had settled on him. It took very little to produce this sense of lazy security, and it took very little to break it. The car smelled somehow like the Bible, like the big leather-covered Bible that lay immovable and somehow obstreperously on the long dining table in the house of one of his uncles. Uncle Saxon too was a preacher, but not a revivalist: a built church and a congregation he claimed. He had a red, rather feline face and a large bald tough head.

Standing steady in his oak pulpit, he seemed neither Shepherd nor Pilot, but rather a huge rock which the tide of the congregation, bowed toward him in the pews for prayer, would recoil against. The summer he was nine years old Paul had spent with Uncle Saxon, and after the Sunday morning sermon, over the fried chicken and rice and the white gravy, the minister would attempt joviality, which fit him about as well as a baby crib would, chuckling heavily, telling Paul the story of the preacher who had put a collar button instead of a cough drop under his tongue. Aunt Cynthia fluttered about the table solicitously, pouring tea into the heavy rough goblets.

It was an old steady house Uncle Saxon lived in there in the eastern part of the state. The ceilings were twelve feet high and on the first floor the rooms were always cool and still. Upstairs you broiled. The temperature stood at ninety-five or ninety-eight degrees on the big RC Cola thermometer on the porch. But on the first floor it was cool and still, the rooms dim in the shadows of the pecan trees. The heavy books on the shelves, the china and the thin glasses in the cabinets, the steady mumbling of a big fly thumping into a window screen: the whole held an air of patient placidity, like a small pool in the woods. Paul used to stand in the center of the hushed living room, breathing deeply through his nose. He walked very softly. In the dining room the Bible lay on the long table. For a game he tried with his little finger to displace the volume, to change its position. He could not. From a long way over the fields came the noise of a dog. His uncle came to the table for the evening meal, opened the book and read from proverbs. "Eat thou not the bread of him that hath an evil eye, neither desire thou his dainty meats: For as he thinketh in his heart, so is he: Eat and drink, saith he to thee; but his heart is not with thee. The morsel which thou hast eaten shalt thou vomit up, and lose thy sweet words." Uncle Saxon closed the book; meditated in silence. "*That* passage," he said at last, "isn't especially appropriate before supper." He opened the Bible again and read some verses from Psalms.

The car was stopping for another hitchhiker. Paul moved over, gathering the pamphlets into a loose handful. The fellow squeezed clumsily into the back seat, grunting a bit under his breath. He was tall and muscular and he badly needed a shave. Khaki trousers and a dirty tee shirt he wore, and a wide leather belt with red glass studs. Settling back into the seat he banged his head against the low roof of the car, and Paul saw that he quickly smothered a curse with his broad hand. On the back of his hand rested a tattooed anchor twisted about with a rope. The little preacher turned in his seat and leveled his fierce gaze at the new rider. He spoke, again with the sharp explosive voice, "What's your name, brother, and which way are you headed?"

"I'm Ray Morris," he said. He put out his hand and the preacher grabbed it. "I'm just going up the road a piece."

"And which way are you headed in eternity?"

"I don't know that," he said. "Are you a preacher?"

The preacher at last let go his hand. "Yes," he said, "that's my calling. For four years now I've been carrying the gospel. But before *that*...." He shook his head disapprovingly and smiled a grim smile. The big fellow nodded knowingly, and the preacher turned around and set the car going again. "You're a Christian aint you, brother?"

"I hope so," he said.

For a moment there was silence. "Brother, you can't hope, you got to know. There aint any ifs or buts. Now, you tell me: are you a Christian or aint you?"

"I try to be."

"What I mean, brother, is, have you been saved? Have your sins been washed away? And have you received the Lord into your heart? That's what I mean. Are you a Christian?"

"I try to be," he said. "I don't know if I'm saved or not." He sat back gloomily in the seat. Paul smiled and winked at him, and he frowned testily so that the boy felt foolish and a bit insulted.

"You're not," the preacher said stoutly. "When a man is saved, he *knows* he's been saved, and there's not the littlest shadow of a doubt in his mind. There's a day coming, brother, a great day of judgement, and on that day the sheep will be standing on the right hand of God and the goats on the left hand. And on that day, brother, there won't be time for you to decide if you're saved or not. There won't be any time left in the world. You'll have done used all your time up. And when you're there at the seat of judgement, you won't be able to say 'I don't know.'"

"I been preached to before," said Ray Morris, "and I still don't know. I been baptized and I been sanctified. But nothing come of it. I still drink and fight and whore around. I still see the jailhouse from the inside. What good does the sanctifying do me then?"

"You have not been saved," the preacher said again. "You never have truly received the word of God into your heart. You have closed your heart against your Lord. Let me ask you something, brother. You talk about being sanctified, but when that happened to you, did you really and truly feel the Spirit move you? Did you feel the Spirit in your heart, in your very loins?"

"I don't know that either," he said. "I don't know how you tell."

"Let me tell you again that you're not saved. When you're truly saved you don't have to worry about the whiskey and the gambling and the painted women."

"Don't call them painted women," he said. "They aint painted no more than the rest of the women you see around."

The car went slower and slower. "You've got your eyes too much on the things of this world," the preacher said, "the things that will pass away. You got to fix your sight on the eternal and everlasting."

"Maybe so," said Ray Morris, "but it's the truth that about every woman you see is wearing face paint. Maybe you don't see any women, or maybe you just see them at revival meeting, but you won't never get nobody to believe what you tell them unless you open up your eyes and look around some."

"Brother, you don't have to tell me. I know this world is foul with sin, I know this world is a vale of filth and misery. My mission is to lift a man's eyes from the sty he's wallowing in to the bright and shining heavens."

"Now you take your wife there, she aint wearing no paint, I'll grant you. But it don't bother me to say, I seen a whole lot better looking women in my time."

The woman turned around and stared, and then—Paul hardly believed it—she gave the big fellow two curt nods.

The preacher pulled the car onto the wide grassy shoulder of the road and cut the motor. Only in the ensuing silence did Paul realize how much noise the motor had been making; it was hard to believe that the old car would run for another fifty miles. At the edge of the shoulder a low bank went up into a pasture, and a barbwire fence straggled along the contours of the bank. The air was still warm. Near and far the crickets pulsed. The grass smelled sweetly musky. No cars passed on the black highway. "This is a good place," the preacher said, jerking his head toward the pasture. "We'll go on up the hill, and I'm going to offer up prayer for you, brother. I'm going to pray to God for your immortal soul."

"Not at one o'clock in the morning you aint," said Ray Morris.

"I am," he said. "You aint got any time to waste."

"I been prayed over before."

"Your ears were sealed and your heart was closed up. I'm going to take the wax out of your ears and I'm going to open up your heart."

"You're out of your head."

"Brother," the preacher said, "I never been as positive in my life." He leaned across his wife and opened the glove compartment and fumbled in it for a moment. When he turned around to face the big fellow again his eyes were hotter and blacker and more hungry-looking than before, and in his left hand he held a big blue-black pistol. He held the gun steady on Ray Morris. "We're going to all go up on the hill," he said. "We're going to all pray for your salvation."

"Sam...," said the woman softly.

"Hush, Martha," the preacher said.

"This is the craziest mess I ever heard of," said Ray Morris. "I never in my life heard of a preacher pulling a gun on a man."

"You didn't give me no choice. I spoke to you with words of honey and you turned a deaf ear. Now I got to use harsher words, I got to use harsh words against the hardness of your heart."

"You wouldn't shoot a man. You're a preacher, aint you?"

"The ills of your body soon pass, but your soul is immortal and everlasting. It's your soul you got to worry about, not your body. The flesh is evil."

"Let's go then," said Ray Morris. "I believe you're just about crazy enough to put a bullet in me."

"Open the door, Martha."

She said again, more softly than before, "Sam..."

"Hush," he said.

She opened the door and got out clumsily; she was much more pregnant than Paul had thought. She was short and her belly was immense. The big fellow scrambled out lithely and stood with one arm outstretched, leaning against the car, resting. The preacher gestured at Paul with his free hand. "You too," he said. "I need all the Christian help I can get." Paul nodded numbly and got out with the preacher, and they went around the car.

"Let's go up on the hill," the preacher said, waving the gun laxly at Ray Morris's chest. The preacher was very short, shorter by about three inches than Paul, shorter than Ray Morris by a head at least. His motions were jerky and quick, as if he had much more energy than he could control. He went up the bank with the tall man before him, holding the gun by his side now, and when they came to the slack rusty barbwire, he parted the strands with hand and foot so the other could shoulder through. They went a few yards farther and stopped. Paul took the woman's arm and went slowly up the bank with her. He held the wire for her when they came to the fence, but she couldn't stoop to go through; she was too big.

"Come on up here," said the preacher.

"She can't get through," Paul said. "There's not enough room."

"You stay there then, Martha. You pray with us by the fence there." He jerked his thumb at Paul. "You come on ahead up here with us."

"I'd better stay here," Paul said hoarsely. "I'd better stay here with your wife."

The preacher hesitated before he nodded. "All right then," he said. "You pray from the fence there too." He turned to the big man. "Let's get on our knees and pray to the Lord."

"Oh, come off it," he said. "This is the craziest thing I ever heard tell of."

The preacher brought the pistol up again; held it unwavering. "I mean it, brother," he said. "I never been as positive in my life."

Slowly Ray Morris went down. He placed one knee on the earth, then the other. "Dammit," he said.

"Brother...," said the preacher warningly.

"I got a horse nettle under my leg."

The preacher chuckled; it was a queer crackling sound, like someone wadding cellophane. "Then shift," he said, "shift your position, brother. That's what I'm trying to get you to do." He gave a downward salute to Paul and to his wife at the fence. "Get on your knees," he said. "We got to pray for this man."

Paul held one of her arms and with the other hand she gripped the fence post tightly, and with great difficulty she knelt. Paul got down too. The grass was damp and he felt very uncomfortable. "I wish he wasn't like this so much," the woman muttered—mainly to herself it seemed.

There was a short silence. Then, "What did you say your name was?" the preacher asked.

"Ray Morris."

This time the silence was longer and more profound. Even the crickets were quiet, and it almost seemed to Paul that the universe had momentarily stopped operating. Although he knelt and the little preacher stood, Ray Morris looked much larger than the man who stood at his right shoulder loosely holding the pistol and gazing up at the warm yellow stars. The preacher didn't kneel, but stood with his feet wide apart, looking at the sky as if there he might find a suitable text.

Then he began. "O Lord," he said, and Paul was surprised to hear how softly he had pitched his voice, "O Lord, here You see before You one of the worst and blackened and hardened sinners I ever seen. Lord, I'm asking You to take the wax out of his ears and melt his heart of stone. I'm asking You to tear the gates of iron off of his heart. And Lord, I'm asking You to forgive this man, Ray Morris, his black dark sins and let him enter in Thy fold. O Lord, make him, Ray Morris, to see and know—"

When the preacher's voice began to rise in volume and intensity, Ray Morris reached up and with a gentle swipe, as if he were capturing a firefly to put into a jar, took the pistol from the relaxed hand. "That's enough of that," he said. He stood up and pressed the catch and flipped the chamber out of the revolver. He looked into the chamber. "I might of knew," he said in an exasperated voice. "Empty." Finding the gun empty seemed to make him angrier. "Empty, by God," he said.

"That's not important, brother," the preacher said. "The gun aint important—"

Ray Morris growled in baffled frustration and slapped the little man across the forehead with the pistol barrel. Immediately the preacher fell back on the grass, like a bottle tipped over. The woman, still kneeling at the fence, cried out. "Don't hurt him," she said. She turned to Paul. "Don't let him beat him up."

Paul struggled hurriedly through the barbwire. Ray Morris kicked the preacher once in the thigh before Paul grasped his shoulder. "Stop," Paul said. "Don't hurt him."

The big man brushed his hand away. "Let me alone, boy," he said. "I ain't going to hurt him." He looked at the gun in his hand. "Empty, by God." He was plainly disgusted. Grasping the gun by the barrel he leaned back and threw it spinning through the dark air. It seemed a long time before Paul heard the faint thump of its impact.

"The gun aint important," said the preacher. He gasped the words out. "What's important is, we still got to pray. Your soul's in mortal danger, sure as God's in heaven."

"Just hush up," said the big man. "You make so much racket a man can't hear hisself think. Don't you never get tired of talking?"

"The word of the Lord is my—"

"Just hush up, I said." He stood with his hands on his hips, looking at the figure seated on the grass. He seemed to be trying to think what to do about the little man. Abruptly he turned away. "Oh hell," he said. "Listen," he said to Paul, "I don't know how far you got to go, but I only got three miles, and I'm going to walk it rather than put up with this buzzard here"—he nudged the preacher with his heavy shoe—"any longer. If I was you I'd walk or either thumb me another ride. This crew here is crazy as hell, and there aint no doubt about it." He went down the hill and clambered through the fence. The woman still kneeling there at the post looked up at him with wide fearful eyes. The big man stopped and looked at her. "Lady," he said, "all I know is, I feel plumb sorry for you." He walked off into the moist darkness, following the black highway, his figure at first a darker shadow on a lighter, and then invisible and soundless.

Paul knelt and looked at the preacher's forehead. The welt was long and dark and it leaked a little blood on one side, the tight skin scraped away. Leaning forward wearily, the little man shook his head. "How are you doing?" asked Paul.

"I'm all right," he said. "Don't worry about me. You got to expect that the righteous is going to be persecuted. This world is a vale of filth and misery, especially sometimes for the chosen of God."

"Can you walk?"

"I'm all right brother, and I thank you." He took Paul's proffered hand and heaved himself up. He walked dizzily down the hill and Paul held the wires apart. Then he went through himself and helped the woman to her feet. She was still scared.

"Sam...," she said.

"Hush now, Martha. I'm all right." His voice was subdued, strained.

They went down to the car. Paul held out his hand for a handshake, but the preacher didn't take it. "Hop in," he said.

"I can walk from here," Paul said. "It's not far now."

"No. No, brother. You get in. I'll take you right to your front door."

"It's all right, I can walk."

"I wouldn't think of it," he said. "Get on in the back there."

Paul got in and they started again. The preacher was driving a little faster now. The car still held the Bible smell, and once again Paul thought of his uncle. Why were these two preachers so different? This little man was so fierce and hot and quick, and his uncle so quiet and steady. The whole fabric of the little fellow's zealous life was unimaginable. He seemed to have no house, no settled pulpit to teach from. Certainly he must be headed for a remote point in this decrepit old car which certainly would never get there.... Paul looked along the road for the sight of the big man tramping along, but he didn't see him. He had probably taken a shortcut through the fields or a back road. There again was another incomprehensible mode of living.

They had come into the suburbs of Beaumont. The white and brick houses sat cool and clean in the light of the street lamps. "I'll get out of here," Paul said.

"I can take you right to your house," said the preacher.

"No, no," said Paul. "It's just down the block." He squirmed out of the back through the door the preacher held open. He turned and shook hands. "Well, goodbye," he said. "You take it easy now."

"Wait a minute." He turned around in the seat and leaned back and came up with a handful of leaflets. He gave them to Paul. "Here," he said, "you can read these and pass them on to them as needs them."

"All right," said Paul. "Goodbye now." He leaned down and waved through the window at the woman. She turned her face away without speaking.

"Goodbye," said the preacher, "and the Lord be with you and bless you." In the light from the street lamp his welt looked larger and angrier. He set the car in gear and it went clamoring down the sleepy street.

Paul walked down the block. He glanced at the tracts in his hand and folded them and put them into the pocket of his tan windbreaker. WHAT IF JESUS CAME TONIGHT? "Not tonight," Paul muttered. "I'm tired."

Unexpectedly, lights were still burning in his house. He hoped that his parents hadn't really waited up for him. If so, he had more lecturing to listen to before he could lie in bed and try to assemble the lovely features of

Helen, those features which the events of the night had almost obliterated from his memory. When he pushed into the living room, his mother and father sat stiffly on the sofa. His father was in one of his newest suits, and his mother wore a black dress and white gloves. They did not look vexed or angry.

"We've been waiting for you," his mother said. Her voice was tired. She pointed to a limp yellow square of paper on the coffee table. "We got the telegram right after supper. Your Uncle Saxon has passed away, and we have to go down there. We'll have to leave right away."

"Uncle Saxon?" Paul was momentarily incredulous.

"A heart attack," she said. "It was very sudden, and we have to leave right away. I've already packed your suitcase for you, and I've laid out the things for you to wear on your bed. So you go change now, and shave. And hurry up, please, we have to leave right away."

"All right," Paul said, "I will."

Interview

Fred Chappell Discusses His Fiction

This interview took place 6 August 2001 at Chappell's home in Greensboro, North Carolina. Chappell has recorded numerous interviews over the years, most of which are quoted in this study. Mindful of his other interviews, I attempted to ask original questions, many of which pertain to his uncollected works and unpublished papers at Duke University. My inclusion of the interview is designed to provide new information from Chappell on certain aspects of his fiction, while also serving as a context for some of the quotations in the previous chapters. In terms of editing, I have left the interview much as it was recorded. When he read the interview manuscript, Chappell offered several grammatical corrections but did not suggest any alterations to the content.

CHC: You once described the widely acclaimed writings of Reynolds Price and Cormac McCarthy as poetically self-indulgent. What is your idea of successful prose writing?

FC: Oh my, that's a very difficult question for me because I think the prose style of any particular piece should conform to the material or subject matter being treated. So when I come across a highly individualistic style, highly mannered style, I sometimes suspect that the writer is more interested in the sound his voice makes than in presenting what he or she is dramatizing or thinking about. So I become very suspicious sometimes of overwrought passages of prose—even Mr. Faulkner seems to me self-indulgent, here and there, in this matter. On the other hand, I understand a writer has a certain style and that he sees and feels the world in terms of this style. So that a great deal of it is not self-indulgent in the least but absolutely necessary: that's the temperament of the artist speaking and interpreting. But sometimes there's a line of distinction that might be drawn perhaps, and the more chances you take in prose style the more likely you are to cross the line and become a little ridiculous, and sometimes a little obtuse. But look at the achievements that can be made by following your own genius to that extent. So it's a trade-off, like most things in art, and I would rather be an artist like Mr. Faulkner than some sort of more measured artist. On the other hand, there's something at bottom that's a little suspicious about it. I don't know.

CHC: James Christopher and Peter Leland are writers working on manuscripts, as are some of the protagonists of your unpublished 1960s fiction. Were these authorial characters attractive because of your own academic background?

FC: Partly that. I could set them in settings that I was familiar with and felt comfortable writing about, but there were other reasons to do that too. In my case, it had to do with a double time-scheme. That is: you have a story in present time and a story in past time, and how do you bring these two stories together? Well, one way is to have your protagonist writing stuff down so that the reader can follow the two stories on double tracks. But undoubtedly my own experiences played a major part in that choice. I guess because I'm always working on some manuscript, I feel like…it's almost as if my inner life is the manuscript I'm working on—whatever kind of manuscript that is. And I use that to project my characters' inner lives on the page too. It's a rather old device but it's one I feel comfortable with.

CHC: More than one reviewer described your second novel, *The Inkling*, as overtly faulknerian. I was impressed by the intricate symbolic structure of that novel, but do you believe the literal narrative flirts with Southern clichés?

FC: I hadn't thought the least bit about Faulkner when I was writing that story. I wanted to tell a different kind of story, almost an allegorical story, about will and appetite, those two large forces. And I lit upon the very famous figures of Rimbaud and Verlaine, but I didn't know anything about

France of that period, though I know the work of those poets fairly well. I felt defeated. I could not have made a historical novel out of them. So I decided to put it in an allegorical setting, a fairy-tale setting in the mountains of western North Carolina and choose a family to act out the drama. When the comparisons to Faulkner came along I was surprised. I partly discounted them because a Southerner can't write a book without some reviewer saying, "Well, Faulkner is present here." And that's simply because Faulkner is such a famous and pervasive writer. But now it does seem to me that there is an element of cliché, or stereotype, in the book, which I hadn't realized. Simply by changing its terms so radically I'd fallen into a kind of Southern framework that's rather familiar to people. The reviews I remember sometimes mentioned incest as coming from Faulkner and I was curious about that, and went back and read in Faulkner, and I couldn't find a single instance of actual incest anywhere in there. I don't know where they get that stuff [laughter]. I think there's some in Erskine Caldwell but those writers are poles apart from each other.

CHC: I enjoyed reading two early unpublished versions of *Dagon*. In one of them the Leland figure is diagnosed with a terminal disease; in the other the protagonist is a Milton scholar who meets the Mina character at an academic party. What other transformations did this difficult novel go through?

FC: I don't even remember those [laughter]. Are those actual versions? I have no idea. I can see why I might have chosen a Milton scholar because I wanted to bring the Dagon material into it. I'm sorry, I don't recall either of those versions. I recall sweating out that novel over here on Spring Garden Street [on the campus of the University of North Carolina-Greensboro] and having great agonies with it, and I think I must have written other versions too and simply discarded them. I'm surprised to hear that there are any of those versions left. I think what I finally had published probably takes from a number of discarded versions, certainly a lot of discarded chapters and pages.

CHC: Two of my favorite stories, "The Lodger" and "Free Hand," strike me as psychological tales, tinged with conventions of horror fiction, possessing some of the psycho-supernatural complexity that appeared in

Dagon. Do you go about writing this kind of fiction differently and do you see yourself producing more of it?

FC: Yes. I think of this kind of fiction in a different way than I ordinarily think about a more realistic sort of short story. I'm very heavily influenced by Poe. I admire his work very much and I like the mode he sets his stories in, which is often not a realistic atmosphere at all, but a heavily symbolic and fantastic one. The advantage in supernatural fiction is the element of moral fable, that's really what it is at bottom. So you're able to illuminate your themes without interference from daily life. You have to keep enough of daily life so that it's believable as a sequence of events, but you don't have to be constrained by characters who are dealing with toothache or tax audits or minor surgery—that sort of thing. In other words, they can focus on the problem that confronts them, which is your theme, generally. I'm very conscious when I write a story of the supernatural that I've got to keep the character focused on theme and I've got to give the story a lot of suspense if it's possible, because otherwise it will be very flimsy and unreadable, as too much fantasy is, I think. Fantasy is very difficult but I enjoy it. I'd like to write more. I've got a ghost story in mind now but I don't know if I'll get a chance to write it or not.

CHC: You have said that your first three novels were partially indebted to specific literary sources. *The Gaudy Place* strikes me as a less overtly "intertextual" novel. Did you have any literary antecedents in mind for that book?

FC: Yes, for the character of Arkie. Sometimes you can't tell what's a literary inspiration and what comes from what you observe, because sometimes those two are very similar. There's a wonderful novel called *Don Sequndo Sombra* about a street hustler and how he makes his way in the world. I must have read that when we were visiting Italy, I'm not quite sure. At any rate, that novel seemed to me to have a lot of energy and a lot of affection for its waif, and I admired the ingenuity of the poor characters, how they made a living in the city in the novel. I had some knowledge of how that worked in Asheville, North Carolina, and so that novel kind of gave me the idea for how to do it. Now the structure of the book—ponderous job that it is—is all mine, as far as I know. I'm not very satisfied with it.

CHC: Most reviewers interpreted *I Am One of You Forever* as a folksy *bildungsroman* involving Jess Kirkman. However, I read that book, and the next two, as being more concerned with the life of the father, Joe Robert. Would you say he is the dominant figure of the Kirkman sequence?

FC: Oh yes, the sequence is about him. He's the dominant figure, the central figure. The themes are manifold in that series of novels, of course, but he is the central character. I think it's a habit of some reviewers to take the first person pronoun as being the center of the novel, but that's not what I intended at all. There was no way to cast this particular sequence of books in third person. That would have destroyed the whole idea of it. So the focus of attention is Joe Robert, he's the pivot. Nothing else can happen in those books without him.

CHC: Before writing the Kirkman novels you remarked to an interviewer that in your fiction you had "not done my area of the country justice."[1] Do you still feel that way?

FC: I think I've made a little more of a stab at it. I don't think I've done it justice. I don't think anyone can quite do a whole region justice, not even the best of us—not even Wolfe or Charles Frazier can get the whole thing down. Nevertheless, I think I made an honorable attempt over four novels and I'm glad I undertook them the way I did in regard to the region.

CHC: In an essay on Allen Tate's *The Fathers* you wrote that Tate achieved a "close poetic analysis of the poetic Southern spirit." Do you think one might replace "Southern" with "Appalachian" in that phrase and apply it to the Kirkman novels?

FC: Well, it would be very flattering. I don't know how accurate that would be. Mr. Tate, I believe, had a better grasp of the society he wrote

---

[1] David Paul Ragan, "Flying by Night: An Early Interview with Fred Chappell," *North Carolina Literary Review* 7 (1998): 114.

about than I have for my more contemporary society. That's one of the advantages of writing historical fiction. When someone's time has passed you can see patterns and tendencies, and you know the result—you know how everything is going to turn out, in a certain sense, so you can illustrate what is pretty well known already, in a way. Allen's novel would match up very well with C. Van Woodward's Southern histories, but I'm not able to do that because the material I dealt with is more contemporary—it takes place in my lifetime. So I didn't have the perspective that would be necessary for me to dissect the "soul of Appalachia" [laughter]. I did try to choose characters and attitudes that I felt could serve as indexes to what I see as the soul of the place. The spirit of the place is poetic, as is the spirit of any place when you come closer to the heart of it. I can't think of any book of real worth, except maybe Dante's *Inferno*, that says, underneath, "This is a horrible, lousy place, nobody should live here, and the people are dumb" [laughs]. On the other hand, every book that deals with place is also a criticism of place, but not simply a wholesale thrashing.

CHC: Do you agree with Will Hickson's claim that the Kirkman novels are overly sentimental?

FC: Yes, I do. There's one critic I can agree with [laughter].[2] I do think that future Appalachian literature will not be as nostalgic as it has been in the past. It will be a little more hard-edged because it will be set forward in time and there will be more clear-sighted analysis of the changes that have been made. I don't think, as far as I know, there's any novel about Appalachia in which the Vietnam War has made a difference. It's all been said mostly in terms of a pastoral versus urban context, although that's not the only one. There are a lot of other contexts too. I'm not smart enough to figure them all out.

CHC: After reading *Farewell, I'm Bound to Leave You*, I read the short story collection *More Shapes than One* before moving on to *Look Back All the Green Valley*. It seemed to me that some of the fantasy element of *More*

---

[2] Chappell, "The Shape of Appalachian to Come: An Interview with Will Hickson," *The Future of Southern Letters*, ed. Jefferson Humphries and John Lowe (New York: Oxford University Press, 1996) 54-60.

Shapes than One spilled over into the fourth Kirkman novel, specifically during the imaginary moon-flight.

FC: Yes, there's a large fantasy element there. I got in trouble with the moon-flight chapter there in the last novel and I knew I was taking a chance when I included it. I made a mistake that's pretty basic, which is to assume that folks would know an area of literature that most readers might not know, or have reason to know. I thought that people would see that it was a kind of parodic fantasy about the optimism and cheerfulness and belief in human ingenuity that characterized the science fiction of the 1940s and '50s, particularly. It's really a parody since the science is perfectly silly; it's just magic, and it's really silly magic. I had thought that readers would recognize that this kind of silliness actually characterized a whole side of Joe Robert Kirkman that, after all, wasn't that silly in a lot of admirable ways. But since most readers didn't know that this was supposed to be silly, they took it to be science fiction and to them it looked like just a chapter of actual science fiction thrown into an otherwise realistic work. So I think I misjudged my strategy there and I hadn't realized how many people are just allergic to the whole thought of science fiction or fantasy. I think a lot of them gave up in disgust at that point. But I meant no harm by it. It was just a miscalculation of my readers' reading habits. But in terms of the book itself, in terms of the book's artistic design, it's a little disconcerting. But now that the book is finished, it seems necessary to me. I'm glad I did it. I can't think of another symbolic, hyperbolic way to show the kind of hopefulness that characterized the American spirit just after the Second World War, at a time when it looked like we might actually be capable of having peace and happiness for a while.

CHC: The fantastic milieu and down-to-earth humor of the space sequence in *Look Back All the Green Valley* are also apparent in your unpublished play "Moonjox." What is different about writing a play?

FC: The difference in writing a play is that I don't know what the hell I'm doing [laughter]. That kind of writing pitches theme forward, center stage, and gives you an opportunity to dramatize it with relative freedom. I can go more or less directly to a philosophical theme, in this case the apprehensions about technology and what might result. And I can do it without preaching a lot, as one has to do sometimes in fiction. Since it was a comedy I was able to put some perspective on it. The play unfortunately fell victim to the end of the Cold War by the time I really got it into any kind of shape. The worry that Russia and the US were going to blow everything up had disappeared, which kind of invalidates the conclusion of the play. I had not realized, as a matter of fact, that it was such a Cold War play, because I had no conception of how a world without that frame of mind would be.

CHC: You have written a respectable amount of historical short fiction with a very wide assortment of historical figures. How do you determine which historical figures to write about and do you have any plans for an extended work of historical fiction?

FC: I've thought now and again about historical fiction, but the more I look at it the tougher it looks to be. You just have to know everything in order to write it and I don't know enough. My grasp of history is not very confident, but I am interested in odd corners of history—things people don't often write about. I wanted to write a whole series of short stories about scientists. For some reason they've been largely neglected in short fiction, but they make very interesting characters and the things they do are interesting. I wrote a few but for some reason just haven't gotten back to that subject.

CHC: I understand that at one time you were working on a comic novel about a man hitchhiking around the South. What was the impulse there and what ever became of that work?

FC: I wanted to write a picaresque novel and it was the one I was working on that became *The Gaudy Place*. I think I had written the first chapter of *The Gaudy Place* and I thought it would be great for Arkie to take off and get out of there, bum around the country. Then, as I was pondering this, the design of *The Gaudy Place*—how it really could be a very tight story and a very wry one—came to me, so I went in that direction. I really would like to write a picaresque novel. I enjoy reading them, but I guess I'll never have much chance to do it. Two of my favorite novels are *Don Quixote* and a novel by Thornton Wilder called *Heaven's My Destination* and, of course, *Huckleberry Finn*. I love the spirit of the picaresque.

CHC: What was the idea behind the string of stories involving Mater Astolpho, the shadow thief?

FC: Just to write a kind of panoramic fantasy novel. I came back to that about a year ago thinking, "You know, this might actually be a long poem rather than a novel or fiction." It was a way to talk about certain philosophical themes with a spirit and freedom, the kind that fantasy allows, in an extended framework, and I think I was struck by one of my periodic jealousies of Edmund Spenser. But I ultimately found that material recalcitrant, either in prose or poetry. I don't know what'll happen to it—probably nothing.

CHC: In addition to being a poet and fiction writer, you are a prolific essayist and reviewer. How would you characterize Fred Chappell's fiction and the direction in which it is moving?

FC: Well, I hope I'm working on a book of short stories. I have three uncollected stories and a few other ones which add up to about half a book. So I guess I'm moving in the direction of short fiction. I find that to be the most challenging of literary forms. Of course, I'm always working on some type of poetry or another. Right now I'm experimenting with the ode. We'll see what happens.

Bibliography

In regard to primary and secondary sources, I list those works from which I quote in my consideration of Chappell's fiction. As a result, many of Chappell's works and a substantial number of scholarly articles about them are not included. There currently exists no published comprehensive bibliography of Chappell's considerable literary output.

Works by Chappell

"Admirer, The." *Black Warrior Review* 6/2 (Spring 1980): 27–32.

"Alien Worlds." *Chronicles* 13/5 (May 1989): 22–24.

"Band of Brothers." *Red Clay Reader* 1 (1964): 34–39.

"Barcarole." *Chattahoochee Review* (Spring 1984): 49–62.

"Blood Shadow." *Memphis State Review* 4 (Fall 1983): 7–9.

Bloodfire. Baton Rouge: Louisiana State University Press, 1978.

Brighten the Corner Where You Are. New York: St. Martin's Press, 1989.

Castle Tzingal. Baton Rouge: Louisiana State University Press, 1984.

Dagon. New York: Harcourt, Brace & World, 1968.

"Darkened Light." *Brown Bag* (1969): 40–44.

"Dreaming Orchid, The." *New Mexico Humanities Review* 5 (Spring 1982): 61–76.

Earthsleep. Baton Rouge: Louisiana State University Press, 1980.

"Elmer and Buford." *North Carolina Folklore* 18/2 (May 1970): 80–83.

"Encyclopedia Daniel, The." *Janus* 2 (Winter 1996): 42–46.

"Fantasia: On the Theme of Theme and Fantasy." *Studies in Short Fiction* 27/2 (Spring 1990): 179–89.

Farewell, I'm Bound to Leave You. New York: Picador, 1996.

Foreword. In *Another Light*, by Marion Cannon, 7–8. Charlotte: Red Clay, 1974.

Foreword. In *The Nightshade Nightstand Reader*, edited by Roy Zarucchi and Carolyn Page, v–vi Troy (Maine): Nightshade, 1995.

"Free Hand." *Death Realm* 11 (Spring 1990): 43–45.

Gaudy Place, The. New York: Harcourt Brace Jovanovich, 1973.

"Good Songs Behind Us: Southern Fiction of the 1990s, The." In *That's What I Like (About the South: And Other New Southern Stories for the Nineties)*, edited by George Garret and Paul Ruffin, 1–9. Columbia: University of South Carolina Press, 1993.

"Gothic Perplexities." *Red Clay Reader* 3 (1966): 44–49.
"Homage to Plato." *Brown Bag* (1969): 1–3.
"Hooyoo Love." *Fantasy and Science Fiction* 105/4 & 5 (October/November 2003): 91–100.
I Am One of You Forever. Baton Rouge: Louisiana State University Press, 1985.
Inkling, The. New York: Harcourt, Brace & World, 1965.
Introduction. In *George Garrett: The Elizabethan Trilogy*, edited by Brooke Horvath and Irving Malin, ix–xxii. Huntsville: Texas Review Press, 1998.
It Is Time, Lord. New York: Atheneum, 1963.
Lodger, The. West Warwick [RI]: Necronomicon, 1993.
Look Back All the Green Valley. New York: Picador, 1999.
"Memorial Poem, The." *The Small Farm* 6 (Fall 1977): 37–41.
"Miss Prue." *Cold Mountain Review* 9 (Spring 1981): 72–74.
Moments of Light. Los Angeles: The New South Company, 1980.
More Shapes than One. New York: St. Martin's Press, 1991.
"Mountain Ghost, A." *Long Pond Review* 7 (1981): 82–86.
"'Not as a Leaf': Southern Poetry and the Innovation of Tradition." *Georgia Review* 51/3 (Fall 1997): 477–89.
"Overspill, The." *Long Pond Review* 3 (Winter 1976): 27–34.
"Powers of Observation: the Stone, the Hawk, and the Solitary I." In *An Open World: Essays on Leslie Norris*, edited by Eugene England and Peter Makuck, 181–90. Columbia: Camden House, 1994.
"Prodigious Words." In *Southern Writing in the Sixties*, edited by John William Corrigan and Miller Williams, 66–78. Baton Rouge: Louisiana State University Press, 1966.
"Property of Hope, A." *Saturday Evening Post* 234/18 (9 May 1964): 62–65.
"Rose and Afterward, The." *Southern Humanities Review* 28/1 (Winter 1994): 66.
"Say It Was Me." *Balcones* 1/3 (Fall 1987): 23.
"Shadow Thief, The." *New Mexico Humanities Review* 3 (Spring 1990): 14–17.
"Simples." *Appalachian Heritage* 31/3 (Summer 2003): 14–26.
"Six Propositions about Literature and History." *New Literary History* 1 (Spring 1970): 513–22.
"Skepticism." *Hemlocks and Balsams* 7 (1986–1987): 7–8.
"Snakehandling." *Now & Then* 14/1 (Spring 1997): 31–33.
Source. Baton Rouge: Louisiana State University Press, 1985.
Spring Garden: New and Selected Poems. Baton Rouge: Louisiana State University Press, 1995.
"Shape of Appalachian to Come, The: An Interview with Will Hickson." In *The Future of Southern Letters*, edited by Jefferson Humphries and John Lowe, 54–60. New York: Oxford University Press, 1996.
"Things Beyond Us." *Quarterly West* 13 (Fall/Winter 1981–1982): 5–19.
"Trout Fishing: Ritual, Not Rapture." *Holiday* 36/1 (July 1964): 122–26.
"Two Modes: A Plea for Tolerance." *Appalachian Journal* 5 (1978): 335–39.
Under Twenty-five: Duke Narrative and Verse, 1945–1962. Edited by William Blackburn, 180–204. Durham: Duke University Press, 1963.

"Visible Allegiances." *Abatis One* (1983): 52–65.
"Visionary Fiction." *Chronicles* 11/5 (May 1987): 19–21.
"What Did Adrian Leverkuhn Create?" *Postscript* 2 (1985): 11–17.
Wind Mountain. Baton Rouge: LSU, 1979.
"Woman One Time, A." *Crescent Review* 2 (Fall 1983): 20–26.
World Between the Eyes, The. Baton Rouge: Louisiana State University Press, 1971.

Secondary Sources

Alhazred, Abdul. *The Necronomicon (Al Azif)*. No publication information available for this private edition (originally published in Damascus, c. A.D. 730).
Andriano, Joseph. *Our Ladies of Darkness: Feminine Daemonology in Male Gothic Fiction*. University Park: Pennsylvania State University Press, 1993.
Bakhtin, M. M. "The *Bildungsroman* and Its Significance in the History of Realism (Toward a Historical Typology of the Novel)." In *Speech Genres and Other Late Essays*, translated by Vern W. McGee and edited by Caryl Emerson and Michael Holquist, 10–59. Austin: University of Texas Press, 1986.
Barnes, Wesley. *The Philosophy of Existentialism*. Woodbury NY: Barron's, 1968.
Barth, John. "The Spirit of Place." In *The Friday Book: Essays and Other Nonfiction*, 127–29. New York: G. P. Putnam's Sons, 1984.
Baudelaire, Charles. "Philosophic Art." In *Baudelaire as a Literary Critic*, translated by Lois Boe Hyslop and Francis E. Hyslop Jr., 186–88. University Park: Pennsylvania State University Press, 1964.
Bayer-Berenbaum, Linda. *The Gothic Imagination: Expansion in Gothic Literature and Art*. Rutherford NJ: Fairleigh Dickinson University Press, 1982.
Beauvoir, Simone de. *The Ethics of Ambiguity*. New Jersey: Citadel, 1948.
Bechler, Michael. "Speaking for Nothing: Michel de Certeau on Narrative and Historical Time." In *Signs of Change: Premodern, Modern, Postmodern*, edited by Stephen Baker, 143–54. Albany: State University of New York Press, 1996.
Benn, Gottfried. "Future and Present." In *Prose, Essays, and Poems*, translated by E. B. Ashton and edited by Volkmar Sander, 154–60. New York: Continuum, 1987.
Benson, E. F. "The Terror by Night." In *The Collected Ghost Stories*, edited by Richard Dalby, 139–45. New York: Carroll and Graf, 1992.
Berry, Wendell. "Family Work." In *The Gift of Good Land: Further Essays Cultural and Agricultural*, 155–60. San Francisco: North Point, 1981.
Bleicher, Josef. *Contemporary Hermeneutics: Hermeneutics as Method, Philosophy, and Critique*. Boston: Rutledge & Keegan Paul, 1980.
Bloom, Harold. "*Clinamen*: Towards a Theory of Fantasy." In *Bridges to Fantasy*, edited by George E. Slusser, Eric S. Rabkin, and Robert Scholes, 1–20. Carbondale: Southern Illinois University Press, 1982.
Boardman, Michael M. *Narrative Innovation and Incoherence: Ideology in Defoe, Goldsmith, Austin, Eliot, and Hemingway*. Durham: Duke University Press, 1992.
Borges, Jorge Luis. "A New Refutation of Time." In *Labyrinths: Selected Stories and Other Writings*, 217–36. New York: New Directions, 1962.

Boyd, Michael. *The Reflexive Novel: Fiction as Critique*. Lewisburg: Bucknell University Press, 1983.

Brinkmeyer, Robert H., Jr. *Remapping Southern Literature: Contemporary Southern Writers and the West*. Athens: University of Georgia Press, 2000.

Broughton, Irv. "Fred Chappell." In volume 3 of *The Writer's Mind*, edited by Broughton, 91–122. Fayetteville: University of Arkansas Press, 1990.

Buitenhuis, Peter. "Desire Under the Magnolias: Review of *Dagon*." *New York Times Book Review* (29 September 1968): 58.

Calvino, Italo. "Two Interviews on Science and Literature." In *The Uses of Literature*, translated by Patrick Creagh, 28–38. New York: Harcourt Brace Jovanovich, 1982.

Cohen, Allen. Review of *Dagon*. *Library Journal* 93/17 (1 October 1968): 3576.

Cozzens, James Gould. *By Love Possessed*. New York: Harcourt, Brace and Company, 1957.

Daiches, David and John Flower. *Literary Landscapes of the British Isles: A Narrative Atlas*. New York: Paddington, 1979.

Davenport-Hines, Richard. *Gothic: 400 Years of Excess, Horror, Evil and Ruin*. London: Fourth Estate, 1998.

De Camp, L. Sprague. *Lovecraft: A Biography*. Garden City: Doubleday, 1975.

Dillard, R. H. W. "Letters from a Distant Lover: The Novels of Fred Chappell." *Hollins Critic* 10/2 (April 1973): 1–15.

———. *News of the Nile*. Chapel Hill: University of North Carolina Press, 1971.

Easa, Leila. "A Conversation with Fred Chappell." *The Archive* 108/1 (Fall 1995): 49–60.

Ellison, Ralph. "Society, Morality and the Novel." In *The Collected Essays of Ralph Ellison*, edited by John F. Callahan, 694–725. New York: Modern Library, 1995.

Faris, Wendy H. "Scheherazade's Children: Magic Realism and Postmodern Fiction." In *Magic Realism: Theory, History, Community*, edited by Faris and Lois Parkinson Zamora, 163–90. Durham: Duke University Press, 1995.

Felman, Shoshana. *Writing and Madness (Literature/philosophy/Psychoanalysis)*. Translated by Felman and Martha Noel Evans. Ithaca: Cornell University Press, 1985.

"Fred Chappell." *North Carolina Book Watch*. PBS. North Carolina Public Television. 1997.

———. *North Carolina People: with William Friday*. PBS. North Carolina Public Television. 1985.

Freud, Sigmund. *The Freud Reader*. Edited by Peter Gay. New York: Norton, 1989.

Gadamer, Hans-Georg. *Truth and Method*. New York: Seabury, 1975.

Gaines, Ervin J. Review of *The Inkling*. *Library Journal* 90/14 (August 1965): 3308.

Gelfant, Blanch Housman. *The American City Novel*. Norman: University of Oklahoma Press, 1954.

Gilman, Richard. "Someone Else Is Living My Life." *New York Times Book Review* (8 September 1963): 43.

Goddu, Teresa A. *Gothic America: Narrative, History, and Nation*. New York: Columbia University Press, 1997.

Goethe, Johann Wolfgang von. "On Criticism." In *Goethe's Literary Essays*, edited by J. E. Spingarn, 140–44. New York: Ungar, 1921.

Gossett, Louise. *Violence in Recent Southern Fiction*. Durham: Duke University Press, 1968.

Graham, John. "Fred Chappell." In *The Writer's Voice: Conversations with Contemporary Writers*, edited by John Graham and George Garrett, 37–50. New York: William Morrow, 1973.

Gray, Amy Tipton. "R'lyeh in Appalachia: Lovecraft's Influence on Fred Chappell's *Dagon*." In *Remembrance, Reunion, and Revival: Celebrating a Decade of Appalachian Studies*, 73–79. Boone [NC]: Appalachian Consortium Press, 1988.

Gray, Richard. *Southern Aberrations: Writers of the American South and the Problems of Regionalism*. Baton Rouge: Louisiana State University Press, 2000.

Guinn, Matthew. *After Southern Modernism: Fiction of the Contemporary South*. Jackson: University Press of Mississippi, 2000.

Haggerty, George E. *Gothic Fiction/Gothic Form*. University Park: Pennsylvania State University Press, 1989.

Hall, Donald. "A Literature of Synthesis." In *To Keep Moving: Essays 1959–1969*, 19–22. Geneva (New York): Hobart & William Smith, 1980.

Hall, John. Review of *It Is Time, Lord*. *Books and Bookmen* 10/11 (1965): 36.

Harmon, William. *Treasury Holiday*. Middletown [CT]: Wesleyan University Press, 1969.

Hegel, Georg. *The Phenomenology of Mind*. New York: Macmillan, 1910.

Heidegger, Martin. *What Is Called Thinking?* Translated by J. Glenn Gray. New York: Harper & Row, 1968.

Hendersot, Cyndy. *The Animal Within: Masculinity and the Gothic*. Ann Arbor: University of Michigan Press, 1998.

Hicks, Granville. "Thirty Years with a Stranger." *Saturday Review* (10 August 1963): 17–18.

Hobson, Fred. *The Southern Writer in the Postmodern World*. Athens: University of Georgia Press, 1991.

Hurm, Gerd. *Fragmented Urban Images: The American City in Modern Fiction from Stephen Crane to Thomas Pynchon*. New York: Peter Lang, 1991.

James, Henry. "The Art of Fiction." In *The House of Fiction*, edited by Leon Edel, 23–45. Westport: Greenwood, 1973.

Jarrell, Randall. "Six Russian Short Novels." In *The Third Book of Criticism*, 233–78. New York: Farrar, Straus & Giroux, 1969.

Jefferson, Thomas. *The Writings of Thomas Jefferson*. Edited by Andrew Lipscomb. Washington, D.C.: Thomas Jefferson Memorial Association of the United States, 1905.

Joshi, S. T. *The Weird Tale*. Austin: University of Texas Press, 1990.

Jung, Carl. "Psychology and Literature." In *Modern Man in Search of a Soul*, 152–72. New York: Harcourt, Brace, 1933.

Justus, James H. Foreword in *Southern Writers at Century's End*, edited by Jeffery J. Folks and James A. Perkins. Lexington: University Press of Kentucky, 1997.

Kroeber, Karl. *Romantic Fantasy and Science Fiction*. New Haven: Yale University Press, 1988.

Lamott, Kenneth. "Deja Vu, Ya'll." *Book Week* (15 August 1965): 10.

Lang, John. *Understanding Fred Chappell*. Columbia: University of South Carolina Press, 2000.

Lee, Ernest. *Discovering Place: Readings from Appalachian Writers*. New York: McGraw-Hill, 1997.

Lovecraft, H. P. *Dagon and Other Macabre Tales*. London: Panther, 1969.

———. *The Lurking Fear and Other Stories*. New York: Ballantine, 1971.

Lutwack, Leonard. *The Role of Place in Literature*. Syracuse: Syracuse University Press, 1984.

Machor, James. *Pastoral Cities: Urban Ideals and the Symbolic Landscape of America*. Madison: University of Wisconsin Press, 1987.

Mailer, Norman. *Cannibals and Christians*. New York: Dial, 1966.

Maltby, Paul. *Dissident Postmodernists: Barthelme, Coover, Pynchon*. Philadelphia: University of Pennsylvania Press, 1991.

Mann, Thomas. "Nietzsche's Philosophy in the Light of Recent History." In *Last Essays*, translated by Richard and Clara Winston and Tania and James Stern, 141–77. New York: Knopf, 1959.

Martin, Robert K. and Eric Savoy, editors. *American Gothic: New Interventions in a National Narrative*. Iowa City: University of Iowa Press, 1998.

Maugham, W. Somerset. *The Art of Fiction*. New York: Arno, 1977.

McDonald, Hal. "Fred Chappell as Magic Realist." *North Carolina Literary Review* 7 (1998): 127–39.

McDowell, Ian. "Fred Chappell." *Coraddi* (Winter 1985): 32–37.

Mill, John. *Utilitarianism*. New York: New American Library, 1974.

Nabokov, Vladimir. *Lectures on Literature*. Edited by General Bowers. New York: Harcourt Brace Jovanovich, 1980.

Nemerov, Howard. "Composition and Fate in the Short Novel." In *New and Selected Essays*, 56–71. Carbondale: Southern Illinois University Press, 1985.

Nin, Anais. *The Novel of the Future*. New York: Macmillan, 1968.

O'Connor, William Van. *The Grotesque: An American Genre and Other Essays*. Carbondale: Southern Illinois University Press, 1962.

Palmer, Tersh. "Fred Chappell." *Appalachian Journal* 19/4 (Summer 1992): 402–11.

Palumbo, Carmine. "Folklore and Literature: The Poetry and Fiction of Fred Chappell." Dissertation, University of Southwestern Louisiana, 1997.

Paz, Octavio. "Literature and Literalness." In *Convergences: Essays on Art and Literature*, translated by Helen Lane, 184–200. New York: Harcourt Brace Jovanovich, 1987.

Percy, Walker. "Novel-writing in an Apocalyptic Time." In *Signposts in a Strange Land*, 153–67. New York: Farrar, Straus and Giroux, 1991.

Prescott, Orville. "Brilliant, but Unsatisfying." *New York Times* (11 August 1965): 33.

Price, Reynolds. "The Thing Itself." In *A Common Room: Essays 1954–1987*, 9–14. New York: Atheneum, 1987.
Rabkin, Eric S. *The Fantastic in Literature*. Princeton: Princeton University Press, 1976.
Ragan, David Paul. "Flying by Night: An Early Interview with Fred Chappell." *North Carolina Literary Review* 7 (1998): 105–19.
Ragan, Sam. *Journey into Morning*. Laurinburg [NC]: St. Andrews Press, 1981.
Redd, Chris. "A Man of Letters in the Modern World: An Interview with Fred Chappell." *The Arts Journal* 14/8 (May 1989): 7–9.
Review of *Dagon*. *Virginia Quarterly Review* 45/1 (Winter 1969): viii.
Review of *The Fred Chappell Reader*. *Publishers Weekly* 231 (13 February 1987): 78.
Review of *The Fred Chappell Reader*. *Tri-Quarterly* 71 (1988): 216–17.
Review of *The Gaudy Place*. *Kirkus Reviews* 41/1 (1 January 1973): 17.
Review of *The Gaudy Place*. *The New Republic* 168/22 (2 June 1973): 30.
Review of *The Inkling*. *Times Literary Supplement* (10 November 1966): 1028.
Rilke, Rainer Maria. *The Selected Poetry of Rainer Maria Rilke*. Translated and edited by Stephen Mitchell. New York: Vintage, 1989.
Rimbaud, Arthur. *Complete Works*. Translated by Paul Schmidt. New York: Harper & Row, 1976.
Rimmon-Kenan, Shlomith. *Narrative Fiction: Contemporary Poetics*. New York: Metheun, 1983.
Russell, Bertrand. *A Critical Exposition of the Philosophy of Leibniz*. London: George Allen & Unwin, 1900.
Santayana, George. *The Life of Reason*. New York: Scribner's, 1932.
Sartre, Jean-Paul. "On *The Sound and the Fury*: Time in the Work of Faulkner." In *Literary Essays*, 79–87. New York: Philosophical Library, 1955.
———. *The Philosophy of Jean-Paul Sartre*. Edited by Robert Denoon Cumming. New York: Vintage, 1965.
Schweitzer, Darrell. "A Talk with Fred Chappell." *Weird Tales* 1 (Summer 1994): 40–43.
Segre, Cesare. *Structures and Time: Narration, Poetry, Models*. Chicago: University of Chicago Press, 1979.
Slusser, George E. and Eric S. Rabkin. *Hard Science Fiction*. Carbondale: Southern Illinois University Press, 1986.
Smith, R. T. "Proteus Loose in the Baptismal Font." In *Dream Garden: The Poetic Vision of Fred Chappell*, edited by Patrick Bizzaro, 35–47. Baton Rouge: Louisiana State University Press, 1997.
Sopko, John and John Carr. "Dealing with the Grotesque: Fred Chappell." In *Kite-Flying and Other Irrational Acts: Conversations with Twelve Southern Writers*, edited by John Carr, 216–35. Baton Rouge: Louisiana State University Press, 1972.
Spender, Stephen. *The Struggle of the Modern*. Berkeley: University of California Press, 1963.
Staggs, Sammy. Review of *The Gaudy Place*. *Library Journal* 98 (15 February 1973): 563.

Stapledon, Olaf. *An Olaf Stapledon Reader*. Edited by Robert Crossley. Syracuse: Syracuse University Press, 1997.

Stephenson, Shelby. "Vision in Fred Chappell's Poetry and Fiction." *Abatis One* (1983): 33–45.

Stirnemann, S. A. "Fred Chappell: Poet with 'Ah! Bright Wings.'" *Poetry Review* (Winter 1990): 41–51.

Stuart, Dabney. "'Blue Pee': Fred Chappell's Mythical Kingdom." *Iron Mountain Review* 2/2 (1985): 13–21.

Tacitus, Cornelius. *The Annals of Tacitus*. Book 3. New York: Cambridge University Press, 1996.

Tate, Allen. "The Profession of Letters in the South." In *On the Limits of Poetry: Selected Essays, 1928–1948*, 265–81. New York: Morrow, 1948.

Terr, Lenore. *Too Scared to Cry: Psychic Trauma in Childhood*. New York: Basic, 1990.

Turner, Frederick. *Spirit of Place: The Making of an American Literary Landscape*. San Francisco: Sierra Club, 1989.

Verlaine, Paul. *One Hundred and One Poems*. Chicago: University of Chicago Press, 1999.

Vonalt, Larry. "Five Novels." *Sewanee Review* 73/2 (April/June 1965): 333–39.

Walsh, William. "Fred Chappell." In *Speak So I Shall Know Thee: Interviews with Southern Writers*, 68–77. Asheboro [NC]: Down Home, 1987.

Waugh, Evelyn. "A Young Novelist's Heaven." In *The Essays, Articles and Reviews of Evelyn Waugh*, edited by Donat Gallagher, 65–66. Boston: Little Brown, 1984.

Williams, Robert Moore. *The Blue Atom*. New York: Ace, 1958.

Wittgenstein, Ludwig. *Notebooks: 1914–1916*. Translated by G. E. M. Anscombe and edited by Anscombe and G. H. von Wright. Oxford: Blackwell, 1979.

Woolf, Virginia. *Orlando: A Biography*. New York: Harcourt, Brace and Company, 1928.

Yardley, Jonathan. Review of *The Gaudy Place*. *New York Times Book Review* (13 May 1973): 36.

Index

www.ingramcontent.com/pod-product-compliance
Lightning Source LLC
Chambersburg PA
CBHW020947310726
48980CB00001B/93

9780865549456